YOU NEED ME

Sharon Bairden

RED DOG
UK

Published by RED DOG PRESS 2021

First Edition

Hardback ISBN 978-1-914480-24-9

Paperback ISBN 978-1-914480-22-5

Ebook ISBN 978-1-914480-23-2

www.reddogpress.co.uk

To Mum, Dad, Anthony, Ashleigh, Logan, Jess, Lynn, Iain, David, Louise and Lacie, you are my world. Always.

Dad, I wish you were here to see this.

Other things may change us, but we start and end with family.

One

Morag

MORAG MCLAUGHLIN PUSHED open the heavy doors, anxious to be in out of the biting November chill. She punched in the code on the alarm pad to shut off the beeping, and flicked a switch. As the lights in the lobby sputtered into life, the spines of a thousand authors stared silently back at her, their presence giving her reassurance. The lights fizzled, the sound of flickering electricity jarred on her nerves, like nails scraping down a chalkboard.

She sucked her teeth and made a note to call maintenance herself to have the bulbs replaced. Her previous complaints to her manager about the faulty lighting had achieved nothing. "It's hardly priority in the current economic climate," he had tutted. Morag supposed this was true, services were being cut all over the place and she should really be thankful that they hadn't affected her yet.

Redundancy terrified Morag, the idea of no longer being needed, of being surplus to requirements. Life had already made her redundant and without her job she would have nothing, she'd have nobody. No, she couldn't imagine her life without it, without them. The thought brought a smile to her lips. They needed her.

Everything is working out the way you wanted it to, it's going to be all right. Morag repeated the mantra to herself, ignoring the twitch in her eye and the fingers of uncertainty tiptoeing up her spine.

She allowed a contented sigh to escape as she pocketed the keys in her oversized Gladstone handbag. She listened to the keys settle down, amongst the clutter. The bag had seen better days. The garnet leather was cracked and dry with age, the floral scent of lavender lingered in the lining. Filled to the brim with the remnants of her life, the stitching showed the strain of the memories and burdens that lay inside. Just like me, thought Morag, memories are pulling us both apart at the seams.

The handbag had been her mother's, and that, and her memories, were all Morag had left of her. Looking at the bag, Morag snorted, as a vision of her mother flashed before her eyes. *Dear departed Mother.* She sneered—memories of her mother were anything but dear.

"Thank God she *has* departed," whispered Morag.

I should clear the damn bag out, she thought, well aware she would not. She hated throwing things away. She liked to keep her memories close, and this bag held her most special memories. Morag's lips twisted into a smile, nobody would ever guess the life hidden inside her bag—her life.

Morag knew others passed her by without a second glance. Nobody would ever guess her secrets. She was invisible to them—a lonely middle-aged woman with nothing to offer but a bag full of clutter. The clutter of a woman old before her time. *If only they knew the truth.* Clutter to some, memories to Morag. Each piece told its own story, and combined they told Morag's secrets. Secrets nobody must ever find out.

Morag closed the door behind her breathed in the atmosphere. The sound of silence filled her ears, while the crisp, clean smell of new books mixed with the sweet but musky smell of the old tickled her nose. She inhaled it, savouring the scent. Nobody would ever understand the pleasure she took from being here, alone with her books, her tellers of stories. They belonged to her, they would never leave her, and nobody could ever take them away from her. The stillness of the building brought a calm to her inner chaos—it soothed her.

She looked around, grateful her library had escaped modernisation—the cuts had saved them from that. Other libraries had been converted into 'hubs' or 'one-stop shops', doubling up as council services—impersonal, soulless shells with their bloody awful machines used to check books in and out. Little human interaction required. She shuddered at the thought. Her library remained as a library should be in her eyes—a place of sanctuary, a place of quiet. A place to be.

As she made her way over to the desk, she ran her fingers along the spines on the shelves, each book with its own stories to tell. The story created by the writer but also the stories of the homes they had been in, the lives they had touched and the memories they had inspired.

The ticking clock reminded her where she was. She looked up. Nine-thirty. Half an hour before opening time. Reaching the counter, Morag switched on the main lights and squinted as the harsh strip lighting lit up the library. Morag would have preferred to replace the lights with old-fashioned reading lamps, little reading nooks and some soft furnishings—things to draw people in and make them feel at home. "But, it's not up to you Morag, is it? You're only the librarian, here to do your job," she parroted her boss. Morag huffed, nobody could stop her dreaming.

Switching on the library management system, Morag reminisced about the old days of library cards and the satisfying *thunk* of the manual stamps checking the books out. But times had moved on, she knew, and she had been forced to move with them. She smiled as the system whirred into life, her library was coming alive, and soon they would be here.

She hurried over to the staff room. Tucked away behind the divider, between the main desk and the admin section, the room was more of a cupboard than a staff room—none of the staff used it to eat their lunch or take their breaks. The small table and chairs provided were laden down with unprocessed books and paperwork and the musty smell of sweat and over ripened food meant nobody ever hung around long. Morag fished a padlock out of her bag, and stuffed the bag into one of the free lockers, locking it and pocketing the key.

Catching her reflection in the mirror on the wall, she stopped and looked at herself. Her critical eye told her that compared to other women her age, she looked frumpy. Her mousy brown hair cut in a no-nonsense bob, her cheeks ruddy from the fresh air. She could not remember the last time she had ever worn make-up, she didn't even own any make up. *Make up wouldn't make any difference to you. Ugly little trollop.* She bit her lip and took in her appearance—her sensible beige polo neck jumper and A-line navy skirt hid her shapely figure, a figure she wished she had the confidence to show off. A figure her mother had taught her to despise. The woman who stared back at her looked at least a decade older than her fifty-five years. Even her emerald green eyes, her one outstanding feature, were dull this morning. They had lost their sparkle. She patted down a stray hair before turning away and hanging up her coat.

Back out at the counter, Morag tutted at the sight of the stack of books lying on the counter. She fumed, none of the Saturday staff had bothered to process them. Probably too busy sitting around gossiping about nights out or some ridiculous celebrity reality show to do the job they were paid to do. *Happy enough to leave me to pick up after them.* None of them cared—about the books, the customers or the library. Not like her. Morag cared.

As she lifted the book from the top of the pile on the counter, the corners of her mouth turned up. *A Suitable Lie* by Michael J. Malone. She could hear her mother now, *a lovely man, a right gentleman, always well turned out. Always had lovely shoes, so he did.* It was probably the kindest thing her mother had ever said about anyone. She had been right as well—he wasn't bad looking at all. Morag had been to a couple of book events in Glasgow where he was speaking and she had to admit she had developed a bit of a soft spot for him. *As if he would be interested in someone like you,* her mother's voice spat in her ear.

Morag's shoulders slumped. She could not escape the sharp end of her mother's tongue, not even when she was long dead and buried.

"Bitch in life, and bitch in death," she muttered under her breath.

Irritated now, she grabbed the book a little more roughly than she had intended. The pages fluttered and something caught her eye as it fell to the floor.

Stooping down, she reached for the sheet of paper. *Probably a shopping list.* She loved to read other people's shopping lists, salivating as she imagined extravagant meals created with the items she read there—the dinner parties with the clink of the glasses and chatter of the guests... or she would pity at the meagre lists where the meat scraps from the butcher's counter were for the non-existent cat. Morag loved to submerge herself in the lives of others. Escaping from her own existence brought her a pleasure nobody else could ever understand.

She turned the piece of paper over in her hand, ready to launch herself into somebody else's life for the next few moments. She soon wished she hadn't. She read the words twice before the meaning sunk in.

Your secret didn't die with me.

Two

Ronnie

RONNIE WHITESIDE SCRATCHED at the bristles on his face. It felt dirty, grubby—the stubble rough under his calloused fingers. He rocked on his feet as goose bumps crept up his arms. Mother didn't like boys who didn't shave. Mother didn't like stubble. Mother thought it was dirty. *Dirty. Dirty. Dirty.*

He paced round the tiny kitchen, his feet treading an already well-worn path on the filthy lino. He studied the clock. Seven fifty-five. Ronnie nodded, satisfied. He trusted the clock. It was about all he could trust in this house. It had to be on time. *He* had to be on time. For Mother. *Never be late Ronnie, he could hear her bark. Mummy doesn't like to be kept waiting.*

He screwed up his face and, in a soft whisper, imitated his mother's nasal twang, sniggering at his nerve before quickly clasping his hand over his mouth, smothering out any noise he might make. Can't have mother hearing me. *What are you laughing at Ronnie? What the fuck do you have to laugh about, you little freak?* He could hear her, her voice raspy after years of chain smoking, thick in his ear even though she was upstairs in her bed. *Mummy always sees you Ronnie.*

He checked the clock again. Only eight a.m. Another two hours before the library opened. He had plenty of time. Should he shave? Did he have time to shave and have something to eat? What about mother? She would want her breakfast soon. She always had breakfast at eight forty-five. On the dot. *ON THE DOT, RONNIE.*

He didn't have time to shave. He shuffled his way out of the kitchen, stopping at the bottom of the stairs to listen for any movement from his mother's room. Silence. Thankfully. He edged his way back through the piles of papers and boxes lining the narrow passage of the hallway leading to the kitchen. He had just enough room to squeeze by, but he had to be careful, he couldn't dislodge any of them. Everything in its place and a place for everything. Methodically he checked the piles four times to make sure. The tension drained from his shoulders when he saw nothing had moved.

Back in the kitchen, Ronnie pulled the fridge door open. He didn't notice the rancid smell of bacon, well past its use by date. Nor did he see the mould ingrained into the shelves. All he cared about was getting his mother's breakfast ready. Exactly as she demanded. Every single day. Two eggs scrambled with one slice of toast, no butter. As Ronnie cracked the eggs into the bowl, he sniggered imagining the fragile eggshells to be his mother's skull, cracking open, wide open, her brain scrambled inside. He snorted.

The clock ticked. Eight fifteen. It was too early to scramble the eggs and eight forty-five seemed a lifetime away. He set the bowl down next to the microwave and stopped. Listening. The house remained silent. But Ronnie could sense something, his head cocked to one side he held his breath and strained his ears. Something was outside—he could hear it. Something shuffling or was it someone? *It's following you Ronnie. It knows you're here. Can't hide from it, Ronnie.*

He shook his head roughly, trying to free the building pressure, the feeling his world had started to close in on him. Ever since he had met… *SHHH Ronnie,* he told himself—the fear that his thoughts could be overhead was so real.

Creeping over to the back door, Ronnie rattled the handle, relieved to find it locked. He lifted the slat of the kitchen blind, oblivious to the thick layer of grease left behind on his fingers. He peered out. Ronnie did not see the planks of wood falling away from the rotten fence, or the small patch of grass, now knee high, the broken plant pots or the rusted bike. His eyes zeroed in on a black shape over in the corner of the garden. He drew in a sharp breath. Something was out there, a dark shadow crouching in the corner. Not something. Someone. Watching him. *Shit, shit! It's here.*

Wringing his hands, he continued to pace the kitchen. *Breathe in. Breathe out. Breathe in. Breathe out.* He stopped and lifted the slat again.

The figure hadn't moved. With one hand holding the slat open, he picked up the kitchen knife from the sink. He lifted it upwards and stabbed it into his hand. Ronnie didn't even flinch. He stabbed again, ignoring the trickle of blood running down his wrist and dripping onto the floor. The figure still didn't move. *It's come for me. It's found me. I'm done for now.*

Ronnie gripped the knife tighter. He stood, his free hand clawing his face, leaving bloody smears. Ronnie scrambled for the door handle and with shaking hands managed to unlock the door. He hurtled outside, screaming: "Leave me alone. Leave me the fuck alone." He rushed at the figure, his arms outstretched, screaming incoherent threats.

He did not notice the woman next door shake her head as she dropped the net curtain back. Ronnie was fixated on the figure before him.

He rushed towards it fuelled by fury and threw himself on top of it. Eyes closed, he sunk the knife in deep, repeatedly not caring what damage he caused. When the figure didn't retaliate, Ronnie's body sagged as the stench flew up to meet his nostrils. He gagged and opened his eyes. The black bin bag was ripped to shreds, the rotten food spewing out onto the ground. He curled into a ball and began to sob.

"RONNIE…"

His mother's voice reverberated around his head as he crawled back into the house.

Eight thirty-five. He tried to ignore the avalanche of thoughts hurtling through his brain and the anxiety stabbing at his gut, as he as he threw the bowl of eggs into the microwave and a slice of bread into the toaster.

He stuck his hands under the tap in an attempt to wash the blood away. He would need a bandage on that he told himself.

Stupid boy. Stupid. Stupid. Stupid.

Each word matched with the dull thump of his head against the kitchen cupboard.

Eight forty-two. He threw the eggs and toast onto a plate ignoring the cracks and the congealed grease from yesterday's breakfast. He picked up the breakfast tray and made his way to the stairs. Foot raised to the first step.

"Mother. Breakfast is coming."

Three

Susan

SNATCHING HER PURSE from her handbag, Susan Bonner yanked it open, praying it had somehow become fuller than it had been the previous night. Two shiny pound coins peeked back at her. Susan groaned, there was just enough to buy milk and bread at the corner shop, or maybe a little extra, if she could hang on—they reduced the prices just before closing time. She swallowed her humiliation, as shame coloured her cheeks. Was this really what her life had come to? how low could she go. She shuddered, knowing she could go much lower. What she was contemplating would take her lower than a snake's belly in her eyes.

She flung her purse back in her bag. *How much would it be worth second hand?* She loved that bag, it had been the only thing of value she had brought with her when she left, a blood red Alexander McQueen bucket bag. He had brought it back for her from some work trip he had been attending. No doubt to salve a guilty conscience. She kicked the bag back under the table making a note to check the value on eBay when she was in the library.

Her belly rumbled as she padded into the kitchen. She pulled open the cupboards, with little anticipation of finding much, but she needed something, anything to take away the hunger gnawing at her belly. Sitting forlornly on the shelves was a packet of supermarket brand noodles which had gone out of date two months ago and a slice of bread with more mould than crust. Hardly breakfast material, but beggars can't be choosers.

The house was quiet—her daughter, Lily fast asleep. If she could heat the noodles quickly, she might be able to eat before Lily woke up. It wasn't as though she would be depriving her daughter of anything nutritious, Susan justified. Besides Lily would get something to eat at the library today. The woman who worked there, Morag, always brought in some little treats for the kids, and went out of her way to slip Lily a little bit extra, it was as though she could sense how bad things were.

Susan gave a silent thanks to Morag and her kindness, it wasn't just the small treats she gave Lily, Morag had also taken both of them to the café on the high street for lunch a few times, always brushing off Susan's protests, telling her they were doing her a favour by giving her some company. Morag was a bit intense at times but, for Susan, it was a price worth paying for what she received in return.

Guilt eating away at her, Susan put the kettle onto boil and crossed her fingers. She cursed as the electricity meter ran out just before the kettle started bubbling. Her heart sank, she didn't have enough money to buy a top-up card. Stomach grumbling, she poured the tepid water over the noodles and scraped as much of the mould off her bread as she could.

Greedily, she shovelled the food into her mouth, trying not to gag as it slid down her throat. The knot in her stomach was growing tighter, her benefits weren't due to be paid for another two days, and she had no electricity left and no food. This meant a call to the electricity supplier for emergency credit and the humiliation of having to ask for another food voucher from Morag at the library.

The solutions to her problems were there, but the humiliation they caused was almost unbearable.

Her cheeks grew warm as she remembered using the foodbank the first time—how she'd cried when she returned home and realised she couldn't use half the food they had given her as she didn't have any money to top up the meter to cook it. Susan threw the remains of her food in the sink and thumped the worktop. Tears of frustration welled up in her eyes. When would this humiliation ever end? How stupid had she been to imagine a new house would be a fresh new start for her and Lily?

When she had been told they were going to be housed in the Waterside Estate in Lennoxhill, a small town in the North East of

Glasgow, she had imagined a neat row of little terraced houses next to a small stream or river, somewhere picturesque she and Lily would be able to make their new home. Instead, she found herself in the bottom flat of a four-in-a-block, in an estate that wouldn't look out of place in Trainspotting. She spent most days staring out the window watching a steady stream of addicts and joyriders slip past, jealous—at least they were moving, at least they had a purpose, while she just existed.

Susan had taken Lily and fled her old life, leaving everything behind her. With no job, her housing options had been severely limited. No leafy suburbs for them. Her thoughts were bitter and full of resentment. The harsh reality of her situation had hit home when she had looked at the price of private lets and realised her budget would only stretch to a couple of nights in a cheap hotel, she had been forced to declare herself and her daughter homeless when they first arrived in Glasgow. She had tried the local shelters for women who had been abused but they were all full. Susan had sobbed, as she begged for their help. They hadn't questioned her but had allocated her a short-term support worker who had been a Godsend, helping Susan navigate the complex maze that was the housing system. A system Susan had never dreamed she would be forced to use.

The support worker had driven them to the estate and had tried to gloss over the state of the place—piles of discarded rubbish, kids running wild on the streets and groups of adults huddled on street corners. Susan had tried to hide the disgust on her face. She knew she should be grateful for a roof over her head for them both, but right now she felt anything but grateful. She was ashamed to admit that more than once she had considered putting a pillow over her daughter's head, taking an overdose herself and ending it all.

Susan tried to push away her thoughts of suicide, instead focusing on the positives. Morag had been a lifesaver and if hadn't been for that awful experience at the job centre she may never have met the older woman. Every cloud and all that jazz, she thought.

She cringed at the memory and the humiliation of her first time in a job centre. For someone who had never had to claim anything in her life, the whole process had been an eye opener for her. From having to pass the security guard on the front door who managed to make her feel two inches small, to having to justify her reasons for being out of work to the stern faced and disinterested advisor behind the counter. Susan had wanted the ground to open up and swallow her.

The advisor told her she would need to submit a claim for universal credit before barking off a list of instructions about setting up an online account which would be monitored closely to ensure she met all the requirements. The advisor had smirked at that point, her eyes telling Susan she didn't believe she was entitled to anything. The words claimant commitments, budgeting advances, sanctions and appeals all went over her head as Susan had tried to take it all in. She had explained to the advisor she had no computer, no internet access and no money to obtain these. The advisor's response had been a shrug and directions to the local library for help. Susan had skulked out the job centre, her face scarlet with shame, and made her way to the library.

The woman behind the desk, Morag, had seemed kindly. She sighed as she explained Job Centre staff should have helped her with the initial set up of her Universal Credit account. Susan had been mortified and gathered up her papers to leave, apologizing profusely to the woman for her ignorance and for taking up her time but she had laughed gently and said: "It's okay love. Why would you be expected to know what to do? You're not the first, nor will you be the last, and I'll do what I can to help you."

Finding the library had turned out to be a blessing. Morag had encouraged her to bring Lily along and to join the group she ran there. Susan quickly realised she wasn't the only person in the small town to use the library to pass time. Most folk gathered there or passed through at some point in the week, borrowing books, meeting friends or just getting in out of the cold. Susan loved to watch the people come and go, and found herself daydreaming about the lives they might lead, wondering if any of them were in the same boat as her. None of them looked like they had her worries plaguing them.

There were the students—full of hope and expectation, the little old ladies who came in for a blether with their cronies and would cackle in time with the clicking of their knitting needles, and of course there were the loners and misfits—those who would shuffle in daily, heads down, avoiding eye contact and doing their best to blend into the background. The invisible ones. Susan wished she had stayed invisible.

Susan had always been a reader, and she could lose herself for hours in a world of imagination as she flicked through books. By filling her head with stories of other places, the library not only provided an escape from her new reality, but on a more practical level it was somewhere to go where she didn't need to spend money, and there was nobody at her back, hurrying her along to move out.

She hadn't been to a library since she was a child, and she had been surprised at the changes—no more frosty librarians with fingers to their lips demanding silence. Lily could play with toys she could no longer afford to buy her, and she could get online without using up all her phone credit. With him, she hadn't needed to borrow books, she had simply ordered whatever she wanted online. A tight smile crossed her face as she recalled his generosity, with both money and his fists.

As she tried, unsuccessfully, to rinse her dishes clean in cold water, Susan's head spun at the pressure she felt. No money, her savings long gone, she had been forced to share a bed with her daughter to try and keep them both warm at night. The thought of ending it all flashed by again, but she knew she couldn't bring herself to harm her daughter, and she wouldn't abandon her to be brought up in care.

The sound of soft steps pattering down the stairs focused her wandering mind. Lily was awake. She came into the kitchen still rubbing the sleep from her eyes. Susan tried to ignore the slight blue tinge to the child's lips, a stark reminder of the chill in the house. Lily didn't stay sleepy for long, and as usual she was full of questions.

Susan sighed as her daughter asked the question she always dreaded. She repeated it at least ten times a day and Susan was teetering close to the edge.

A small hand tugged at her arm. "Mummy, will we see Daddy today?"

Susan blinked the tears away as her eyes dropped towards her daughter and she caught her breath. The child was the spitting image of her father—the same deep blue eyes that crinkled when she smiled, but quickly narrowed to slits when she was angry, and a wide mouth with a welcoming smile, but one that could cut her in two when crossed. She wished she did not see his face every time she looked at her daughter. She wanted to look at Lily and see her own reflection instead.

Shaking her head, she crouched down to Lily's height.

"No sweetie, I told you, we can't see Daddy. He's had to go away for a while."

"But why? It's not fair…"

Susan sensed the rumbling of a tantrum and, wanting to stop it in its tracks before it exploded, she swooped her daughter up in her arms and firmly placed on her 'happy mummy' mask for the day. It wasn't Lily's fault they were in this mess, she had to keep going for her.

"Why don't we go to the park and feed the ducks, then we can stop at the cafe and buy a cake before we go to the library," she asked, as she swung her daughter round trying to shake all pictures of that bastard from her head.

Giggling now Lily nodded, "Yessssss! And can I get a bouncy ball to play in the park?"

Glad her daughter could be so easily distracted, she knew the two pounds she had earmarked for food would need to go towards the treat she had promised Lily. She crossed her fingers in the hope she might find some loose change down the side of the sofa.

"But first, young lady, you need to put some clothes on. Now quick." She chased Lily up the stairs and managed to persuade her the outfit she had worn yesterday would do again today.

What the hell was she going to do? They couldn't carry on like this.

She heard her phone ping from downstairs. A reminder. She had a choice. She had been given some options, but had baulked at the suggestions before. She couldn't consider lowering herself to that level... could she?

Four

Alan

ALAN AITKEN LAY on the filthy mattress in the middle of the bedroom floor, oblivious to the fact he was lying in his own urine—self-care and dignity the furthest things from his mind. He stared vacantly towards the empty light fitting swaying from the ceiling in the draught from the open window.

His 'friends' had stripped everything they could from the flat, including all the lightbulbs, selling it off to pay for their next hit. He wondered what the going rate was for a used lightbulb these days? Definitely not enough to pay for the gear they had turned up with at the weekend, that was for sure.

Alan wasn't daft. He knew where the money for the gear came from. He'd got the cash the same way himself plenty of times, but wasn't proud of it. He didn't get the same buzz from thieving as his mates did, but it did provide him with the money he needed, as well as the chance to escape his living hell every now and then.

Alan had always made sure he left behind some sort of calling card on the jobs he done, a stray hair, fibres from his clothes, the distinct footprints of a size fourteen trainer. He ignored his mates' taunts of 'useless fucker'—the words running like water off the proverbial duck's back. He didn't care and neither did they when he gladly took the rap for them.

He was probably the only thief in Glasgow who prayed for one of the tougher sheriffs to hear his case at court, and his heart sank when he found himself in front of one of the bleeding hearts who believed in rehab and second chances. Alan wanted to be sent to prison—he craved it, almost as much as he craved the drugs. He wanted the safety prison gave him. Inside, he had regular meals, clean clothes, heating, and a bed to sleep in at night. In many ways, it felt safer than the prison his house had become.

Alan stared at the walls, closing in around him—the damp seeping through the plaster, ripped curtains swaying from the rail like shredded tissues. Drug paraphernalia littered the floor—used needles, and syringes, skins, rolled up balls of tin foil, and spent matches. On all fours, ignoring the cramping spasms in his stomach, he crawled across the floor in search of an escape from reality. He needed something, anything, to take the edge off his jitters. But he was wasting his time. He knew those bastards would have left him nothing.

His mates weren't 'friends', they were hangers on—leeches, using him and his flat as somewhere to get stoned. They had first latched on to him when his gran had been diagnosed with dementia. Poor old soul hadn't known if it was New Year or New York, and they had threatened to hurt her if he didn't let them use the flat as their base. Bastards, that's what they were, scummy bastards. A little voice inside his head told him he was just as bad as they were for not standing up to them, for not looking out for his gran.

His gran was long gone now. Somebody must have grassed him up to the social. One of them came knocking on his door, demanding to see his gran. He had tried his best to deflect the social worker's shock at the state of the house and of his gran. He had done his best to keep on top of things, to look after her, he had protested, but his words had fallen on deaf ears. The social worker had bandied about words like vulnerable adults and adult protection. Alan had to draw on his full charm reserve to convince her his gran was not at risk, and he'd just been struggling to care for her as her dementia advanced.

He *had* tried his best, he reminded himself, but those bastards had made it clear they were his priority, not his gran. And so the poor old dear had languished away in the back room. It had been a relief when the social worker had assessed her as needing to move into care. At least she would be safe from them. Alan screwed his eyes shut at the memory of telling his gran she was just going on a wee holiday, her gnarled old hand clutching his, begging him not to let them take her away. He never saw her again.

It hadn't been the end of it though, the social worker had come back, sticking her nose in. She wanted to know how he was coping.

"Get rid of her," one of his new mates had growled, not wanting to lose their base. He had briefly considered taking the chance, telling her the truth and finding a way out of his mess, but the lure of the drugs proved too much for him and, once again, slipped neatly under the radar.

He only had himself to blame for where he was now. He had no pity for himself—he didn't deserve it. A solitary tear slid down his cheek, freedom was killing him, he had only been out of prison a couple of months, and he already knew he wouldn't last much longer.

Alan would have robbed again to wangle a return to prison, but the woman in the library, Morag, had taken him under her wing. Morag had found him prowling outside her house one night. He'd been looking for a way in. He had tried to run but Morag was stronger than she looked. To his surprise, she hadn't called the police. Instead, she had taken him into the house, fed him, and gave him some money. Alan couldn't remember the last time anyone had treated him with such kindness, the last time anyone had cared enough—had cared about him.

Morag wasn't like others in the town. She didn't look down her nose at him. She had welcomed him into the library and listened to him—properly listened. She had even persuaded him to stay for one of her group meetings, and he had gone back every week since. Somewhere to stay warm, a respite from his mates. He laughed to himself. A group. What sort of a wanker goes to 'a group'?

Alan stayed quiet about it in front of his mates. He didn't need to guess what their reaction would be. Secretly, he had enjoyed going along on a Tuesday morning—he had felt like he belonged. But even in the state he was in, Alan realised something wasn't quite right about the relationship between them both. Morag had become needier, always on at him to go round to her house for dinner, wanting to feed him up. Never one to pass up on a free meal, he had been happy to go along with it, but lately she had started to creep him out. Calling him son, wanting him to stay overnight, and full of talk of them being family and being together forever.

As the months had gone on she began to confide in him, little things at first about her mum, about her family, about her past. He had to admit some of the things she told him had freaked him out a little, he'd never have guessed it looking at her. Not wanting to give up his free meal ticket, he had played along with her, but then something had opened his eyes to Morag's level of manipulation. *She* had opened his eyes. He quickly realised life with Morag would be just as dangerous as life out here with his mates. *She* had persuaded him he had only one way to escape it all.

Alan had wanted to slip away quietly, unnoticed. But *she* had convinced him otherwise. She had a plan and if he agreed to go along with it, she had promised him the trip of a lifetime, the last trip he would ever have to take. All he had to do was give up his secrets, a cheap price to pay for the gear she had given him. *There's more where that came from, I've got something that will blow your mind, take you on a trip you never want to come back from. All you need to do is tell me.* Unable to turn down one final glorious hit, Alan had done as she asked.

He had gone to the library and slipped the note inside the book just before closing time. *You need to teach her a lesson,* her voice had whispered to him. *She has used you and she will keep on using you until she destroys you.*

THE CRAMPS WERE growing worse now, he needed something and he needed it quick. He huddled in the corner of the room. He was rattling, the rats gnawing at his flesh as the cravings intensified. He started to drift in and out of reality—his vision blurring as memories flitted in and out his mind like some kind of horror movie. The shadows in the room were morphing into monsters. It was almost time. His bedroom door opened and the sound of footsteps clipped across the floor. A pair of feet appeared by his head. He could hear her words crystal clear, his angel.

"Shh Alan. It's going to be okay now. I'm here." She'd whispered, as she had placed a small package under his mattress. "I promise, I won't tell a soul."

He had wrapped the tourniquet around his arm. Safe injection methods were the furthest thought from his mind as he picked up the dirty syringe lying on the floor. He drew it back, and watched as the answers to his prayers filled the grubby barrel.

He sank back into the mattress and closed his eyes. *Shit, this stuff is good.* The echo of her footsteps faded as the front door clicked over. Would she come back with more? He smiled, it didn't matter anymore—he wouldn't need it now, not where he was going.

Alan closed his eyes and welcomed the oblivion that sucked him under. One last time.

Five

Jess

TWENTY-FOUR YEAR old Jess Wishart stood behind the counter of Café Marianna's, watching the customers as they trooped through the door—the relief clear on their faces as they hurried in out of the cold. It might be bitter outside, but inside the cafe was like a furnace with the coffee machine and grills on their never-ending conveyer belt of serving.

Jess pushed a strand of lank hair away from her face as she welcomed the short blast of cold air slipping in with each new customer. Her regulars, along with some new faces, filled the small space, and she groaned at the prospect of yet another shift serving an endless line of caffeine-deprived addicts. The eternal crash of metal against metal, the satisfying spurt of steam escaping the coffee machine drawing them in.

"Sitting in or taking away?" Tap, tap, tap.

"Small, medium or large?" Tap, tap, tap.

"Would you like some of our special roast today?" Tap, tap, tap.

"Anything else for you?" Tap, tap, tap.

The same chat every day, alongside the constant hissing and tapping from the coffee machines. Jess went through the motions, making the appropriate facial expressions and noises in response to the same phrases she heard on repeat, day after day, hour after hour, minute after minute. Occasionally broken up by a snippet of small town gossip or one of the lonely regulars looking for a chat to fill their empty days. None of it interested her. Her responses were vague and bland.

She pictured her mum's face. "I'll bet this wasn't the life you imagined for me mum, was it?" She wiped away a tear as she thought about how her life could have turned out. Her mum had been gone a long time now, and the life Jess had once known had disappeared along with her. No point dwelling on the past, she mulled, as she put on her best smile and carried on with pretending she gave a toss about the customers waiting.

Jess hated her job in Café Marianna's—a small café on the main street of Lennoxhill. Well, that wasn't strictly true. She didn't hate it, it just bored her, she was overworked, undervalued and underpaid. Marion, the owner, took advantage of her good nature—she hardly ever showed face until the morning rush had passed, and was far too tight to employ another assistant, so the graft was left to Jess.

She rolled her eyes and yawned as she looked at the queue of customers—it was never ending. She smiled wanly at the next in line, as she reminded herself the job was just a means to an end, she wouldn't be there forever. She had come to Lennoxhill in search of something, and although things hadn't quite worked out as she had wanted, Jess remained determined to stay there and see it through. Whatever it took.

"C-c-can I have a small coffee please?"

Jess recognised the nasally twang of the local weirdo, Ronnie. She looked up. It was him. He stood at the counter fidgeting as usual and rocking from one foot to the other.

Ronnie had latched onto her not long after she moved to the area. She felt sorry for him but at the same time found his neediness irritating and, today, she didn't have the time nor the inclination to indulge him. Noticing the grubby rag serving as a bandage wrapped round his hand Jess nodded in his direction but made no attempt to engage him in any conversation about his injury. However, Ronnie had other ideas.

"It was there this morning, Jess. I saw it… I saw it there." His voice was low. He thrust his bandaged arm towards her.

Jess leaned backwards, trying to avoid any contact with the grubby bandage. "Did you Ronnie? That's great. One pound seventy-five please." She tapped her fingers against the counter.

"But Jess, it was there… in my garden… it was… it made me…" He spun round, as though searching the café for whoever it was he believed to be following him, before turning back to her, his eyes wide, the panic clear on his face. He waved his arm closer to again, and she shrunk back, wrinkling her nose at the smell emanating from it.

"Ronnie, I'm a bit busy this morning. The money for your drink please, eh?" She cut him off before he started rambling again. Jess was used to Ronnie's paranoia and obsessions. If it wasn't someone following him, he would be prattling on about bloody Morag from the library. She could see he was more agitated than usual this morning but she wasn't in the mood for indulging his paranoia today.

Jess watched as he hovered nervously, stepping from one foot to the other, his pupils darting around the cafe, looking to see if anyone was listening to him. All he needed was the tin foil hat, she thought unkindly. Jess held out her hand, wishing he would hurry up and pay for his coffee and leave. He wouldn't hang around long today.

"Ronnie, its one pound seventy-five for your coffee." She pushed her hand further out and stared pointedly at the clock. "And it's already ten to ten, Ronnie. You're gonna be late if you don't get a shift on."

"Late. Can't be late. It's Tuesday. Can't be late." He threw the change on the counter, grabbed his coffee and shuffled out the door, still muttering under his breath.

Jess smirked. He sounded like the bloody White Rabbit from Alice in Wonderland. Today was his group meeting at the library. He never missed it, and would have a meltdown at the mere thought of being late.

Jess had tagged along to the group with him not long after she had moved to Lennoxhill. She had stood hovering about at the edge, watching Morag welcome everyone along and fussing over them. Following Ronnie's lead, Jess had sat down to join in. She would never admit it to anyone, but she missed being a part of a family and wanted someone to fuss over her too. But Morag had pointedly ignored her all through the meeting, other than asking her to introduce herself. She had also shifted the seating around, making sure Ronnie wasn't sitting next to her.

When the group had finished, Morag had approached Jess and told her, in a sharp tone, that the group was full, and they had no space for new members. At the time, Jess had brushed off the obvious rejection, but inside it had hurt her deeply.

A movement caught her attention. She looked up and saw two women sitting in the corner table, it was Annie Boyle and Mary Martin. Jess folded her arms and watched as they stared at Ronnie's retreating figure, before looking over at her and pursing their lips in disapproval. Jess glared back at them. She had no time for the two women. They were nasty, bitter, small-minded gossips and tight with it. They came in most days and would spend the morning nursing one cup of coffee each and a cake between them.

Annie, the larger of the two women, rubbed her thumb against the vinyl tablecloth, as though trying to erase the bright sunflower pattern. Jess sensed the woman's eagerness to impart what she believed to be her words of wisdom.

Taking her eye contact as an opportunity to engage Jess, Annie sniffed loudly.

"See what happens when they close all the institutions? Care in the community they call it. It will have us all murdered in our beds, Mary, just you wait and see." Eyes narrowed she glanced back over at Jess as she said it, gauging her reaction. Jess didn't rise to the bait.

Mary nodded her agreement. "Aye, I know Annie. It's no right. People like him should be away for their own safety."

"Aye, closing down The Overton was the worst thing they ever did," grumbled Annie, before launching into a spiel about her time spent working in the old psychiatric hospital that had dominated Lennoxhill until it closed in the early 1980s.

Jess grinned, Annie Boyle had never been a nurse in her life. Marion had told her Annie had been a domestic in the hospital, and she had been moaning about its closure ever since she lost her job there and had never been able to find another position. Anyone listening to Annie would have thought she ran the place single-handedly.

"Deluded old bat," muttered Jess under her breath.

Annie spun round and snapped, "What did you say?"

"Nothing," smiled Jess. "Just wondering if you two ladies would like a top up?"

Annie huffed and turned her back on Jess.

Giving Annie a virtual two-fingered salute, Jess tried to bite down her irritation towards the woman. She hated judgemental people, and Lennoxhill seemed to be full of them. She only had to look at the reaction towards Ronnie to know that.

Jess had spent enough time on the wards to recognise all the classic signs of paranoid schizophrenia and understood Ronnie was at more risk of being hurt himself, than of him hurting anyone else. But that wasn't the way other people perceived it, especially people with small town mentalities like those two. She had tried before to explain this to Annie and Mary, but they were having none of it. 'Lock him, and the likes of him, up and throw away the key,' had been their response to her protestations. She didn't bother trying anymore, she left them to their ignorance. She had met plenty like them and knew she was wasting her energy trying to change their minds.

The door swung open and a small girl burst into the café. She ran up to the counter and threw a smile at Jess—a smile that would melt even the coldest of hearts.

"Can I have a big cake please, one wiff cream on the top?" The words tumbled out of her mouth as she pointed to the cakes on display. Behind the child stood a woman. Jess recognised her from around the town. She looked harassed as she tried to grab the child by the arm.

"Lily, I told you, stop running away from me, and no, you can't have a cream cake. We don't have enough..." The woman stopped abruptly, her face flushed. She smiled a weak apology in Jess's direction.

"Sorry, she's a bit over excited this morning. Don't know what got into her. Come on Lily." She grabbed the child again. "Can we just have one of those please?" She pointed to the cheapest cake on the counter, fishing out some coins from her purse.

"It's okay." Jess returned the woman's smile. She could see the stress beneath the half-hearted grin.

Jess studied the woman's face. Behind her pretty features, she looked a bit like a rabbit caught in headlights. She had been into the café plenty of times with that woman from the library. *Another one of her bloody weirdos*, thought Jess, *what draws them all to her? Everyone apart from me.*

She returned her attention to the woman in front of her, remembering overhearing her talk to Morag about her ex-husband, the child's father. She remembered thinking at the time, he sounded like a right bastard.

Uncharacteristically, Jess felt a rush of pity for the woman, clearly struggling to make ends meet, and on her own with a kid. It couldn't be easy.

"You okay?" Jess offered

The woman's eyes widened at Jess's question, but she nodded hesitantly.

"You don't look okay. Anything I can do? I'm Jess by the way." She thrust her hand across the counter and then snatched it back again. What a twat, who shakes hands these days? Her face coloured.

The woman threw her a grateful smile. "Thanks, er… I'm Susan. Sorry, I think we're just having one of those days. Lily here is a bit hyper today. Kids eh."

"Yeah, don't envy you that. Not got any myself, but I guess it must be hard, especially if you're on your own and that?"

Susan's eyes dropped to the floor, and she muttered something Jess could not quite make out.

"Sorry, I didn't mean to be nosey. But listen, if you ever need anyone to talk to, you can usually find me in here."

Susan smiled gratefully and nodded. She turned to leave the café.

Stuffing a cream cake into a brown paper bag, Jess thrust it across the counter.

"Here, give it to the kid."

Susan's face flushed. "I can't... I don't... honestly, please, it's okay."

"It's on the house," Jess winked. "Go on, my treat. I won't tell anyone if you don't."

Lily having witnessed this transaction between the two grownups stood with a look of expectation on her face, eyes wide as she stared at the brown paper bag containing the cake she so desperately wanted.

"Go on, take it, please, I can't sell it now anyway. It's second hand." She winked again.

This time Susan's face broke into a smile. A genuine smile. It gave Jess a small rush of pleasure. It was not often anyone showed her any gratitude.

"Thank you. Thank you so much. Lily say thank you to the nice lady please."

"Thank you, nice lady."

Jess laughed. "You're welcome. But don't be telling everyone, you'll get me the sack."

She watched them leave the café and a small pang of jealousy hit her. At least she has the kid. At least she has somebody.

The morning rush finally over, Jess poured herself a cup of tea— nice and strong with two sugars. *Builder's tea.* She smiled, just the way... then it dawned on her, he hadn't been in for his usual order this morning. 'He' being one of the Tuesday Club, as she called them.

She recalled seeing him the day before when he had come in looking for food. She had given him a bacon roll and tea on the house, loving getting one over on her tight-fisted boss. Marion would be furious if she knew Jess was giving her profits away, especially to someone like Alan. Everyone in Lennoxhill knew Alan, and everyone avoided him like the plague due to his addictions, but Jess had a bit of a soft spot for him. Nobody got themselves in that sort of state unless they were trying to escape from something inside their heads. She used to give him the leftovers after the morning rush, always under the guise of shooing him out the front door before pressing a bag of food into his hand. Annie and Mary would have taken great delight in grassing her up to Marion if they had caught her.

The café had grown quiet. Jess looked around. Apart from the two women gossiping in the corner, the place was empty. She guessed from the pursed lips and nodding heads that Annie and Mary were too caught up in their chatter to want anything else from her right now. Deciding to give herself a well-earned rest, Jess plonked herself down at the table next to the counter with her tea. She pulled her phone from the pocket of her grubby tabard, and scrolled through her social media feeds, biting down her jealousy at the perfect lives of the people she followed online, or the lives they liked to say they lived. She hated them all, liars and fakes, every single one of them.

When she had finished here, people were going to remember her, and at least they would remember her for being real. Her phone flashed, the icon indicating an unread text message—it had come through late last night. Probably another one of those ambulance chasers or someone offering her a PPI claim. Hardly anyone ever texted her. She opened it up, ready to delete it when the name of the sender made her stop. She read it, twice to make sure.

"It's started, Mum. Payback has begun," she whispered.

Six

Morag

HER HAND FLEW to her mouth and her eyes darted around the library, expecting to see the writer of the note staring back out at her from behind the shelves, or to hear her colleagues sneer at her stupidity at falling for a silly hoax. But she was the only person there. She already knew that.

Morag clutched the sheet of paper and swallowed down the lump in her throat and cursed her own stupidity. She had let her guard down, she was too trusting, that was her problem. Her mother's voice whispered, *you stupid bitch, did you really think you could keep that secret forever.* The note fell from her shaking hands and fluttered to the floor. Had he finally done it? Killed himself?

The clock was ticking, Morag ignored the impulse to grab her stuff and run. Her days of running were over. Her library was due to open up soon. People needed her.

Hands trembling, she clicked on the library management system. Her fingers ran over the keyboard bringing up a list of borrowers. If she could find out who had last checked out this book she might be able to confirm who had written the note.

She called up the book title, scanning the list of borrowers, but nobody had taken it out recently, which meant someone had deliberately come into the library and left the note in the book, placing it on the table for her to find. She was the only person who worked early on a Tuesday morning, the others weren't due in until eleven. Any regular visitor to the library would know this. Someone had wanted her to find it. Morag had an idea who had written the note, but she wouldn't be able to confirm it until the group started.

If one of them didn't turn up, she would know for sure who had written the note.

Her spine tingled as she heard her mother's voice grate in her ears. *See, nobody needs you girl. Nobody cares whether you are here or not. Stupid little girl. No wonder you are on your own after everything you have done.*

She put her hands over her ears to drown out her mother's taunts. Her eyes flickered as she ran through the faces of the library visitors. There were so many but only three of them mattered to Morag. Her fingers worked anxiously at the cuff of her jumper, time was running out for her, she couldn't stand the thought of her mother's words becoming the truth.

Feeling faint, Morag slumped to the chair. She sat for a moment before rushing back to the staff room. Hands trembling, she unlocked her locker and reached for her bag, rummaging about the contents. Her hand settled on the photograph. She took it out her bag and held it against her cheek. Her heart settled. It was still there, all would be well. It was a good omen, wasn't it? They wouldn't have left her. They couldn't have left her.

She breathed a gentle kiss to the photograph and placed it carefully back into her bag. She clasped the bag to her chest and gave a small silent prayer of thanks to a God she did not believe in.

Trying to quell her growing anxiety, Morag put her bag back in the locker and busied herself getting ready for opening and more importantly for her group. When Morag first started working in the library she watched people.

Morag liked to watch people, that's how she found her special ones. The ones who needed her. She watched the customers who came in day after day, the ones with nowhere to go and nobody to talk to, and the ones like her. The idea of the group came to her as she tried to come up with ways to connect with them, ways that would not get her into bother like before. Her manager, though, had not been so keen on the idea, reminding her, her job was to deal with books and not solve the town's social problems. "You're not a bloody social worker Morag, you're a librarian," he had snapped.

Morag hadn't given up though. Giving up wasn't in her nature, and she had persisted until her manager had agreed, with the stark warning that it would be her responsibility and she couldn't expect extra pay for setting it up or running it. Morag hadn't been looking for extra money, she had been looking for something much deeper.

Her manager's reaction had set her opinion of him in stone. She had always believed him to be arrogant and lacking compassion and this simply confirmed it. She suspected he didn't think much of her either, and that he wasn't alone in his views. Morag cringed as she recalled some of the things she'd overheard her colleagues saying about her.

Plenty of times, she had gone into the staff room only for the conversation to stop abruptly. She refused to let them see it bothered her. She had spent most of her life as the butt of other people's gossip.

Oh, but you do care, don't you Morag? Her mother's voice came from within her head.

"I do not," she retorted. "Just you wait and see Mother. I'll show you. I will have a family who needs me."

Morag shook her head. *You're going absolutely bat shit crazy, having imaginary conversations with your dead mother.* She laughed. If they could all see her now, they would nod their heads—her behaviour affirming their view of her as a crazy old woman.

When she had returned to Lennoxhill, Morag had been determined to put her past behind her. She just wanted to be normal, just like everyone else. She had made a real effort to be friendly. She bristled as she recalled how she would take the other girls in treats and not just any old treat. Morag had gone out of her way to find out the things her colleagues liked, their favourite perfume, chocolates, and music. She always took the time to complement their hair, their clothes or the way they looked. She had even gone out of her way to go to the same hairdressers as they did, to visit the same shops. Yes, she thought, she had tried her very best to make friends. But it hadn't been enough for them. Their whispers in the staff room, the closing down of any conversation she started or tried to join in, invitations to nights out dried up completely. Morag hadn't worried about that, Mother would never have allowed her to go on a night out. But she could not work out why her colleagues had turned their backs on her efforts to make friends.

Over the years, she had grown used to her own company, but it didn't take away her aching loneliness. After her mother had died, returning home to the empty house had just compounded her loneliness. Returning to an empty house, night after night, had not been the life she had planned for herself. All she wanted from life was to be accepted and for someone to need her for a change. She didn't think she was asking for a lot. So why did everyone continue to let her down, why didn't they understand? They knew what it felt like to be on the outside looking in, to feel you didn't belong anywhere. They needed her. Didn't they?

Morag looked up at the clock: one minute until opening time. She grabbed the keys, plastered on what she hoped would pass as a welcoming smile, and made her way to the front door to open up. Pleased to see a small queue of people already forming, she opened the doors with hope in her heart.

The small crowd shuffled in, their faces showing their relief at getting inside and away from the sharp nip in the air. Morag watched them all fondly, smiling a greeting at each person as they came through the door. She knew their habits and watched them as they each gravitated towards their preferred area of the library.

Old Helen Boyce made her way straight to the home and garden section. Morag smiled, Helen lived in the small block of maisonettes at the edge of the town, where the debris of her neighbours' lives adorned the small concrete block that served as a garden. She also knew Helen lived on a small pension and depended on the reduced section at the supermarket to see her through the week. She came to the library to escape into her imagination.

Graham Smith came through the doors next. He had once been the proud proprietor of the long closed down "Writers Arms" pub. Graham loved to relay tales of the writing groups he had run in the pub until the combination of the smoking ban and minimum pricing of alcohol proved to be final nail in the coffin for his ever-dwindling profits. Profits that hadn't been helped by his fondness for supplying his friends with a never ending source of free beer. The pub was now a fancy wine bar called The Lennox Arms. With no job and little else, to pass his time, Graham was a regular visitor to the library where he always headed straight for the crime fiction section. Another one, who used imagination and escapism to flee the reality of life.

Then there were the twins, a strange pair, Katie and Katrina, ethereal in appearance, Morag knew little about them other than they appeared to exist in their own little world. They came along to the group every week but never joined in. She had tried hard to befriend them, sensing a vulnerability about the girls but they had rejected all her offers of friendship, preferring to keep their own company. Shame, thought Morag, they would have been ideal.

Morag was pleased to see Jess, from the café on the Main Street, was not among the crowd. She had been so persistent a few months ago, trying to wheedle her way in, but something about the girl caused Morag's hackles to rise, and she had done her best to show her the cold shoulder. She didn't need the likes of Jess coming along and spoiling her group.

As the small group spread out to their own little worlds, Morag stood behind the counter anxiously awaiting *her* customers: Susan, Alan and Ronnie. Her family. Ten minutes late, Morag's fists clenched tightly at her side and she chewed at her lip. She reached into her pocket and rooted around for the note she had stuffed there earlier. Finding it, she clutched it tightly unable to ignore the overwhelming feeling of dread building up in her stomach.

The sound of soft footsteps approaching caused her to glance up and a huge grin of relief spread across her face as Ronnie slouched towards her.

"Ronnie, I'm so glad you are here," she gushed.

She beamed at him taking in his wringing hands and jittery body language. He was more agitated than usual.

"Are you okay, love? What happened to your hand?" She looked at the grubby handkerchief acting as a makeshift bandage around his hand, her eyes widening at the sight of fresh blood seeping through the dirt. "Do you need that looking at?"

Ronnie yanked his hand away, stuffing it in his jacket pocket. He shook his head and his eyes dropped to his feet before looking up and scanning the library. His fingers were picking at his clothes, and she could see a nervous tic at the side of his eye. Something had obviously spooked him today. Morag laid her hand gently on his arm.

"Ronnie?" she whispered.

He stared up at her and she recognised his panic, his body dancing a nervous jig.

"I thought it was there this morning. I thought she had sent it after me. In the garden. I saw it. Waiting for me!"

His face was inches away from hers, his voice shrill. She took care not to recoil at his breath. She had to keep his trust. She knew exactly how to deal with this.

"Has it gone now love?"

He nodded. "Yes, I took my knife out... It r-r-ran," he stuttered, as though not quite convinced he was telling her the truth himself.

"Oh, Ronnie love. You need to be a bit more careful, you know that, don't you? You can't go running about the garden with a knife. Did your mother see you, Ronnie?"

Her words came out a little harsher than she had meant. Ronnie flinched as he shook his head, backing off.

He mumbled something unintelligible, his eyes trained on his tattered old trainers, scuffing across the floor.

Damn, I've scared him.

She approached him slowly, careful not to frighten him further. She had to take things slowly with Ronnie or he would close down completely.

Laying her hand gently on his arm, she reached up and whispered gently into his ear.

"Don't let your mother see you with the knife Ronnie. You know what happened last time?" She fixed him with a meaningful stare.

At her words, Ronnie shuddered. Morag laid her hand on his arm again, though her touch was a little firmer this time.

"Why don't you take a seat Ronnie and I'll make you a wee cuppa, eh?"

He peeked at his watch. "It's not eleven o'clock yet. Tea is at eleven. They will see if you break the rules." His voice still had a sense of rising panic about it.

"Shh, it's okay Ronnie. Remember? I told you—they can't see what happens in here. I'm in charge in here, Ronnie. It's our safe space…"

"Safe space," he repeated slowly.

Morag busied herself making Ronnie a cup of tea. She kept an eye on him as she stirred the sugar into his cup. Her warning about his mother seemed to have done the trick. He had followed her over to the chairs and sat where she had told him to. *Such a good boy*, she thought, as she stirred the sugar into the tea.

He had been visiting the library for as long as she had been there and others had told her he'd been coming long before that. She hadn't liked their tone when they talked about Ronnie. Their mockery of his unkempt appearance, the words 'psycho' and 'nutcase' often accompanied any tales they had about him. Most people crossed the street to avoid him if they saw him coming. Not her though. No, she had taken the time to get to know him, to nurture him, to build up his trust and he was almost ready to become part of her family.

But lately she had sensed a change in Ronnie. He had become more distant as though his mind and his thoughts were elsewhere. *And not on you.* Just as she thought she had him where she wanted it felt as though she was losing him. Even her threats of his mother to control him were beginning to lose their power. She suspected the girl from the café had something to do with it all. She had seen him hanging round the café, sniffing round the little bitch and now his chat was usually full of what Jess had said, and what Jess liked. Morag felt her fingers grasp the handle of the spoon tighter. Little trollop, batting her eyelashes at him, trying to take him away from her.

A splash of boiling water on her hand jolted her out of her thoughts. She hadn't realised she'd been stirring quite so briskly.

Smiling, she walked over to Ronnie, taking him his tea and one of his favourite chocolate biscuits, relieved the note hadn't come from him. He still needed her. It wouldn't have done for him to leave her just yet, would it?

She left Ronnie drinking his tea and taking comfort from his familiar surroundings. Another glance at the clock only seemed to confirm that time was slowing down, her stomach clenched in knots and she drummed her fingers against the counter. Where were Susan and Alan?

The library doors burst opened and in rushed a brightly coloured bundle of chaos.

"Missus Library Lady… guess what?" The bundle rushed out a stream of words as she ran towards Morag.

Dressed in pink leggings and a bright green jacket that had clearly done the tour of all the charity shops before it had ended up on her back, she had a ring of cake crumbs around her little mouth, which flashed a wide smile, displaying a row of tiny baby teeth. It was difficult not to notice the paleness of the child's skin and the dark shadows circling those big blue eyes—circles that didn't belong on a child so young.

Morag's heart contracted, she yearned to reach out and touch the child, to take her hand… but she couldn't. Not yet. Pulling herself together, she smiled back at the little girl, trying to ignore the tight grip her mother had on her.

"Good morning, Lily sweetheart. What are you wanting me to guess today? Is it that you have just had a cake?" Morag laughed as she leaned forward to wipe away the crumbs from Lily's mouth, but inside she was judging a mother who thought it appropriate to feed a child cake for breakfast.

Lily laughed.

"No Missus Library Lady. Well yes. I had cake, but guess why we are late… guess… can you guess? The man came to see mummy yesterday and he told her she could…"

Her words were cut off by her mother's sharp tone.

"Lily," Susan snapped. "What have I told you about being such a tittle tattle? Come here, now!"

Morag raised her glance and saw Susan's face flush red. Morag couldn't quite work out if it was with anger or embarrassment. Susan dragged the child roughly by the wrist, offering Morag a small, apologetic smile.

Inside Morag fumed. How dare that woman treat her child like that? She ought to be grateful she had a child. But a part of Morag was also intrigued as to what Lily had been about to disclose. Masking her face with a smile, she welcomed Susan and Lily anyway.

"Come away in out the cold, you two. It won't be long until the group starts, that's everyone almost here now." She lowered her voice to a conspiratorial whisper. "I've got a wee treat for you both in my bag for later." She winked as she directed them across to the area of the library where the Blether group met.

It was a little after eleven now and still Alan had not appeared. Morag desperately wanted to leave—to rush over and check on him. But she couldn't, she had the group to run and none of her colleagues would help her out. Her loyalty torn, Morag spent the next few minutes moving between the group and the door, before she had to give in and admit defeat.

She spent the morning on autopilot, going through the motions. At the end of the session, she pushed some food parcels into Susan's hands, reassuring her they were leftovers. Morag suspected Susan knew she was lying, but she didn't care. She made a mental note to take the two of them for lunch at the café one day soon, and try to probe a little more about what the child had said.

Rushing over to her colleague, Lynn MacDonald, she announced she was taking her lunch break. Lynn shrugged her shoulders and grunted something that sounded like "Whatever", her eyes glued to her phone.

Morag glanced back at Susan, Lily and Ronnie. Ronnie appeared mesmerised by Lily's antics and had a wide grin on his face, while Susan stared at the phone in her hand. *What's she up to?*

She didn't have time to find out right now, first she had to find out why Alan hadn't appeared and then she would turn her attention to Susan.

Seven

Morag

OUTSIDE THE LIBRARY, Morag pulled her scarf tighter around her neck and stuffed her hands into her pockets as the cold snatched her breath. Anxious to get to Alan's flat she scurried along the street, then turned right and stepped straight out onto Barrhill Road, narrowly avoiding being hit by a white transit van. She didn't hear the horn blasting, nor did she see the two fingered salute from the driver. Morag could only think about getting to Alan's flat before anyone else. Hurrying through the streets with apprehension gripping her stomach, her gut instinct screamed what she already knew. She quickened her pace until she was almost running.

At the end of the road, she turned right into Waterside Road, which took her into the Waterside estate. She slowed a little, it wasn't the most salubrious of areas in Lennoxhill and she didn't want to draw any unnecessary attention to herself by running along the street like some crazy woman. She clutched her bag a little bit tighter, it wouldn't do for someone to mug her and steal her precious belongings.

Morag stopped outside the four-in-a-block at the top end of Waterside Road and stared up at the window at the top left. She could see no sign of life. A tattered bed sheet served as a curtain remained motionless, and no prying eyes peered out onto the street below. Morag grimaced at the debris littering the streets. *Thank God, I didn't end up somewhere like this.* She gave thanks that her parents had at least had the foresight to buy a house in the Rosehill estate at the outskirts of the town. *At least they got something right.*

Soiled nappies, used condoms and discarded toys formed a small mountain in the middle of what served as a garden. She could even see a couple of used syringes peeking out the pile of rubbish. She shuddered at the idea of children growing up in a place like this. An image of Susan and Lily living here popped into her head and her heart lurched at the thought of that wee girl growing up in a place like this. Although she had only known Susan a short while, she believed she knew enough about her to know the estate was not the kind of place she had been used to. Morag could not imagine Susan adapting to life here and all that it entailed.

Looking around again, Morag shook her head in despair, it was all wrong. Where were the social workers, the support agencies? The police? Where were the families looking out for each other? Nobody cared anymore, nobody acted until it was too late and then the headlines all screamed. *Lessons would be learned.* But Morag knew better, professionals did not seem to learn their lessons and carried on making the same mistakes repeatedly. She should know. She could hear her mother in her ear, chiding her for getting herself involved in things that were none of her business. Morag pushed the voice away, her mother had a cheek, *she* was still interfering in *her* life, even now.

Making her way into the close, she stepped gingerly over the used needles and wrinkled her nose against the stench of stale urine and god knows what else. Alan's flat was on the top floor and she climbed the stairs as fast as she could, praying she would not meet anyone on the stairwell. As she glanced at the closed doors, Morag could hardly imagine the lives behind them, she pictured the wasted bodies of addicts lying waiting for their next fix, hungry kids crying in filthy cots. Her upper lip curled as she almost ran up the middle of the stairs avoiding contact with anything solid. How could anyone live like this?

Reaching Alan's door, she knocked tentatively, before taking a step backwards and listening for signs of life. There was no reply. Not a sound came from the flat. Reaching out to try the handle, she stopped. Should she really be doing this? What if someone was inside, someone who wasn't Alan? What if she was putting herself in danger?

"Oh for goodness' sake Morag," she scolded herself. "You are a grown woman. You have been here plenty of times before. You will be fine."

She took a deep breath and tried the handle, not surprised to find the door unlocked. She sighed, Alan never paid any heed to her warnings about keeping himself safe and locking his door. She pushed the door open and stepped inside.

"Alan?" she called, gently. "It's me, Morag... Morag from the library."

Nothing. She had not really expected a reply.

She peered into the living room first but, even in the dim light, she could see the room was empty, other than one large cushion and a scattering of syringes and tinfoil. She pulled the door closed. The kitchen came next—a pile of empty beer cans and half-eaten takeaways littered the floor. She moved onto the bathroom, where the stench caused her to gag. But still no sign of Alan. That left one room, his bedroom.

Bracing herself, she took a deep breath and pushed the door open. Morag held onto the door for support as she took in the sight before her. Alan lay face down on a mattress on the floor. Her eyes filled as she saw the needle hanging from his arm. She moved closer. His face was softer, relaxed even, as though he had escaped the dark, dark place he had inhabited for so long.

She brushed her lips against his cold blue face before pulling back and slapping him hard

"Who have you told, you stupid, stupid boy? You've ruined everything. I'd have taken care of you. You needed me. You told me you needed me."

She wanted to shake him awake, to rewind the clock, and take back her secrets. Instead, she took a small pair of nail scissors from her bag and snipped off a lock of his lank, brown hair. She wrapped it up tightly in the note she had found in the library and shoved it to the bottom of her bag. She would keep that for later.

Morag tidied up a little before calling for an ambulance. She did not want anyone else judging Alan, she didn't want them seeing what she could see. She didn't have to wait too long for the emergency services to arrive. She heard the thud of their boots as they traipsed up the stairs to the flat, as though there was a sense of inevitability about Alan's death. No importance or significance given to the waste of a life, no words of comfort were forthcoming. Just straight down to business.

"Was there anyone else in the flat when you arrived?" the young constable had asked Morag once they had formally declared Alan dead. The paramedics had ushered her out of his room, telling her to wait in the living room, they were oblivious to her need to be with him.

"No, just me." She wiped away a tear.

"Are you a relative, love?" He offered her a tissue.

"No, I'm the librarian. Alan used to come along to our group on a Tuesday. One of our regulars, never missed a week. I knew something was wrong when he didn't turn up this morning."

"Librarian? Do you always visit your customers at home?" His eyebrows raised.

Morag smiled. "No, not as such, but Alan was different. He had no one to look out for him. Someone had to take an interest. Nobody else cared. He was just another addict to all the services around here. Just another junkie. But they didn't know him like I did, he was a good kid underneath all this." She indicated their grim surroundings. "He had a sorry background, what with his mum and dad dying when he was a kid, then in and out of care until he found his gran. Then when she moved into nursing home and died..." Morag's voice choked.

"What can you do, eh?" The constable shrugged his shoulders.

Morag stiffened at his tone. She did not like his attitude at all— he was just like all the rest. He didn't care. This was just a job to him. She bit down her frustration at his cavalier attitude as he continued.

"I don't suppose you know if he had any other relatives?"

"No, I told you, he had nobody. Apart from me. The only others were the wasters who hung around and used him. He hadn't been long released from prison, you know? They were sniffing around within hours of him getting home. I tried to tell him they were no good for him. But... well... he didn't listen. I guess he must have thought they were better than nobody. And now look..." She swallowed down her tears.

"Yeah, Alan was well known down at the station. A bit of a character, and a bit of a poor soul too." He shrugged. "But people make their own choice in life don't they? Nobody forces them to do this... Mrs... sorry I didn't get your name?"

"It's Miss... Miss Morag McLaughlin."

"Thanks. Well, Miss McLaughlin, I'll need you to give us a statement. We can do it today down at the station, or I can get one of my colleagues to come and take it at your house if that's easier?"

Morag shook her head. "No, I'll come to the station if you don't mind. I can come down this afternoon. I don't think I could face going back to work today. Not after this..."

The tears began to flow freely down her cheeks. She could sense his discomfort, he didn't know where to look, clearly not sure what to do with a middle aged woman in floods of tears.

He placed a hand awkwardly on her arm. "Is there anyone I can contact for you, to sit with you?" he asked, attempting to inject some kindness into his tone.

"No... there's nobody. Just me. A bit of a loner myself really." She smiled. "Like Alan, but without the addiction. That's why I liked to look out for him."

TWO HOURS LATER, Morag had left the station having given her statement. The nice young female constable she spoke to seemed satisfied with the information Morag had given her, and she had even made sure she got a cup of tea and a biscuit. She had been much more sympathetic than her colleague had. Morag left making a mental note to find out what the funeral arrangements were—she wanted to say goodbye properly, it was the right thing to do for family.

Eight

Susan

SUSAN LOOKED UP, trying hard to ignore the tremor in her hands causing her phone to shake. There had been fifteen new messages when she had turned her phone back on after the group finished. Fifteen messages. All from him. All demanding a reply. His final message had given her to the end of the week to give him an answer. A bead of sweat formed on her forehead, what real choice did she have?

She watched Lily, and questioned again if she had made the right decision taking her away from her old life. Maybe if she went back, maybe if she spoke to him, maybe… she shook her head. Going back to Colin wasn't an option, he would never change. And as for talking to him, that was a joke. No, if she went back, she would be signing her own death warrant.

She glanced down at her phone again. Another message pinged through. It was him, not her ex, but him, reminding her she had four days to make her choice. A choice Susan knew would be a way to escape the mess she found herself in, but it was also a choice she didn't know if she had the stomach to make. How had she reached rock bottom so quickly?

She swallowed down the lump in her throat, stuffed the phone back in her bag, and looked over at her daughter. Lily was sitting beside that young guy, Ronnie, chattering away, oblivious to the fact he was giving her nothing in return. She watched them for a moment, smiling at just how easily kids accepted difference. Life was so simple for them. She wished she had the same outlook. She looked at Ronnie, trying not to screw up her face at his dishevelled and filthy appearance.

He was a bit odd but seemed harmless enough. Susan had seen him around the town centre but had always tried to avoid him if she could. She was ashamed of her reaction to him—the poor guy had never done anything to upset her, but the tension radiating from him had made her wary. It reminded her of Colin and his quick temper. His agitation when he came home from work, his irritation at her for any little thing—for not having dinner ready, for having the wrong dinner ready. She could never work out what he wanted and then he would...

A memory flashed before her eyes as she recalled one incident, when Lily was one, when he nearly... she pushed the memory away not wanting to remember how close to death she had come.

"Lily," she called. "Come back here now. Stop annoying the man before he..."

Lily turned towards her mother.

"I'm not annoying him, mummy. I'm telling him about the nice lady in the café who gave..."

"Lily, I told you, come over here now."

Lily's bottom lip began to tremble, her eyes threatened tears.

"Lily, *now* I said!"

"But mummy..."

"NOW!"

Heads around the library popped up, faces glowered, disturbed by her shout breaking their silence. A few disapproving tuts could be heard.

Susan's face flushed. "Lily," she hissed. "Come here this minute."

Lily reluctantly made her way over to Susan, but not before standing on her tiptoes and giving the young man a kiss on the cheek.

Susan saw him put his hand to his cheek and watched her daughter make her way over to her. He raised his eyes to meet hers and she recognised the hurt in them. Her cheeks burned as she saw him mouth 'thank you' at her daughter's retreating back.

He stood up and moved towards her. She recoiled in her seat. He must have sensed her apprehension. She watched him as he picked up his stuff, head drooped, and shuffled his way out the library. Her chin dropped to her chest.

"Come on, Lily. Let's go over to the park for an hour. Mummy's got a sore head and she needs some fresh air."

She could hear the frantic buzzing of her phone from inside her bag.

Nine

Jess

JESS TOOK ADVANTAGE of Marion's early return and told her boss she was taking a break. Marion's face had broken into a scowl, but she could hardly refuse, given that Jess had just agreed to stay on for the rest of the day.

"I'd love to know what she does with her time, because it sure as hell isn't spent on this place," Jess muttered to herself, as she threw her apron in the back shop. "I'll be back in an hour," she yelled to Marion, skipping out the door before her boss could reply.

She took a deep breath of fresh air, trying to clear away the smell of grease and cleaning fluid. It was a waste of time—she would need at least an hour under the shower to get rid of that lot. Jess nipped across to the park and sat on the bench at the furthest end, seeking some quiet time to collect her thoughts.

As she reached the bench, she spotted Morag hurrying away from the library towards the Waterside Estate. Even from this distance, she could tell from the woman's hunched up body language she was worried. She bit down a laugh as she watched a transit van almost hit her. It gave her a small sense of satisfaction.

Serves the stupid old cow right. Hope it's bad news she's got. See how she likes it, old bitch that she is.

Jess's fists clenched tightly at her side as she recalled her attempts to try to befriend the woman. Jess had moved to Lennoxhill in search of acceptance and belonging, but instead she had found herself living in a community so tight knit that a DNA sample was considered the only evidence of belonging there. With no family of her own, all she wanted was somewhere to belong.

Hunched up on the bench, the tears pricked at her eyelids, was she that unlovable? Was she that prickly, that even a sap like Morag wouldn't take her under her wing?

"Oh Mum," she cried. "What's wrong with me? What's wrong with wanting to belong? I'm not asking for the world am I? I'm not going to give up Mum, I promise you, I'm not a quitter, I won't let you down."

Lighting a cigarette, Jess sat back and inhaled deeply. The cloud of nicotine reminded her of her mum at the kitchen table of an evening, chain smoking as she filled Jess's head with the life they would have together. Her fingers flicked the lighter on and off as she found herself thinking about what might have been. She couldn't help thinking that despite everything, it would never have been this bad. 'Oh mum, I bloody miss you. I'd give anything to turn the clock back, if only...'

Jess sat up, giving herself a shake—she could not afford to let herself go down that road again, wallowing in self-pity got her nowhere. What was done, was done. She just had to make the best of it and focus on putting it all right for her mum's memory. Then she could move on, find some closure.

She dropped the cigarette to the ground and, ignoring the bins, she ground her heel against the cigarette end. Jess stood up to make her way back to the café, the thought of a long afternoon stretching out ahead of her. A small bundle careered into her legs, knocking her backwards back on to the bench.

"What the f..."

"Oh God, I'm so sorry. LILY!"

She recognised the woman from the café, Susan. Jess looked at her, her face red, as though she was about to burst into tears.

"Hey, it's okay. Just an accident, and no bones broken," she rubbed at her knee, hiding the grimace of pain. The kid had jarred her kneecap and it hurt, but one look at the other woman's face told her she had more on her mind than her kid running riot around the park.

"Hey, it's Susan, isn't it? I'm Jess. From the café. You were in this morning?"

Susan nodded, her eyes downcast, "Yeah, I remember. You gave Lily a cake. Thank you."

"No worries. Anytime. She's a wee cutie. Must be a handful on your own though, eh?"

"Yeah, you can say that again."

Jess glanced down at the other woman's hand clutched tightly around her mobile phone, which seemed to be taking on a life of its own with the vibrating she could hear coming from Susan's fist.

"Someone's popular, eh?" she grinned.

"No, no, nothing like that, just those sales calls…" Susan's face coloured as she said it, and Jess had a feeling she wasn't telling the truth.

"Never known them to be that persistent," Jess replied.

Susan shrugged.

"Listen, you can tell me to mind my own business if you want, but it seems like you've got more on your mind than unsolicited sales calls. You don't need to tell me what's going on, but if you ever need anyone to talk to just give me a shout, I'm always around and I'm a good listener."

"Thanks, I appreciate it," Susan said, shyly. "I'm grateful, there are some really decent folk around here, and I need to remember that."

"Yeah, I suppose, I'm pretty new around here too, and I've not found it so easy to make friends."

"Oh you should come along to the library. We go to a group there on a Tuesday. Morag who runs it, she is lovely."

Jess rolled her eyes. "Well my face clearly doesn't fit, does it? She wouldn't let me join."

"I'm sorry. She's nice to me, maybe… oh I don't know… sorry."

"Hey, it's not your fault, just one of those things I guess. It's fine, I'll find my own way to fit in." Jess shrugged.

Susan didn't say anything. Instead, she stared at her phone, which continued to buzz in her hand.

"Tell you what, why don't you turn that thing off, stick it in your bag and we can go grab a coffee or something?"

"Thanks, but I can't. But thank you. Sorry."

Jess didn't want to push it, she'd already guessed Susan probably didn't have any money for coffee and she didn't want to embarrass her by offering to pay, besides she wasn't too flush herself.

"Cool. Some other time. I'm going to head back to work now, anyways. But I'll give you my number and we can do something some other time."

"I don't have a pen."

Jess laughed, "What century are you in, who needs a pen?"

Jess took out her own phone and rhymed off her number. "Text this, and then you will have my number and you know where I am if you ever need to talk, right?"

"I'm sorry, I didn't catch that... look it's okay... I can get it some other time... honest...I'm..."

Jess grinned and shook her head.

"Here give me it." She reached out and grabbed Susan's phone from her and punched in her number. She handed it back. "And Susan, do yourself a favour and quit apologising to everyone for everything, eh? Now send me a text."

Jess waited until her phone pinged. "See? That wasn't so hard, was it?" Jess winked and turned away.

She heard Susan's phone ring again, and this time she answered it. Jess slowed down on the pretence of tying her shoelace.

Susan spoke in a hushed tone "Please, I don't want to. I can't do that. Please can you just leave me alone?"

Interesting, thought Jess. *Doesn't sound much like a sales call to me.*

She whistled as she walked back to the café, her mind doing overtime as she thought about the strange lives of those who lived in this small town.

Ten

Ronnie

AS RONNIE LEFT the library, he lifted his hand to touch his cheek on the spot where the kid had kissed him. He wanted to feel it again—the unconditional acceptance she had given him. She hadn't stared at him like he was crazy. She hadn't backed away, disgusted by his smell. She hadn't shrunk back in fear like the rest of them. Even now, Ronnie could see the few people around the main street backing off as he walked towards them. He saw them cross over to the other side of the street. He heard the sly whispers as they watched him shuffle his way home. Not that kid though.

The tears pricked his eyelids. He was twenty-six years old and, in another life, he could have had a kid of his own, a family, a proper family.

He could have been the same as everyone else. Normal. Nobody staring at him every time he left his house. His skin began to prickle, why couldn't he just be like other people. The buzzing inside his head grew louder. Morag loved him. Didn't she? Jess loved him too. She understood.

He placed one foot in front of the other, he had to get home. He had to get inside. Snippets of his past flitted in and out his head. His mum had always been more interested in her next fix of smack than getting food in his belly.

She's a monster, Ronnie.

His family had been around back then, they had looked out for him.

They stopped us looking after you, Ronnie.

He knew he was lucky, he could have ended up in care.

But they're all gone now Ronnie.

One aunt had died of cancer when he was fourteen, and the other overdosed six months after that. A year later, and his gran had died of what he believed to be a broken heart—her three daughters all gone before her.

At sixteen he'd been left with no choice but to go back to his mum. By then the drugs had well and truly taken hold of her

He felt himself shiver as he remembered the first time going out on the streets to score for her.

That's when we stepped in to help Ronnie.

The weed had taken the edge off it, just like they had promised him it would.

His stomach lurched as a memory crashed its way inside his head. He had been about eighteen and had been hanging round the estate all day with his mates, smoking, but had been getting bad vibes from them. He'd left and gone home to find his mother out of her bed in the kitchen, standing over the cooker with a cigarette in her mouth.

"What are you doing?" he blurted.

His jaw dropped when she turned round. Her face was gone, replaced by a blank faceless mask like some weird waxwork figure. He had taken a step backwards.

'I'm making your dinner you idiot, what the fuck do you think I'm doing.'

She had never made his dinner in her life.

She's not your mother Ronnie. She's come to take you away.

He had looked round to see where the voice was coming from, but there was nobody there. *She's going to hurt you, Ronnie,* it persisted.

He had put his hands over his ears trying to drown out the voice, but it grew increasingly shrill, drilling through his fingers and slicing into his brain.

"What's happened to your f-f-face?" he stuttered, as the figure in front of him started to morph into something dark and dangerous.

Cowering back, he pushed himself into the kitchen counter whimpering, but the creature kept inching closer and closer as the voice in his head grew to a screech inside his head.

She's coming to get you, Ronnie. She'll send you away.

"Stop!" he had yelled at the thing… no, the devil, advancing towards him. But it had just kept coming, a manic laugh escaping from the space where its mouth should have been.

She's going to hurt you Ronnie. The insistent whisper galvanised him into action.

Ronnie had picked up the knife lying out on the counter and waved it at the thing before him

"Get the fuck out our house before my mum comes back!"

It had laughed again. Louder this time.

"I am your fucking mother, you crazy bastard. Put the knife down now."

It's not your mother, Ronnie. It's not, it's not, it's not! The voice had grown louder until it screamed inside his head.

The creature came closer to him, face grotesquely twisted, the cigarette in its outstretched hand. He heard the hiss as the cigarette scorched his arm.

His world grew red, the pressure in his head about to explode, every nerve ending on red alert as he screamed and rushed at the monster masquerading as his mother, and brought the knife down, slashing her across the arm. The blood staining the sleeve of her white jumper spread out, and he'd watched, fascinated, as it formed the shape of a blood-red flower, before he looked up and saw his mother staring back at him, her mouth opened in a round O. The knife had dropped from his hand and then she ran, right past him and out the back door screaming, "He's trying to fucking kill me, the crazy bastard is trying to fucking kill me."

Ronnie could not remember much after that. He had woken up in a hospital bed and had stayed there for six months. Six months spent with people trying to get inside his head and forced into a room with other patients to paint bloody pictures and talk about his feelings. He had left the ward armed with a diagnosis, medication and an appointment with a psychiatrist.

They had not wanted him to return home to his mother, but he had nowhere else to go, and besides his mum needed him. Nobody else would look after her. Eventually they had agreed, and for the first twelve months, he had regular contact with the mental health team. Like a good boy, he had taken the pills and done what they told him to do. Life returned to normal.

Trust earned, the professionals began to back off. They had other people to look after, more urgent cases. People who needed them. He didn't need them now. In the beginning Ronnie stuck to the routine they had helped him make. He kept popping the pills. He was a good boy. He felt better. He didn't need them anymore. He began making excuses for his follow up appointments. He kept himself under the radar and they left him be.

Just be a good boy Ronnie. Don't make a fuss. We'll look after you. You don't need those pills anymore. They just slow you down. Trust us Ronnie. The voices promised him everything.

At first, they would send letters, make a few phone calls, pop round to the house to check up on him. However, the check-ups soon fell away too, and they left him and his mum alone. Ronnie had been glad. He did not need them anymore. He could control the devil himself now. The voices were there to help him.

RONNIE LOOKED UP, surprised to find himself looking at his house. He had no recollection of his journey home, which wasn't unusual. He quite often zoned out of the world around him. But today he felt more anxious than he had for a long time. There was a bad feeling in his belly. Touching his cheek again to remind himself of the little girl in the library, of acceptance, Ronnie took a quick look around to make sure nobody was watching him and made his way into the house.

Inside the door he stopped and listened for his mum's usual yell. But only silence answered. He let out a sigh of relief and bent down to pick up the mail. He sifted through it, discarding the junk, until his eye caught the handwritten envelope addressed to him.

"Ronnie, is that you?" His mum's voice screeched down the stairs and into his ears.

Sticking his fingers in his ears, he yelled back up. "Yes Mum, it's me."

"Where the fuck have you been, you lazy bastard? Bring me up a cuppa tea and a fag, now."

Her voice managed to find its way through his fingers and he grimaced. He knew she could get her own tea and fags and she probably had been out of bed while he had been out. He wasn't late, the clock read four-thirty p.m. and she wasn't due her dinner until six. He still had ninety minutes, but it wouldn't be good to go against her. Not today. Not now. The anxiety in his belly niggled away and the voice in his ear whispered, *she'll make IT come for you Ronnie, better be a good little boy for Mummy.*

Ronnie shuffled into the kitchen and put the kettle onto boil, he took a cigarette out the packet lying in the mess he had left that morning. He popped it between his lips letting it hang there. He opened the envelope while waiting for the kettle to boil.

Meet me at the park at seven tonight. It is important. Don't be late.

He stuffed the note in his pocket and took the tea upstairs. The cigarette dropped to the floor.

Don't be late Ronnie, don't be late. You had better not be late, Ronnie. You know what happens if you are late.

Eleven

Jess

JESS LET OUT a sigh of relief as the last of the customers left. The café had been busier than usual, and now she felt dirty and sticky. The sooner she tidied up, the quicker she could be out in the fresh air. She'd mopped half the floor when she heard the door chime ring.

"We're closing," she barked, not looking round. There was no reply, only the sound of heavy breathing. Her hands clenched around the handle of the mop, she swung round ready to give whoever it was the sharp edge of her tongue. Jess could give as good as she got and she was well used to the neighbourhood neds trying it on. There was no way she was about to let some wee scrote rob her. She stopped in her tracks. It wasn't kids, it was the woman from the library, Morag, and her face was as white as a sheet.

"Here, sit down, quickly," Jess let the mop fall to the floor and rushed forward and pulled out a chair. Morag allowed her to help her sit down. She could feel her tremble under her touch. "Are you okay? Has someone mugged you? Do you need me to call someone? Ambulance? Police?"

Morag shook her head, her hand at her throat. "No, no. I'm fine. I'm not hurt. Just had a bit of a shock, that's all. I'll be okay. I just needed a seat and I noticed you were still open… I thought Marion might be in… it's okay… I'll just go…" She made to stand up.

"Don't be daft, just stay where you are. I'll get you some tea or would you prefer coffee? Water?"

"A glass of water would be fine, thank you."

Jess closed the café door and pulled down the latch, turning the sign from Open to Closed. She poured a glass of water from the tap, feeling guilty at her earlier reaction seeing Morag rushing from the library. Taking the drink over, she pulled up a chair next to Morag.

"Here, drink this. Take your time." She watched as Morag took small sips of water, the colour slowly coming back into her cheeks.

"What happened? Are you sure you're okay?"

"I'm fine, honestly, I'm fine," insisted Morag, and promptly burst into tears.

Jess rubbed Morag's shoulder at the same time keeping her distance. She felt awkward in the older woman's company and sensed that she was probably the last person Morag wanted giving her comfort, given the way she had treated her in the past.

"What happened? Is there anything I can do to help?"

Morag sniffed, "No, there's nothing anyone can do. I've lost someone close to me, so close. I can't believe he's gone, left me…"

Jess mumbled, "Sorry." She didn't know what else to say.

"I don't need sorry, and I don't need your pity. And no offence, but I hardly think anyone has ever needed someone like you in their life."

Shocked at Morag's response and her sudden change in manner, Jess drew back. "I was only trying to be nice, there's no need to be so rude."

Morag shrugged.

"I've seen you try to wheedle your way in with the others, poking your nose in where it's not wanted, where the likes of you aren't wanted." she snapped, pulling herself up from the seat.

"You know what? You bloody well deserve to be on your own. No wonder you run that group, probably the nearest thing you'll ever have to family or friends." Jess's hands were shaking, and she had to clench her fists to stop her slapping the woman in front of her.

Morag stood at the door. Turning around, she glared at Jess.

"Stay away. We don't need you, and we don't want you," she snapped as she unlocked the door and disappeared outside.

Jess shook her head in disbelief, where the hell had that come from? Crazy old bitch. She could bloody well whistle if she ever turned up here again looking for sympathy.

"Fuck you, Morag. And fuck your poxy group. This place is full of freaks and weirdos, sooner I'm out of here the better," she muttered. "Won't be long mum, I promise you, it won't be long."

GIVING THE SHUTTERS a sharp yank, Jess satisfied herself the café was securely locked up for the night. Though she didn't know why she bothered so much. It was no skin off her nose if someone broke in and robbed the place overnight. That was Marion's problem, she was just the hired help. The sap that Marion took advantage of, playing on her good nature knowing she needed the money—she was always leaving Jess to lock up

Jess turned away from the café, deliberating what she should do now. She rubbed her forehead, trying to ward off the tension headache caused by Morag's outburst. Her eyes stung with tears remembering Morag's harsh words. She might give the impression of being thick skinned and hard faced but the truth was that Jess desperately lacked any self-confidence and the encounter had left her feeling uncomfortable. It had taken a lot for her to move here, to make a new start and try to work things out for herself and she hated how that woman left her feeling small. Unwanted.

Jess kicked the café shutter and cursed under her breath. She didn't want to go home now. Being cooped up in the flat, staring at four walls, getting herself angrier wouldn't do her any good.

She briefly considered replying to the text she had received earlier. He would have whiled away a few hours for her, but she couldn't even be bothered with him tonight, his neediness was becoming suffocating.

At times like this, Jess wished she was like other folk her age— with a bunch of friends and plans to look forward to. But she wasn't like other folk her age, she had way too much baggage weighing her down. *Christ, I haven't even had a proper boyfriend yet.* She didn't count the quick fumbles she'd had in the past as relationships. And her current status would most definitely be 'it's complicated' on social media, if she could be bothered to update it

She recalled her past and the nights that turned into giant piss-ups and the offer of a walk home at the end had always seemed like a good idea with the beer goggles on. But something had always stopped her from going too far and she'd always managed to sober up before she ended up in bed with some waster. Jess had no intention of ending up pregnant and stuck in some crappy flat with a kid on her own. She had plans, and that wasn't one of them. While she had managed not to land herself with a kid, she hadn't been able to stop herself spiralling into a life out of control. She had ended up in Stobcross Hospital in the Southside of Glasgow. Jess had partied hard and paid the price, the staff there looked down their noses at her, writing her off as just another junkie. Nobody bothered to try and find out what had led her to that dark place and so she had learned just to build her walls higher. But she had been determined to turn things around and to prove them all wrong and to make her mum proud of her from the grave. She had bided her time, got herself clean and she had planned. By God she had planned, searching for a long time for the right place to live, the place where she would lay her ghosts to rest. And now she was here, she wouldn't let anyone stand in her way.

She stood for a couple of minutes trying to work out what she could do to fill the next couple of hours. Her options were limited, the shops were either closed or pulling down their shutters for the night. Other than the only two pubs in the area, the library was the only place still open, and Jess didn't have the balls to walk into a pub by herself and risk everyone staring at her.

Library it is then.

She passed the library every morning on her way to work, and had been in a few times, but hadn't got round to joining or borrowing any books yet. The building looked out of place amongst the ugliness of Lennoxhill. Dating back to the 1800s it was one of the few older style buildings in the town—the gold sandstone standing proud at the edge of the park. *Maybe I'll go and get myself a book, something to lose myself in for a while,* she thought.

Mind made up she strode quickly along the main street, shivering against the cold seeping through her thin jacket. She considered cutting through the park for quickness, but Radio Joe sat on the park bench and if she got waylaid by him, she would never get away. Everyone in Lennoxhill knew Radio Joe, he had earned the nickname because he carried about an old transistor radio. He could talk the hind legs of a donkey. He was harmless enough, but he never knew when to shut up.

Pulling her jacket tighter around her, she glanced up at the Cancer Research shop thinking she might pop in over the next few days to buy herself something a bit warmer to do her over the winter. She turned right onto Parkview Road and hurried along it, her footsteps echoing sharply on the deserted pavements. She became acutely aware of the empty houses in this area, no more than concrete shells. The street was derelict, the streetlights long gone, and it wasn't somewhere she wanted to be lingering on her own for too long. She imagined evil peeking out at her through the dark windows

Crossing the road at the library, Jess let out the breath she hadn't realised she'd been holding, relieved to be away from the empty streets. She contemplated the building before her, the lights beckoning her, inviting her in. She hadn't picked up a book since her mum had gone, the memories of her mum's love of reading too much to bear. At the bottom of the stairs, she hesitated again—*she wasn't a member, she didn't have a card. Maybe this was a dumb idea.* But the thought of going home to an empty flat felt like even more of a dumb idea so, bracing herself, she climbed the steps and pushed open the heavy door.

The warmth and hush of the library caused a sudden rush of memories from her childhood and a sense of familiarity washed over her. Apart from the computers at the front desk and signs displaying free e-books and magazines, it was a step back in time. There was no sign of Morag and she found herself relax a little—she didn't feel like another run in with her tonight.

Sorting out a membership took minutes, and soon Jess had lost herself in the bookshelves enjoying the peace and quiet the library brought her—a rest from the thoughts swirling around inside her head. Before she knew it, the girl at the desk had shouted a reminder the library was closing in fifteen minutes.

"Christ," Jess muttered to herself. She hadn't meant to spend as long in there. Armed with a pile of books, she checked them out and made her way outside. Jess shivered as the cold night air penetrated her thin jacket again. Her stomach grumbled, reminding her she hadn't eaten all day. She fished in the pocket of her jeans and found a fiver, her tips from last week. Maybe she could treat herself a bag of chips and even throw in a pickle for good measure.

Jess left the library, debating her route. If she nipped through the park, it would be quicker. She pulled out her phone and checked the time. It was ten to seven, if she took a shortcut through the park she should be home in time for the soaps starting.

She slipped through the park gates and disappeared into the night.

Twelve

Morag

MORAG STOOD ON Waterside Road, she frowned as she looked around. Her thoughts and memories jumbled inside her head. How on earth had she ended up back outside Alan's flat? Where had she been? And what had she been doing since she left the police station all those hours ago? She had a vague recollection of a run in with the girl in the café, but she couldn't for the life of her remember what about. *God, I must be losing it.*

She peered at her watch, surprised to see it was already seven-thirty. She had been wandering for hours. Glancing back up at Alan's flat, she blinked back the tears as the shadows stared back at her. She hoped none of his so-called friends would take over the flat now he had gone. She prayed they would leave him to rest in peace. She made the sign of the cross, shivered, and wrapped her thin coat tighter around her. She watched the sky as day bled into night. She hated this time of year, the oppressive, cold, dark November nights, reinforcing her loneliness.

Another shiver ran down her spine. Not cold, this time—she was fearful of being alone on the Waterside estate at night. It wasn't the kind of place she wanted to be wandering about in the dark. With a last look at Alan's flat, turned round and began to make her way home, anxious to leave the estate behind her. The light of a downstairs lamp shone weakly behind the thin curtains framing the windows of Susan's flat as she passed, but Morag kept her head down and rushed ahead. She did the same as she passed Ronnie's house, not wanting her thoughts to linger on the man inside.

As she trudged home, away from the town, the familiar sights and sounds of a world she recognised flooded in. The brightly lit homes, with the blue flicker of TV screens and the rich glow of lamps, the shadows of family life, teasing her, always just out of her reach. Sometimes she would stop and watch from the darkness, drinking in the lives of those she watched. She had nobody to go home to, nothing in her home but darkness and emptiness.

As she walked along the street, she found herself seeking out certain houses—the ones with their own dark secrets to hide. Morag knew all of their secrets. Always watch out for the quiet ones, the ones others dismissed as insignificant. It was this ignorance that allowed her to fly under the radar—always watching, always listening, stealing their secrets and keeping them close. Oh yes, everyone had secrets but not everyone knew how to keep them. *Not even you, you stupid bitch, she heard her mother's voice in her ear.*

The streets grew quieter as she neared her own house, in Cedar Drive in the more upmarket Rosehill Estate. Rosehill sat on the edge of Lennoxhill, a quiet area, the houses were larger and set back in their own expansive gardens, shielded from prying eyes. She only had two neighbours on Cedar Drive and both were elderly, she never saw or heard them, which suited her fine. *They wouldn't want anything to do with you anyway Morag, they know how crazy you are,* her mother whispered in her ears.

She was glad to reach her front gate. The sight of the detached house set in a perfect garden served as a stark reminder as to how lucky she was, in comparison to those living on the Waterside estate. The weed free lawn and flower beds, which were a riot of colour come summertime, were her pride and joy. She smiled, picture perfect. She stopped at her gate and considered the heavy net curtains framing her windows. Perfect for hiding the truth.

Morag trembled, her cheeks felt as though they had been rubbed raw. She wanted nothing more than to get inside and warm up with a cup of tea. reached into her bag for her keys. As she fumbled about the contents, her hand brushed the small jar lying at the bottom of her bag. She normally left it at home, but her sub conscious must have made her put it in her bag this morning. Her hand closed around it and she felt a sudden rush of sadness. Her jar of hearts.

She let out a breath she hadn't realised she'd been holding, she would need to add another heart tonight, one for Alan. God bless you son, she sighed.

The key slid into the lock and she pushed her front door open. Glancing down at the floor she groaned at the usual junk mail waiting for her—fliers for local takeaways and the familiar brown envelopes containing bills. Picking them up, she made her way down her narrow hallway, not bothering to switch on the light as she hadn't replaced the bulb which had blown in the summer.

Reaching the kitchen, she flicked on the light switch and a dim yellow glow warmed the miserable room. She filled the kettle and skimmed through her mail while she waited for it to boil. Just the usual rubbish. She'd deal with it later. And then the white envelope caught her eye. It had the NHS Scotland logo stamped on the back and her stomach plummeted. Hands shaking, she tore the envelope open and shook out the contents. She scanned over the words a couple of times, not wanting to acknowledge what they were saying. Blinking back tears, she placed the letter back on the table, and busied herself making her tea.

Tea made, the letter glared out at her from the table, so she stuffed it into a drawer, slamming it closed. Out of sight, out of mind. Morag busied herself with her usual after work routine. She flicked on the heating for an hour to take the chill from the air. A small lamp cast a yellow glow over the living room, highlighting the chaos Morag had found herself living in. Newspapers and unopened mail littered the floor, while the coffee table was buried under a mountain of magazines and unwashed dishes. Any surface not covered in clutter had an almost velvet like covering of grey dust. Even the idea of tackling it gave her palpitations—she wouldn't know where to begin.

Since her mother had died, Morag had neglected the house, there had been no point, it wasn't like anyone ever came to visit. She closed the door and made her way towards the stairs, she needed to get up and switch on her electric blanket to take the chill off the air. At the bottom of the stairs, she stopped and picked up her shoes to take them with her. She tutted at the mud and leaves sticking to the soles and threw them in the porch to let them dry intending to brush it off in the morning.

Upstairs, Morag paused by the bedroom that had once belonged to her mother. She cursed under her breath at the woman who had ruined her life before offering a silent prayer of forgiveness. She pushed the door open and slipped inside.

The air was dead, suffocating, as she stood absorbing the quiet. She imagined she could hear her mother's voice, cold and vicious as it stabbed out words designed to hurt her.

"You are nothing but an embarrassment girl... your father would be ashamed of you. You have brought shame upon this family and upon yourself. You will die alone girl, mark my words."

Morag bristled. Her mother still managed to exert her control and wound her even after her death.

Perhaps she had been right all along. After all, here Morag was, as she'd predicted, on her own. Had her mother's prophecy come true? Morag sat on the bed, the dust rising as she lowered her slight frame on to it. She trailed her fingers along the pillows where her mother's hair used to fan across the soft cotton. Reaching under the pillows, she pulled out a pair of scissors. They had been her mother's favourite dressmaking scissors. She raised them high above her head and with a gasp plunged them deep into the pillow, exactly where her mother's face used to stare up at her...over and over again she plunged, coughing and sneezing as the feathers filled the room.

Sated, she placed the scissors back under the pillow. Standing up, she brushed down her skirt, fixed her hair and spat out the word "Bitch," before turning and leaving the room.

Thirteen

Susan

SUSAN HAD GOT Lily off to sleep after wrapping her up in every spare bit of clothing she had, just to keep her warm—the poor kid had been chittering with the cold. Susan sank down on the threadbare sofa and stared into the darkness as misery enveloped her. With Christmas in little over a month, she stressed about how she could make it special for Lily. She had no spare money to splash out on a present, and Lily wasn't the kind of kid who asked for a lot but she could not bear the thought of her daughter going without. The guilt at taking her daughter away from everything she had ever known combined with her relief at getting out of it alive ate away at her on a daily basis. She was desperate to make things alright for her daughter and she would do anything to make it happen. Chewing what was left of her nails, she churned the only possible solution she had around in her head, but the images it invoked made her gag. Would she go that far to ensure her daughter didn't miss out?

She tried to convince herself she could do it, just a couple of times, just to make enough money to get back on an even keel. But she wasn't stupid. If she went down that road, there would be no way out for her. She wrapped her arms around her body, tormented by her fear of the future, and a dark reminder of the last time she had felt this way.

Life hadn't always been like this, Susan had lived in a detached villa with her ex-husband, Colin, on the outskirts of Aberdeen. Theirs had been a whirlwind romance—he had swept her off her feet when she was only eighteen. Susan's parents had died in a car crash when she was thirteen, and at seventeen her gran had passed away.

Alone in the world, she had been ripe for the picking for someone like Colin.

Some ten years her senior, he'd lured her in with promises of family, love and happy ever afters They had married not long after her twentieth birthday, and by twenty-one she had fallen pregnant with Lily. Colin had insisted she gave up work. He would provide for his family, he had assured her. In her naivety Susan thought he was being protective, caring, and loving even. The perfect man. This side of him had compensated for the flashes of temper she had witnessed soon after their marriage. She had even stupidly convinced herself her pregnancy would signal a new start for them both.

Colin had a good job as a Detective Sargent Inspector for Police Scotland—highly respected and going places. Well, that's what he had always told her, as he put the boot in. Shuddering, she relived the memories of nights where he would come home in a foul temper, which she always managed to exacerbate by doing the wrong thing. It had been impossible to please him. No matter what she did, she would get it wrong—from the way, she dressed, to her skills as a wife and mother. She had tried everything she could think of to please him. She would cook him a slap-up meal and leave it waiting for him when he came home, late as always.

"Useless cow. Who the fuck wastes food like that? And look at it, all dried up. It's disgusting. I wouldn't even feed that to a dog." The plate ended up smashed against the wall.

She left him sandwiches to eat when he returned home.

"Fucking bitch. What sort of a meal is that to leave a man coming home from work?" He rammed the sandwiches down her throat until she had begun to choke.

She tried to make an effort with her appearance for him, taking care with her hair, clothes and make-up.

"Little tart, who the fuck have you been seeing behind my back? Who is he? I'll fucking kill you... and him." A kick to the ribs accompanied each word he uttered. "Do... you... know... who... I... fucking... am?"

The beatings had been relentless. There had been times where she honestly thought he was going to kill her and there were times she prayed he would. However, Colin was not stupid. He knew when to stop. He knew where to strike her. He knew how to make sure it all stayed behind closed doors.

It never became easy to live with, it just became easier to block it out, to numb the pain with a bottle. Drink became her friend.

There had been no point in reporting him to the police. Colin *was* the police. Colin knew people. Nobody would believe her—he had told her so often, she believed it. She was nothing more than a mess—the alcoholic wife, the embarrassment, the one all his colleagues down the nick commiserated about with him. She knew this because he told her, every single day he told her, reminding her of the nothing she was.

But there was another side to her husband, and that's what had made it so difficult for her to leave, to stand up for herself. Watching him with Lily only served to reinforce everything he told her. His wicked side was all her fault—she made him behave that way. 'Good Colin' was the best father to their daughter. She only had to see Lily's eyes light up when he walked through the door, or watch her wee face shine with happiness as they played together. She would toddle over to him, ignoring her mother completely and clamber up on his knee, wrapping her tiny little arms around his neck. It broke Susan's heart. The look he would give her over their daughter's head would chill her to the bone. They belonged to him.

It had taken Susan a long time to pluck up the courage to leave him. It had not been easy. Colin watched her every move. Not long after Lily's birth, she had begun to squirrel away every spare penny and started to hide some of her belongings in an emergency grab bag. She never believed she would have the courage to use it. There had been times where she had considered leaving Lily behind. It would be easier to get away without her daughter in tow. She would have had more freedom without her. Colin loved Lily, didn't he? He wouldn't hurt her, would he? But in the end she could not leave her daughter, she couldn't take the risk… the risk she would be compelled to go back for her.

Colin had begun turning Lily against her. It had been little things at first—encouraging Lily to disobey Susan, to laugh at her when she was drunk before moving on to teaching Lily to repeat the foul insults he used on her. It had not been long before Lily had started playing up on a daily basis. The final straw had been Lily kicking her and calling her a stupid cow when she had not liked the snack Susan had given her. There was something quite chilling about the vile words and aggression coming from a child so small.

For the sake of their marriage and in a bid to put things right, Susan tried to tell Colin it wasn't right, allowing their daughter to act in this manner. He laughed and said she must have done something to deserve it. A switch had flicked inside of Susan's head, she couldn't let Lily grow up believing this was normal behaviour. She could not leave her behind, and risk Colin using her as his human punch bag when she grew older and began standing up to him. She could not risk Lily ending up in the same mess as she was.

So she spent months getting herself clean. She cut out the drink but was careful not to let him know. She would still buy bottles of vodka emptying most of them into the sink and over her clothes, to stop him suspecting anything. Acting the drunk had come easy to her.

Biding her time, Susan had waited until Colin had been attending a police conference. It was a prestigious event where all the top brass would be out in force. Organisers had invited Colin to give a keynote speech at the event and Susan knew he would never turn down such an opportunity. She could still remember him gloating about the invitation. How he had pinned her down on the bed, pushed his face in close and reminded her of how lucky she was to be married to him. She buried her face in her hands as she remembered how he had made her show her appreciation.

She recalled the day they left with perfect clarity. Friday, 12 August, just over a year ago now. The sun had been shining and Colin had left at nine a.m. sharp, giving her strict instructions not to leave the house. She couldn't leave the house without his permission. He didn't even need to lock the door anymore, he knew she would not dare disobey him. Giving Lily a huge hug, he had stage whispered, 'Look after mummy Lily, make sure she behaves herself. You know what a bad mummy she can be.' And he'd winked. Lily had giggled and made the promise. Three years old and he had turned the child into her jailer.

For two hours Susan had busied herself around the house. She plonked Lily in front of her favourite TV programme with crisps and snacks, while upstairs she gathered their stuff together. She had not dared leave until after his first phone call, which he had scheduled for eleven in the morning, then she would have time to make her escape. He would be caught up in his ego trip until dinnertime.

At eleven on the dot, the phone went. His voice gave her the shivers, even safe in the knowledge he was over a hundred miles away.

"Remember what I told you, bitch. Don't leave the fucking house. And get it tidied up while I'm away, it's in as much of a mess as you are."

He had laughed as though it were all some big joke, but there was nothing remotely funny about his warning. Colin was deadly serious.

As soon as she had put down the phone, she had run upstairs and grabbed hers and Lily's bags. She had not packed much, just a couple of changes of clothes and a few of her daughter's toys. She had stuffed them all in a small suitcase they had stored away for rare family breaks. She went to the bathroom and prised back the bath panel, reaching in and ignoring the spider's webs, she snatched the pile of money she had squirrelled away. She counted it quickly, just under three hundred pounds, enough to get them away and to buy a cheap untraceable phone. She had taken her mobile out her bag and put it in her bedside drawer. He would search for it and find it but at least without it he could not track her down. She had found the app he had installed on her phone to monitor her. Well, she calculated, if it's in the house, then he will think I'm still here, for a little while anyway.

Susan had gone downstairs to get her daughter. Using the remote control, she turned off the television, causing Lily to turn round.

"Come on. Get your jacket on, we're going out," she urged her.

Lily's mouth had dropped open, aghast at the idea of betraying her father. "But Daddy said we were not to go out. He told me to make sure you did as you were told." The look on her face had been just like Colin's—the mean sneer and screwed up eyes.

"I just spoke to Daddy. He said I could take you on an adventure. A special treat because you've been such a good girl."

Lily hadn't looked convinced, but had allowed Susan to help her on with her jacket.

"Are you sure Daddy said it was okay?" She had huffed as Susan quickly zipped her up.

"Yes, I'm sure. Now come on Lily. Quickly now love, we're in a hurry."

The child looked at the case by the door and gazed at her suspiciously. "Why have we got the holiday case? Are we going on holiday? Why's Daddy not coming?"

"Stop asking so many questions and just do as you're told," she had snapped, losing her patience, terrified they would miss their only chance to escape.

Lily screwed up her eyes and took a deep breath. Susan sensed a tantrum brewing and she certainly couldn't deal with that. She said the first thing that came into her head in an effort to appease the child.

"Daddy is going to come and join us tomorrow. It's a surprise for him. I've booked us all a holiday as a surprise... okay?"

She almost crumbled as the child peered up at her, her eyes wide with uncertainty. She could sense her desire to obey her father's wishes fighting against her childish desire to go on an adventure.

"Are you sure?" Her voice sounded little now.

"Yes, I'm sure sweetie. Now come on. I'm going to call him later and tell him. He'll be so happy, just you wait and see."

Apparently satisfied, Lily had smiled and allowed Susan to lead her out the house and into the waiting taxi. A taxi she could ill afford, but she couldn't risk getting a bus and having anyone see her and report back to Colin. As Susan locked the door and slipped the key through the letterbox, she had muttered under her breath. "Goodbye, you bastard."

Now, she cast her eyes around the living room again, taking in the stark differences from where she had come from and found herself questioning it all again. Had she done the right thing leaving Colin, after all? Had moving here been stepping out of the frying pan into the fire? Her head was a mess. She thought about Morag, and the friendship she had shown her and Lily. And then the girl from the café this morning—she had been kind too. Maybe she should confide in one of them? Maybe they could help her? But how could she ask for help? What would she say? How could she tell them she had even considered doing what he wanted?

Her phone pinged an incoming message, she did not need to read it, she already knew who it was from.

Fourteen .

Ronnie

GASPING FOR AIR, Ronnie slammed the front door behind him. He sunk to the floor clutching his head in his hands and thumping it rhythmically against the door, trying to rid himself of her voice, but her words played on a loop inside his head. He could feel himself being sucked into a dark hole as he fought his rising panic. He didn't want this to happen again. He didn't want to be sent away.

You should have known. You knew it was there in the garden the other morning. She brought it here. That bitch upstairs.

"Noooooooo!" Ronnie began to scream. He crammed his fist into his mouth, trying to stop the noise escaping, terrified his mother would hear.

She's been planning this all along. Thinks you're stupid, Ronnie, thinks you're crazy, Ronnie. Just like the rest of them do Ronnie. They want to lock you away Ronnie.

He leaned forward and threw his forehead against the banister. The loud crack only made the voices in his head clearer.

You need to kill the bitch, Ronnie. Kill her before she kills you. We'll look after you, Ronnie. We'll always be here for you. Kill her, Ronnie. Do it. They bounced around incessantly, taunting him.

He had gone to the park as the letter had instructed him. He had even been there ten minutes early. Never ever be late, Ronnie. The warning had run through his head all the way there. He had sat on the bench and waited. Seven o'clock had come and nobody had appeared.

He'd wanted to leave then, wanted to run away, but he couldn't. He couldn't move. Not until it came. Look what had happened to

Alan. It had got him, hadn't it? Alan was dead now. Dead because he didn't do what he was told?

That's what happens to bad boys, Ronnie. Dead. Dead. Dead. And so he had sat on the bench and waited.

He had sat rooted on the spot for what seemed like hours. A soft rustle in the leaves behind him indicated a presence. He had turned his head but a warning was hissed.

"Don't look round, Ronnie. Just listen."

"U-u-huh," he stuttered

"If you look, it will know and it will come for you. It can see you everywhere, Ronnie."

He grabbed onto the bench, his knuckles white. "I-I-I won't l-look r-round."

"I need you to listen, Ronnie. I need you to pay attention. You know how important that is? You know how important you are to me, don't you, Ronnie? You know how much you mean to me, don't you? How special you are to me, Ronnie?"

He had nodded. The voice sounded familiar He relaxed a little, feeling safer now. It was going to be okay.

And so Ronnie had listened.

The disembodied voice told him to wait for five minutes before moving.

"I'll know if you move, Ronnie. I always know what you have done. It will know too."

He had stared at his watch. Five minutes slowly ticked by. He had slowly raised himself from the park bench.

And then he had run. All the way home from the park, not stopping for a breath.

Now, he glanced towards the stairs leading up to his mother's room. Shadows danced on the walls, whispering in the silence. He tried to convince himself he would be safe.

You will never be safe, Ronnie, not while I'm here, the voice whispered in his ear.

Ronnie started to fall, slipping further into the black hole that existed inside his head. The one where IT lived—the monster from his childhood nightmares. The nightmares had become his reality. The monster wanted to take over, the monster made him do bad things. Ronnie closed his eyes, searching for his safe places, clinging onto the pictures in his head—the library, the café, Jess, Morag. He reached out to touch them, to cling on to them, but still he kept falling, spinning round and round as they disappeared into nothingness. Nobody could help him. His heart tore at his chest, hammering its way out, and the voice inside his head screamed. He put his hands over his ears. His lips mouthed, "Shut up... shut up... shut up."

"Ronnie, is that you?"

He opened his eyes and looked around him wildly but there was nobody there. It had gone quiet again. Safe again.

"Ronnie!" This time the loud screech bounced off the walls and into his head.

"Yes mother," he whispered "It's me."

Slowly he clambered up and stumbled up the stairs to his mother.

He stepped inside the room and the stench instantly hit his nostrils. Mother had soiled herself... again.

"Where have you been? You left me here half the day on my own. You bloody halfwit. You know I can't be left on my own. You are an ungrateful little bastard. What are you?"

"I'm an ungrateful little bastard mother," he repeated, not daring to lift his eyes to hers.

"Well, stop standing their like a useless prick and get me cleaned up," she snapped.

Ronnie reached under the bed and grabbed the cleaning supplies. He took a deep breath and pulled on the rubber gloves. His heart sank when he saw the look of grim satisfaction on her face. He knew she took some sort of perverse pleasure in this.

She beckoned him over, her bony finger sticking out of the covers like something wicked from the fairy tales she had read him as a child. *She's the monster Ronnie.* His feet moved of their own accord, slowly edging him closer.

He trembled.

She smiled.

He tried not to gag as he began the task of cleaning her up.

Finished, he watched her hand dart under the covers and pull out a cigarette. He took a step backwards.

"Come closer," she hissed

She nodded towards the lighter on the bedside cabinet.

Ronnie shook his head.

"Light it, you little fucking bastard."

His hand reached out and picked up the lighter. Three times he tried to spark it, three times he failed—his hands were shaking too much.

She hoisted herself up from the pillow and snatched the lighter from his shaking hands.

Putting the cigarette into her filthy mouth, she took a draw as it lit and smiled a smile of grim ecstasy.

He moved backwards. She shook her head and patted the side of the bed.

Liquid trickled down the inside of his leg, its warmth comforting until it turned cold and the stench hit his nostrils.

"Put your hand out," she snapped.

"P-p-please…" The trickle became a stream.

"Dirty little bastard. HAND! NOW!"

Ronnie thrust his hand forward and squeezed his eyes closed as tight as he could.

The acrid tang of singed hair hit his nostrils as the cigarette hissed down on the back of his arm. It would leave a small bullet like hole next to the rest of them. He bit down on his lip to capture his screams.

"Now clean yourself up, and fuck off out my sight," she snapped as she flopped back down on the bed.

HALF AN HOUR later, and Ronnie was back downstairs. His mother fast asleep. The sleeping pills he had crushed up into her drink had knocked her out. He tried the front and back door repeatedly in a bid to reassure himself he had locked them. He then went round drawing closed all the curtains and shutting off the lights. It would not know he was here in the dark. *Darkness is safe.* He repeated this over and over, trying to convince himself it was true.

He sat on the sofa and rocked back and forth, clutching his arm. It hurt. *Will the scars go green like the others?* He fought back the compulsion to roll up his sleeve and start picking.

He tried to block out the pain by thinking about her. The voice had gone now but he could not stop worrying. What if they had got to her? What if he couldn't trust her anymore? He had to trust her though. He had no choice. She was the only one who could keep him safe. She had promised him she would, as long as he did what she told him to.

He sat there, rocking, until the night turned into morning. Only when daylight broke did he sleep. A dark tortured sleep.

Fifteen

Jess

JESS LET HERSELF into the flat. She kicked off her shoes, ignoring the muddy footprints and leaves she had trailed in with her. Housework was not high on her list of priorities. The steaming hot chips warmed her hands, causing her stomach to growl as her hunger made itself known. It had taken much longer to get home than she had anticipated and she was starving. Working in the café had ruined her eating habits. By the time she had cooked and cleaned for everyone else, she had little appetite left. Caffeine and nicotine tended to be her staple diet these days, although she had to ration the nicotine intake given the cost of a packet of fags. Still, Ronnie was usually good for a loan of a roll up when she was desperate.

Back home, she was buzzing for the first time in a long time. The evening had turned out far better than she planned, and the light was finally starting to shine at the end of the tunnel. Just the boost she needed. Things were going to work out, she was convinced of it. Okay, perhaps not quite how she had envisaged it at first, but hey, closure was another step closer. She had a little dance to herself around the flat. Today had been the first step in what felt like the rest of her life.

She didn't bother with a plate for her chips—she ripped open the paper and savoured the hot steam carrying the aroma towards her, the tang of vinegar making her mouth water even more. A picture of her mum popped into her head. Both of them, on the beach. A day out to the seaside. It might have been Ayr. She couldn't remember. But what she did remember was the chips wrapped in newspaper, the seagulls attacking them both, her mum's hair blowing in the strong gusts of wind, her mum's head thrown back as she laughed at something she had said. Her mum's arm thrown round her, protecting her, and the promise their life wouldn't always be like this.

Jess reached into her handbag and dug out the small photograph album she carried everywhere with her. Flicking through the pages, her smile was wistful. She ran her finger over the photos, lingering on her mum's face longing to feel her for real again. She ignored the jagged edges where she had carefully ripped out the others, erased them from her mind, from her history.

"This is what it's all for, mum. It's all for you, I promise I'm going to put everything right. I'm doing it all for you."

She lifted the album to her face and kissed the photo of her and her mum on the beach, the wind blowing their hair, their smiles wide, caught in that moment forever.

Mum was right when she told me life would not always be like that, thought Jess bitterly. Life had changed alright, but not in the way her mum had promised her.

Her mood plummeted. She pushed the chips away from her and balled her hands into her eyes in an attempt to stop the tears. She did not want to remember—the memories made it all harder. No, she had to focus on the here and now. On her future. Her plans.

Come on Jess, get a grip. You can do this. You can bloody well do this.

She threw the chips in the bin. She couldn't face them now—the taste spoiled by the memories they had invoked. Instead, she grabbed a packet of crisps from the cupboard and a can of diet coke from the fridge. Throwing herself on the sofa, the books she had borrowed from the library caught her eye. Two true crime books and a police procedural, she smiled at the irony of her choice of reading material.

The sight of the books distracted her from her melancholy enough to find her thoughts returning to the library. She had not felt out of place when she had gone in earlier. The girl behind the desk hadn't looked much older than her. She had been really chatty too. Jess had probed her about Morag, referring to her as the 'old woman'. The girl at the counter had rolled her eyes and made a face, making Jess laugh.

"Old?" she had replied to Jess's question. "Morag isn't really that old. Well, she is in her fifties but, seriously right, what woman in their fifties goes around dressed like that these days? I mean, my gran is nearly seventy now and she has more style than Morag has. She's a right weirdo her. Always walking about with that bloody stupid bag of hers, looking down her nose at the rest of us... and her hoity toity voice, grinds my gears."

The girl would have gone on forever, if Jess had not interrupted.

"It's fine," she had replied. "I only wanted to know because I know she runs that group and it's just because I'm kinda new around here, I thought..." She'd let her sentence tail off, realising how lame she sounded. The look on the girl's face said she agreed. She had bombarded Jess with questions about where she had lived before Lennoxhill and what had made her move here. Jess had managed to be as vague as she could—the less folk knew about her the better.

Jess had made her excuses and wandered away from her, not wanting to draw much further attention to herself.

Now alone in the flat, her thoughts wandered back to Ronnie. Jess knew it was a shitty thing to do, to let him think he was in with a chance with her. She wouldn't normally do stuff like that but sometimes in life the end justified the means.

It hadn't been her fault Ronnie had placed himself firmly in her sights. He had latched onto her when she first started working in the café. Used to everyone avoiding him, he had clearly taken her empathy as a sign of something else. In the beginning she had tried to put him off, but he was like an eager little puppy, always hanging around her.

Jess had seen the dark looks Morag had thrown her when she caught her talking to Ronnie, and recognised the green eyed monster for what it was. This had simply fuelled the fire for her. And after Morag's little outburst today, Jess was determined to do anything— whatever it took—to put things right and lay her ghosts to rest for once and for all. Nobody in this god forsaken little town would stop her.

Sixteen

Ronnie

RONNIE LAY IN the middle of his bed, the sheets rising and falling in time with his sobs. Curled up in a foetal position he held onto himself, trying to stop the last dregs of reality leaving him. His body ached, and his mind was in chaos.

Ronnie didn't know anything other than this way of living, his mother had been subjecting him to physical and mental abuse ever since he had returned home to live with her. She knew how to press his buttons and manipulated his fear of being sent back to hospital. He knew he wouldn't dare tell anyone what went on behind closed doors and she knew that. Ronnie wasn't stupid, he knew everyone else believed he was the crazy one. If only they would realise it was his mother who needed locking up, not him.

"Tell anyone about this, you little freak, and I'll see you locked up for the rest of your fucking life," was her daily threat. "I'll tell them it's you that is battering me, me, the poor old defenceless woman who can't get out her bed. The woman who's terrified of her crazy son, the psycho who burns himself with cigarettes and hits me. Don't think I won't, freak. 'Ohhh please Mrs nice social worker, I'm so scared of him, and he doesn't give me any food and leaves me lying in a soiled bed all day'." Ronnie did not doubt she would carry out her threats.

He pushed himself backwards into the thin mattress, ignoring the sharp tips of the springs digging into his back. He wished the bed would swallow him up, make him disappear. *You are a coward, Ronnie,* the voice niggled in his ear. Those voices, the ones that made other people avoid him. It wasn't too hard to work out what ran through people's minds when they heard the word schizophrenia. He knew people thought he was going to lose his shit at any time and start randomly attacking strangers. He had thought the same until it happened to him.

If only they could understand—the voices didn't want him to hurt anyone else, they only wanted him to hurt himself. He would give anything to open up his skull and rip them out. But he couldn't do anything. He was frozen into a situation he didn't know how to escape from.

He checked the clock, the ticking sound reverberating around his head like a countdown—a cluster bomb ready to explode in his brain as the clock hands slowly moved. He saw the clock face twist and laugh at him, taunting him as he cowered under the blanket in his bed. He called on the distraction techniques he had learned in hospital, he tried to challenge the voices by escaping from inside his head, but the techniques were not working anymore. The pressure was building and he wouldn't be able to take much more before he gave in.

He threw back his blanket and gazed down at his arm. The perfect little circle resembled a blistered bullet hole., He compared it to the other circular scars covering his arm. The yellow bubble of blister pulsed the longer he stared at it. The last time he'd been in hospital, staff had questioned him about the marks on his arm. He had been afraid to tell them the truth. Instead he told them he had done it himself. After his confession he was only ever allowed to smoke supervised by staff. He had wanted to tell them the truth, but he couldn't. Now the scars had become a part of his life.

Life with Mother.

Ronnie turned to the cardboard packing box he used as a bedside table and grabbed the pencil lying there. The pencil he used to write the list for his mother's messages. He stared at the burn again. It seemed to be glowing, drawing him in. He could feel the heat sear his face, it made him feel alive. Taking the pencil he hovered it above the burn. *Do it Ronnie, do it!*

The clock ticked louder.

He had breakfast to make, and he had to get up.

The clock ticked louder.

His legs were heavy. They did not want to move.

The clock ticked louder.

He wanted to stay in bed, pull the duvet over his head and pretend he didn't exist anymore.

The clock ticked LOUDER.

Maybe he would be better off dead.

THE CLOCK TICKED LOUDER.

Maybe he should go jump in front of train, take an overdose, anything, maybe dying would be his only way to escape all this. He didn't want to die but he did want the voices to stop.

LOUDER.

The wound continued to pulsate, throbbing as he dug the pencil in deeper and deeper. He smiled, embracing the pain as the voices faded away.

Ronnie inhaled deeply and the tension drained away.

BREAKFAST DONE, RONNIE paced around the house like a caged tiger. His mother's mood had been dark this morning—she had refused to eat her breakfast and had thrown it against the wall in a fit of temper. He had been distraught and his tears only made her temper worse.

"You're nothing but a fucking useless little freak," she had spat at him, as he had dropped to all fours trying to retrieve the mess from the floor. "Pathetic little runt. Should have drowned you at birth." On and on she had ranted until he'd ran from her room with her threats ringing in his ears.

Her voice had slowly faded away. Ronnie opened her bedroom door cautiously, relived to see she had fallen into a deep stupor.

Back downstairs, Ronnie chewed at his frayed nails as he contemplated the day stretching out in front of him. He paced around the small living room, his steps becoming faster and faster as the voice began to creep back inside his head.

He had to get out of the house.

It did not feel safe here.

He was not safe.

His mother's purse lay on the worktop, his hand hovered over it... she wouldn't notice if he took a couple of pounds, it was full of loose change anyway—no notes, just coins. Coins meant he could go to the café, he could see Jess, she would make him feel better. Just thinking about her made his stomach flutter. He snatched up the purse quickly, before he could change his mind, but his hands were trembling so much the purse fell to the floor. The coins clattered as they bounced off the tiles, scattering everywhere. He stopped and listened. Holding his breath, he waited for her to roar his name.

Nothing came.

He bent down and scrabbled to pick the coins up, shoving two pound coins and some silver in his pocket. His mouth was dry as he returned the purse to the worktop. He listened again, still no sound. He grabbed his jacket and slipped out the house, clicking the door closed softly behind him.

Out on the street he fought the panic rising in his belly. *What if they saw him? What if she saw him?* He pushed himself against the wall, trying to make himself invisible. It was only nine, hardly anyone around. On this estate, nobody got up before lunchtime unless they were going to court.

The streets were empty apart from Ronnie, but he could still feel its eyes on him, watching him. He inched his way slowly along the street until he came to the block of flats at the top of Waterside Road. He glanced up in the direction of the top floor window. The curtains were blowing out in the wind, the window battering back and forth. He remembered Alan, the wee junkie who used to live there. He was dead. Drug overdose, she had said, with a smile on her face. But Ronnie knew better—it must have got to Alan, and if he wasn't careful, he would be next.

He broke into a shuffle, he wanted to run but his feet were wading through quicksand, the pavements trying to suck him in, his feet heavy and his body refusing to obey him. He wanted away from here, away from this flat. What if they were still up there? Watching him… waiting.

When he reached the café, he stopped and bent forward with hands on his knees. He took long deep breaths until his breathing returned to normal. He peered through the steamed up window and caught sight of her. She sat with her back to the door. Morag. He let out a breath.

His heart lurched as his gaze turned to the counter and the sight of Jess's poker-straight, black hair bobbing up and down as she served the customers She looked like an angel. Beautiful.

Jess spotted him through the window and winked. His face flushed in response, his mouth turned up at the corners. But his grin quickly turned to a frown as the awkwardness of the situation hit him. Morag and Jess would both expect his attention and he could not talk to both.

He bounced on the balls of his feet looking back and forward at them both.

Who should he talk to? Jess or Morag?

Should he ignore them both?

He moved away from the door and then back again, oblivious to the irritated grunts from customers having to step around him. Ronnie peered up and down the street. Should he go home? Should he go into the café? Both options twisted the knots in his stomach as he darted nervously from one foot to the other, the buzzing inside his head getting louder. He stared through the window again and made his mind up, he needed to be amongst people, and he needed their noise to drown out the voices echoing in his head. He stepped forward and pushed the door open.

Jess lifted her head up and smiled at him, he smiled back.

Ronnie liked Jess. He liked her a lot. She often invited him round to her flat to hang out, watch TV and chill, but she had warned him against telling anyone else about his visits. "Our secret, Ronnie," she'd whispered to him. He could still feel the tickle of her breath against his ear.

Jess was special. She didn't treat him the same way others did. Yes, she could be a bit short with him at times, like when he took too long to pay for his order or when he didn't answer all her questions quickly enough. She asked him lots of questions, mostly about Morag and her group at the library.

"Why don't you ask Morag yourself?" he'd blurted out one day, regretting it as soon as the words left his mouth.

"Because she hates me Ronnie. That's why."

Morag's eyes had narrowed into slits when he asked her why she hated Jess. She'd grabbed his arm tight, "That little bitch is trying to take you away from me, Ronnie. Don't you dare let her. You know how much you need me. You know what will happen to you if I'm not there to look after you? Don't you Ronnie?" Her nails had left little half-moon imprints on his skin.

Hovering in the doorway Ronnie watched them both, his head darting back and forth, his hands wringing. He faltered and moved towards Jess at first but quickly changed his mind and shuffled over to the table where Morag sat. He hesitated before taking a seat at the table next to her.

He picked up the menu and turned it over repeatedly in his hands, his lips moving silently as a stream of worry escaped them. He ignored the two older women in the corner, he could feel their stares but he fixed his eyes straight ahead. He could guess what they would be saying about him, and he didn't want to hear it.

"Ronnie," whispered a voice in his ear, and he turned around and saw Morag staring at him. He glanced over to Jess but she was busy with customers and so he moved closer to Morag.

Her eyes were puffy and red. He shuffled about in his seat awkwardly, not quite sitting at either table, wishing he hadn't come in now. She looked upset, he didn't know what to say or to do. He started to shuffle backwards.

"Och, Ronnie, don't be daft. Come over here and sit down next to me. I was just thinking about Alan there, such a shame, eh?"

Ronnie nodded his head. "It must be true. It must have got to Alan too," he wanted to tell Morag, but the words stuck to the roof of his mouth. *Don't say a word you little freak.* He dug his nails into the palms of his hands and said nothing.

"Sit down properly Ronnie, love. You're making me nervous, shuffling about in your seat like that."

He dragged the chair over roughly hitting the leg of Morag's table, causing it to rattle and Morag's tea to slosh over the side. She wiped at the liquid with a hanky, gawping at him. He held his breath anticipating her yelling at him like his mother did.

But her voice was kind.

"You okay, love? How's things?"

He shrugged. "Okay." His head pitched back and forth watching Morag and Jess, waiting for a reaction from either of them.

Morag caught him staring at Jess and he sensed her disapproval as her lips stretched into a tight grimace and she shuffled round a little, as though trying to block his view.

She reached out and touched his arm and he winced.

"What's wrong with your arm?"

He focused on the table, "Nothing, just banged it."

"Really Ronnie? Banged it?"

"Aye. Banged it."

She reached out again. "Let me see it?"

He jerked his arm back but she persisted and, reluctantly, he let her look at it.

He saw the look on her face and followed her gaze to his arm. He grimaced and bit down on his lip as the pus oozed from the wound from under his sleeve and the dull throbbing pain began to intensify. He felt Morag pull back his sleeve.

"Ronnie, what the hell has happened? Who did this to you?"

"N'bdy," he muttered, unable to meet her eyes as she pushed his sleeve further up. He heard her sharp intake of breath, he didn't need to see her face. He wished he had never come here.

"Jesus, what the hell happened?" exclaimed a loud voice from behind him.

Ronnie looked up at the same time as Morag. Jess stood behind them, studying Ronnie's arm.

He wanted the ground to open up and swallow him, he could feel everyone staring at him, eyes boring into the back of his skull, laughing at him, he wanted to run but he could not move. He sat rooted to the spot.

"Ronnie, has somebody been hurting you… your mo…" started Morag.

He squirmed as he forced out the words. "No, not mum. Not mum. She wouldn't hurt me."

"Shh. Okay, Ronnie. It's okay," Jess knelt down in front of him now.

"Ronnie, have you been hurting yourself?"

His mouth wouldn't open.

"It's okay Ronnie, you can tell me. I'm not going to judge you, and I'm not going to say anything."

He stared at Jess. Her eyes never left his. He was compelled to speak and the words spilled out his mouth.

Seventeen

Susan

"MUMMY, LOOK!" Lily tugged at her mother's arm. "Mummy look, look what I've found." She tugged harder.

"Shh Lily, mummy is busy just now. Go and play please."

"But mummy…"

Susan's head snapped up, her phone gripped tightly in her hand.

"Lily!" she warned.

Seeing the tears fill her daughter's eyes, she felt a pang of guilt. She looked up at the clock. Almost lunchtime. Poor kid would be getting hungry and probably a bit bored by now. Although they usually spent most of their days at the library, Susan usually took Lily out at some point during the day, to let her run off a little of her energy. It wasn't fair to keep her cooped up all day. Her phone pinged again.

"Time's almost up. You need money and I need an answer. Quit messing me around."

Susan died a little inside. Time was running out and she didn't know if she had the guts to stand up to him. Besides, he was right, she did need the money. But her stomach churned at what she would have to do it earn it.

She had first come across Kris outside the foodbank not long after she had moved to the area. Mortified at having to rely on a foodbank to feed herself and Lily, Susan had been in a rush to get in and out without anyone seeing her. All she wanted was to get in, grab some stuff and get back home again. As she approached she was aware of someone watching her and she looked up to see him leaning against the wall smoking a cigarette with not a care in the world. His gaze had settled on her as she had neared the door and Susan had hurried by him, eyes downcast. Life with Colin had left her feeling uncomfortable at any form of attention, particularly the attention of men.

Kris had still been standing there when she came out forty minutes later with a bag of essentials and reeling from the experience He had thrown a lazy smile in her direction and a little shiver whispered down her spine. That should have been all the sign she needed. His arrogant smile should have told her he was the type to be avoided, cocky and oh so very sure of himself. She should have kept walking. Why hadn't she kept walking?

"Alright, love?"

Susan felt obliged to return his smile with a polite one of her own, while inside willing him to turn and walk away. She didn't know how to ignore him. She didn't want to speak to anyone. Her insides clenched at the desire to be back home behind the safety of her front door. She felt her nails dig into her palms as she kept on walking.

"Sorry. It's just you look like you've got the world on your shoulders," he persisted, matching her step.

"I'm fine, thanks. Sorry, I… we just need to get home." she quickened her pace a little.

"Hey, no worries. I wasn't trying to hit on you. Just thought I recognised a kindred spirit." He grinned as he nodded towards the foodbank.

Susan felt her face grow red as worry settled in her belly, what if she had offended him? He was only saying hello. After all those years with Colin, she had been left with a genuine fear of offending anyone, especially men. She felt compelled to stop. She looked up. He wasn't bad looking—brown eyes framed with smile lines. Her shoulders relaxed. He looked harmless.

"Sorry, I didn't mean to be rude, it's just…" she looked back at the foodbank and let her head drop.

"Hey, it's okay, love. Don't be embarrassed, you'll not be the first and you won't be the last. I've been there too, you know."

"Really?" she replied, not quite believing anyone as self-assured as him would have ever needed to go cap-in-hand to a foodbank.

"Yep, a while ago now, but I still remember feeling mortified too." He stuck out his hand. "Kris, by the way."

She took it weakly and smiled, "Susan."

He gave a mock curtsey. "Pleased to meet you Susan, and this is...?" He nodded down at Lily.

"My name's Lily," she beamed, and stuck her hand out for him to shake.

"Cute kid," he laughed.

She'd pulled Lily closer to her, suddenly unsure of this man's interest in her and her daughter. Her eyes had darted around the street, seeking an escape.

He must have sensed her discomfort. His face fell, "Oh God, sorry, I'm not some sort of weirdo... y'know... like..."

"It's okay." She hadn't known where to look, and had found herself frozen to the spot.

"Sorry. I didn't mean to frighten you both. I'll just go, and maybe I'll see you around?" He held up his hands in mock surrender and backed off slowly. He gave her a wink before turning on his heel and striding off.

Susan watched him leave, not quite sure what had just happened.

She didn't see Kris slip into the alleyway, she didn't see him pull out his phone and she didn't see the smile on his face as he whispered, "She's going to be putty in my hands."

AND SURE ENOUGH, Susan had seen him again. Kris would often appear from nowhere, randomly popping up in the same places as her, taking her for coffee, giving her a wee hand with her shopping and insisting he could do some odd jobs around the house. He was charm personified. Slowly he wormed his way in, he was easy to be around, he never pressured her or made her feel uncomfortable, he was just always around to lend a hand and never asked for anything in return. He had even slipped her some cash every now and then, ignoring her protests that she couldn't pay it back. At the start, she had been grateful for his help but it wasn't long before his mask began to slip.

She wished she had kept on walking the first time she had met him. Because now, he would not leave her alone, he bombarded her with texts, piling on the pressure, demanding an answer. What had initially felt like friendship became something much darker. He wanted to know where she was all the time, who she was talking to and what she was doing.

Kris had wheedled his way into her life before she had known what he was doing. He'd got under her skin and used his charm to cajole information from her. While she hadn't told him everything about her past, he had worked out she was running away from something and, sensing her desperation, had made his move. At first, she had laughed aloud at his suggestion. But when he had grabbed her wrist tightly, she knew it wasn't a joke. Kris didn't laugh as his fingers dug deeper.

"You owe me, after everything I've done for you. You owe me back." His warm brown eyes had turned black, a glittering angry dark.

"B-b-but it's…"

"It's what?" he had spat. "All you need to do is go out for dinner, play nice and you'll get your money at the end of every week, what's wrong with that? I can even get you a free babysitter for the kid. It's a win-win situation. You get a few nights out, some money at the end of it? What's not to like?"

"It's prostitution," she'd cried. "You're asking me to sell myself to these men."

"Don't be so fuckin' stupid, prostitution… Do I look like a fucking pimp? It's a service. There's guys out there—lonely, wives gone and left them, just wanting a wee bit of company, that's all. A service, that's all it, giving something back to your community." He'd smirked.

Susan had turned and fled. But Kris hadn't given up. He'd used her weakness to control her. "I'm giving you a choice," he'd leered, as he slipped a photocopied newspaper cutting into her hand. She had choked back the bile as Colin's face peered out at her. The headline screamed: *Top Cop in plea for his missing wife and child.*

Eighteen

Morag

MORAG SUCKED HER breath in behind pursed lips as she watched Jess fussing over Ronnie. Her jaw clenched tightly and her eyes narrowed, watching the girl fawn over him. Although she couldn't prove it, Morag was convinced Ronnie was lying about the self-harm. She suspected his injuries came from the abuse she knew his mother doled out to him on a daily basis. Everyone knew what that little trollop was like, she had heard all the rumours. Women like her didn't deserve a family, she fumed.

When Morag had first got to know Ronnie she had used the rumours and her suspicions to her advantage. People like Ronnie were easy to manipulate, little lost souls, crying out to be wanted. It had been so easy to worm her way inside of his head, playing on his insecurities and fears, feeding his paranoia, making him believe being with her was the safest place for him to be. He had needed her, almost really needed only her. They could have been a family. He could have been her family. Until Jess. Until that little bitch came along.

Batting her eyelids at him, luring him in. Morag recognised her type—the type her mother had always warned her about. *Wanton little tramp,* her mother whispered. *Just like you, Morag. Nothing but a little tramp.*

Morag sat rigid in her seat, knowing she was staring, but neither Ronnie nor Jess were paying her any attention. She might as well have been invisible, they were so caught up in their own little bubble. She balled her fists by her side, wanting to smash them down on the girl's head. She recognised her feelings as jealousy, but she didn't care. She didn't like this Jess, sneaking in and trying to take what was hers, wheedling her way into Ronnie's life and closing her out. Jess was obviously trying to take her family away from her. Morag had been right not to let her join their group.

She shuffled backwards in her chair, deliberately clattering the chair into the table behind her, but not even that caught their attention. She pushed back her seat further and snatched up her bag.

"I'll be off, then," she huffed.

They glimpsed up at her and smiled briefly before turning back to each other. *Looks like you're not wanted... again,* her mother sneered. Morag shrugged her shoulders and stormed out the café letting the door slam behind her.

"That little bitch best be careful," she muttered under her breath as she stepped out into the cold winter afternoon. She checked her watch. It was only lunchtime, and she didn't know how to fill the rest of her day—she felt completely out of sorts.

Wandering up the main street with no real interest in what was happening around her, she wandered into a couple of the shops to pass the time, but quickly left as soon as she caught sight of anyone she recognised. She didn't feel like speaking to anyone. She crossed the road and stood at the park gates.

Spying an empty bench, she sat down, and tried to slow her breathing, to rid herself of the anxious niggle in her stomach. Looking for a distraction, she pulled her phone out of her bag. The message icon flashed.

"What about my money?" The text read.

"I told you, you'll get it when the job is complete." Morag replied.

"I'm not waiting much longer, this shit is dragging on too long. Unless you want me to make the call? Get him involved?"

"No. Don't, don't do that. Nothing stopping you pretending you've made contact though?"

"I'll be in touch, but I'm warning you, I'm about done with this and you owe me for the work I've already done."

She stuffed the phone back in her bag as a shadow fell across her.

"Alright Morag," a voice boomed.

She looked up in dismay. Radio Joe stood in front of her, with a stupid grin across his face and his radio stuck to his ear as usual.

"Just listening to the news, did you hear…?" He stopped abruptly as she cut him off with her glare.

"I'm not interested in the news Joe, I came here for some peace and quiet," she snapped.

Joe's face fell. Morag knew she should feel guilty but Joe wasn't one of hers. He didn't need her. People like Joe weren't as vulnerable as people thought. She felt him see through her. He was wiser than he looked. Joe shook his head and ambled away, radio still glued to his ear.

Morag walked through the park to the entrance nearest the library. It was quieter there and she looked around to check Joe had not followed her over. Satisfied she was alone, she sank down onto the bench oblivious to bite of the cold November air, completely lost in her own thoughts, her rage keeping her warm. She reached into her bag and picked out the photograph. Holding it to her cheek, she let the closeness soothe her a little.

"My most precious, special one. You didn't leave me did you? Family never leave. They took you away from me. It wasn't my fault. I'd have never let you go." She brushed her lips over the photograph.

A sudden movement caught her from the corner of her eye. She quickly stuffed the photograph back in her bag and squinted, expecting to see Joe again. Morag smiled to see Susan and her daughter Lily instead. Her smile quickly turned to a frown as she noticed Susan was glued to her phone, ignoring the child tugging frantically at her arm in a bid to catch her mother's attention. Her teeth clenched in frustration, why did parents ignore their children, why were they so obsessed with the gadgets in their hands than the little ones who needed them. Some people didn't know how lucky they were, they didn't deserve children if they couldn't bring them up properly.

She swallowed the words she wanted to say, it wouldn't do to tell Susan what she really thought of her parenting skills, she needed the young woman on her side. Morag needed her even more now Alan had left and Ronnie was slowly slipping further away from her. Besides, perhaps Susan was even better than Alan and Ronnie. She had Lily. Lily was perfect. *Yes,* she thought, *I need to be careful how I approach this one.* She didn't want to scare her off, but she did need to teach her a lesson. How to be a better mother, to give Lily the attention she needed.

Morag could help her, she could look after them, just like family were supposed to do. After all, that's all she was trying to do, watch out for her family. Wasn't she?

But Morag was worried, women like Susan were weak, they ran away thinking they could make it on their own but, without the trappings of a fancy lifestyle, they would often cave and go crawling back to their exes. She had seen it before, wasted so much time on women like Susan. Women who could have been part of her family, but had not been up to scratch.

But Susan was different, Morag worked hard to convince herself, she was getting desperate now. She was worth the effort. Susan had Lily. Lily had been the sign Morag had been searching for, and she had known it from the day she had first set eyes on the child. The mass of blonde curls and big blue eyes. Yes, Lily had been the sign, and Morag had to make sure things would go to plan. This time. Nothing could stand in her way. She needed family around her now.

"Library Lady… Library Lady," the child's voice dragged her back to the present. Lily ran over to her with a huge smile on her face, quickly followed by a breathless and crimson-faced Susan who was stuffing her phone back into her handbag. She looked to be on the verge of tears.

"Lily," smiled Morag pretending to be surprised to see them. 'How nice to see you. What have you been up to today?'

The child burst into an itinerary of her morning's activities, hardly stopping for a breath. Morag's heart was fit to burst, in such a short time she had grown to adore this child, she couldn't let Susan take her away. Not now.

Letting the child chatter on, Morag turned to Susan, she stood rigid, not saying a word, staring into space. Morag reached out and touched her arm gently. She ignored her real wish to dig her nails deep into the young woman's skin.

"Are you okay love?"

Susan shook her head, tears now falling freely.

"N-n-no I'm not. I d-d-don't know what to do anymore. I've made such a mess of everything, I-I-I…"

"Shh," said Morag, looking over at Lily who stared back at them both, open-mouthed. Morag leaned over and patted the child on her arm, loathe to remove her hand relishing the surge of protectiveness she felt for the girl.

"It's okay, Lily. Mum will be okay. Listen, why don't you go over to that patch of grass and collect me some leaves, and we will see if I have some spare glue and paper in the library and you can make some winter pictures this afternoon, if you want."

Easily distracted, Lily obeyed and ran over to the grass where the adults could still see her. Morag nodded encouragingly to the child, keeping her gaze firmly on her, while speaking to Susan at the same time.

"Is it Colin? Is he back on the scene? Has he found you?"

"No, not Colin, it's…"

"Susan, you need to tell me if you want me to help you. You can't be getting yourself into a state like this, not when you've got a wee kiddie to look after. There is nothing that cannot be sorted, you know."

Morag felt Susan appraise her as though trying to decide if she could trust her. Morag tore her gaze from Lily reluctantly, turning to face Susan.

"You can trust me Susan, there's nothing you can say that will shock me. And who knows, I might even be able to help you both," she smiled.

Susan took a deep breath and the story came tumbling out. Of how she had met the man outside the foodbank, of his kindness at first and how his kindness had quickly turned to demands. How he said she owed him for everything he had done for her. She thrust her phone in front of Morag's face.

"This just came through."

Had a nice chat with hubby last night. Don't worry, didn't tell him anything, but if you don't get your finger out soon, bitch, I'm spilling the lot. You owe me big time.

"Maybe he's right, I do owe him. He did do a lot for me, maybe if I do this just the once then I will have paid him back… and it means I'll have some money for Lily's Christmas presents." The words tumbled out of her mouth.

"Susan! You can't think like that. What he is doing is illegal. He's trying to get you to have sex with other men for money… A prostitute, Susan!"

"It's n-n-ot…"

"It is, and you know it is. Otherwise you wouldn't get yourself in such a state about what he is asking you to do. Would you?"

Morag didn't wait for a reply, she moved straight in with her plan—a proposition she didn't think Susan could turn down.

"Do you need money?"

Susan's faced reddened. "Yes, I do. But I'm not asking you for…"

"And I'm not giving you money for nothing either. I do have a proposition for you, though."

Morag told her how she had let things go at home after her mother's death.

"I've tried to keep on top of things, but I just don't have the motivation or the energy to tackle it all. And now it is a so much of a mess I wouldn't even know where to start."

She watched for Susan's reaction, not sure if the woman could read between the lines. Susan's face remained blank.

"I guess what I'm trying to say is, it would help me out a great deal if you could come round to mine a couple of times a week and help me sort things out, and then maybe just help me keep on top of things?"

"I don't know…"

"You can bring Lily, and if you want to come in the afternoons, you could both stay for your dinner? It'll give me some company, if I'm honest. I get pretty lonely rattling about that house on my own." Behind her back, her fingers were crossed.

She could see the cogs turning inside Susan's head and she recognised the temptation shining from her eyes.

"Cash in hand. Our secret, nobody needs to know," she smiled.

Susan was quiet for a moment, before smiling herself. "Only if you're sure? I don't want you to be doing this because you feel sorry for us both. We don't need anybody's pity you know."

"I'm not doing it out of pity. I'm doing it because my house is a tip, I need help to clean it. I trust you to do it and you will be doing me a big favour. And I'm paying you, so it's a working relationship." She added in her mind, *and you don't know just how much I need you both in my life.*

Morag watched Susan carefully, but she already knew what her answer would be. Lily came running back over to the two women.

"I've got lots and lots and lots of leaves, Mrs Library Lady," she chuckled. Morag ruffled the child's hair and turned to Susan raising an eyebrow.

"But what about Kris?" Susan whispered, "What will I tell him? He's not going to take no for an answer?"

"Leave him to me. I'll sort it."

Susan raised her eyebrows, her face twisted.

"I'll sort it. Trust me." Morag's voice was firm. "Men like Kris don't frighten me. I'll look out for you Susan."

"It's a deal," she smiled weakly.

"Excellent. Now Lily why don't you and your mum go over to the library, I won't be long. It's my day off today, but I can pop over and get you the craft stuff I promised you."

Susan took her daughter's hand and smiled at Morag.

"Why don't you come round tomorrow morning and we can go over what needs doing?" asked Morag.

Susan nodded. "Thank you. Thank you so much."

Her gaze followed Susan as she walked towards the park gates, she looked lighter than she had twenty minutes ago.

"No, Susan, thank you, my dear. I'm only doing what families are meant to do—watch out for each other."

Nineteen

Jess

JESS BREATHED A sigh of relief as Ronnie's snivelling had eventually subsided. It had been a narrow escape trying to stop him blubbering out all his secrets for all and sundry in the café to hear. She chuckled as she recalled Morag storming out, clearly in a huff. Serves the stupid bitch right. She doesn't deserve to have anyone around her. She deserves to be on her own, the stupid cow.

Jess had gone back to her work behind the counter, but Ronnie had been super clingy, reaching out to her every time she stepped out to clear the tables. Even now, she could feel his eyes boring into her back as she moved around the café. She had tried her best to reassure him, especially when that stupid Annie fucking Boyle had had a right strop about Ronnie 'making a show of himself.'

Jess had been raging at the woman's ignorance, and had to bite her tongue to stop herself giving Annie a mouthful back. The daggers she had thrown in the direction of the older woman left Annie in no doubt as to what her true feelings were.

"Costs nothing to be kind Annie," Jess had snapped at the woman's retreating back, as she had marched out the café muttering about 'locking up the nutters and throwing away the key.'

And now her head was all over the place, she couldn't focus on what she was meant to be doing. Orders had been muddled up and she had dropped more than she had sold as her fingers had seemed to turn to butter. The final straw had been when she spilled a full cup of coffee over her favourite bag. It was only a cheap one she had picked up in a charity shop a few years back, but the bright patchwork colours had caught her eye and it had been with her ever since. She had cursed, ripped off her apron and told Marion she was done for the day. Ignoring her boss's protests that she still had an hour of her shift left, Jess grabbed her stuff and walked out, desperate to feel some fresh air on her face.

Ronnie had shuffled out the café after her like a lost puppy.

"I'm going over to the library. You can come if you want?" Her irritation had swayed to pity. None of this was his fault. He had just been caught up in the crossfire.

"No, it's Wednesday. I don't like going on a Wednesday. Morag's not there."

"What is it about that bloody woman? Why does everyone follow her around? She's like the bloody Pied Piper." Jess snapped, her pity for Ronnie quickly evaporating again.

Ronnie's face fell. "She's kind, Jess. Honestly, she is. She treats us like family, she looks out for us."

Jess shrugged her shoulders, mimicking him. "She looks out for us." She snorted. "Aye right, Ronnie, whatever. Believe that if you want. That bitch doesn't deserve family. She's a manipulative old cow. But hey, if you think she's 'family' then good luck to you. She wouldn't be the family I'd choose for myself."

Jess turned her back on him and marched off, her shoulders rigid with rage. *It's not fair*, she thought. Bloody family. Morag wouldn't know what family meant if it hit her between the eyes.

Oh mum, I miss you so much. Jess felt as though she was losing it, her emotions were all over the place and not for the first time, she began to doubt herself. Maybe she should just pack up and leave. Start all over again? Hot tears stung her eyes, as she remembered how the family she had known and loved had been torn apart. No, she thought, no way was she giving up now. She owed her mum that much.

She stopped at the park gates and turned around, watching Ronnie shuffle away, shoulders slumped but his head darting all over the place. His weakness shone out like a beacon, it was no wonder Morag had found it so easy to manipulate him.

Jess had been watching Morag for months, the woman was like a vulture, circling around the weak and the vulnerable before swooping in for the kill. She couldn't fathom why no one else could see this. Maybe they did and they just didn't care. People like Ronnie were invisible, their lives didn't matter. Anyone with half a brain can see she doesn't want to be on her own, thought Jess. And that lot are the only ones who will give her the time of day.

Rather than making her feel better, her thoughts made her question her own value more. *What's wrong with me? Why doesn't she want me around? Why does everyone leave me?*

Feeling herself sink into a bout of self-pity, Jess took a deep breath and swallowed hard.

No tears Jess, just put on your big girl pants and get on with it. She pulled her shoulders backed and lifted her face towards the sky and mouthed the words 'for you mum'.

SHE CROSSED THE park and ran up the steps to the library. Opening the doors, a blast of warm air met her—a welcome relief from the biting cold outside. She stepped inside, pleased to see the familiar face of the young girl on the desk who had been there on her first visit. As she approached the desk she spotted Morag leaving. She looked around and saw Susan and her kid sitting doing some crafts, the kid waving to Morag with a huge smile on her face.

Jesus, even the kid gets the special treatment. Jess barely hid her sneer, before turning her back on them before they spotted her, she wasn't in the mood to pretend she was pleased to see them.

"Hi… Lynn, isn't it?" she said, peering at the girl's name badge, which read Lynn MacDonald, Senior Library Assistant.

Lynn lifted her eyes. "Oh hi. You were in the other night weren't you?" The smile on her face had widened as she recognised Jess.

"Yeah, back again. Like everyone else in here, I guess," she laughed. She nodded over to Morag who was making her way out the front door. "Looks like your staff can't even keep away from the place on their days off."

Lynn Followed Jess's gaze and her lip curled, "Oh her, she's never away from the place. Mind you, she's nothing else going on in her life, has she? She just hangs about here all the time… with the weirdos." She slapped her hand across her mouth, "God, I'm sorry, I didn't mean that."

"Hey, no worries, I know what you mean though. There's plenty of them around here." The words Jess really wanted to say remained firmly behind her lips. Inside she cursed the silly bitch for her crass use of language to describe people. Jess knew she might not have the same education as some people but at least she knew how to treat people with a bit of dignity and respect. Her face hid her true feelings as she applied her fake smile and carried on the conversation. Apart from Susan and the kid, the library was nearly empty and she sensed Lynn was the type who liked to gossip.

"So, she not got any family of her own then?"

"Nah, she lived with her mum until she died. Mind you, she only turned up a few years ago, to care for her mum. Nobody knows where she had been up until then. My gran said she used to live here, as a kid. Her mum and dad were weirdos too, right religious nuts. At church every day. Then her dad upped and left one day and never came back, apparently. Weird if you ask me. They were the talk of the town after that, according to my gran, them being so churchy and all that."

"So how come she moved away?"

"Nobody knows. She disappeared one day, same as her dad, only she came running back with her tail between her legs. My mum reckons something must have happened wherever she had been. She came back even stranger than before. Like she had some sort of dark secret."

"Ha-ha, did you not ask her? I would have, if I worked with her," Jess retorted.

Lynn was settling into her story. Jess could tell she was happy for someone to gossip with—in a dump like this, folk had to make their own entertainment.

"Well, I've not been here as long as she has, obviously, but the other staff in here said they tried at the beginning—tried to invite her out on nights out, include her in things, but she was having none of it. She kept saying she had to go home and see to her mother and clammed up when anyone asked her where she had been living before. She was really weird, too. Apparently she used to bring presents in for the other staff, but not in a nice way. In a creepy way... like she had been stalking them or something, cause it was always stuff they really liked but nobody else would have known about. They kind of stopped talking to her after that... so no one really knows if she had been married, shacked up with someone or whatever... hey, maybe she had been married and killed him off," she snorted.

"Yeah, maybe. People are strange. You never know what goes on behind closed doors, I guess." Jess winked.

Lynn pulled herself forward, elbows on the desk, checking nobody was listening. She was clearly settling down for the long haul. Jess stifled a yawn and changed direction of the conversation to cut her off.

"Can I book a slot on the computers? My internet's slow back at the flat and I've got some stuff to do?"

Jess smirked as Lynn's face dropped, but fair play to the girl, she quickly adopted a bright smile. "Course you can, you can have as long as you want. It's normally an hour max, but there's nobody about today looking to use them, so fill your boots," she handed Jess an access code.

Jess turned to walk away when Lynn called her back, "You're pretty new around here, aren't you?"

"Yeah?"

"Well if you're ever stuck for a night out give me a shout. Some of us go down the local, The Toby Jug, at the weekends and you're welcome to come along if you want? Nothing worse than living in a new place and being Billy-no-mates is there?"

Jess smiled. "Thanks. I might just take you up on that once I get paid, cheers."

She walked away smiling, building this little network of 'friends' was turning out to be useful indeed, but she had to be cautious—she didn't want to get too close to anyone and risk them prying too closely into her life.

Twenty

Morag

MORAG LEFT SUSAN and Lily in the library, her mood lighter than it had been for a long time. At last, a family. A real family, all for her. She shivered with excitement as she imagined them being with her happily ever after. The perfect fairy-tale ending.

With her mood lifted Morag decided she would take a trip out to the retail park. She usually avoided the place, full of families and smiling faces it just served as a bitter reminder of her own loneliness. But now she had something to look forward to. She had a family to shop for. She made her way to the bus stop with a smile on her face.

As she waited for the No.88 to arrive, Morag ran through a list of everything she would need for her guests—no, family. The smile on her face grew wider as she hummed tunelessly to herself, her plans running a marathon inside her head. She was oblivious to the stares of the others waiting in the queue.

The bus arrived and Morag settled herself down for the half-hour journey. Taking her phone out her bag, she gave a surreptitious glance at the other passengers. Satisfied none of them were paying her any attention Morag, pulled up her Facebook page, and scrolled quickly through the posts. Her lips puckered as she flicked through the lives of those she followed and she tasted the bitterness at the faces smiled back up at her. Perfect lives. Perfect families. Then, the corners of her mouth turned up as she remembered, she would soon have her own family around her. Morag stifled a snigger as she imagined the look on her colleagues faces if they could see her now. They all thought she lived in the dark ages. Oh, she'd heard their pointed remarks at how long it took her to do things on the computer, and their pointed stares when she took out her old brick of a mobile. If only they knew just how much she knew. If only they knew she could see their ugly truths hiding behind the lies they told online. She heard them in work bitching about their kids, their husbands, their parents. Nobody ever bothered with her—they all just wrote her off as an old has-been, nobody worth bothering about. None of them would ever have believed she would be capable of creating a whole new online persona to watch them with, reinventing herself was nothing new for Morag.

The ping of an incoming text message interrupted her internal rant. She opened it up and frowned. Quickly, she stabbed out a reply. "You will get what you're owed when the job's done. I need you to deliver a message tomorrow."

The phone beeped almost immediately in response. "I'm out of pocket now. I need paying."

Morag replied: "I've told you. You'll get your money. I'll sort it. Will message you tomorrow." She stuffed her phone back in her bag, a dark shadow cast over her happiness. She was completely unaware of the stares and whispers from her fellow passengers and completely oblivious that her dark mutterings were not as quiet as she had thought they were. she

The bus slowed as it neared the retail park and she followed the rest of the passengers off, careful to keep her head down and make no contact with them. She didn't need anyone else now—her family was coming home to her.

Morag lost herself for the afternoon mooching around the shops. She embraced the busyness of the place, soaked up the sounds of families and people as she wandered through the aisles. She sighed as she stroked the soft fabrics of clothes she would never have the confidence to wear. Clothes that would make her stand out, make people sit up and take notice. *Plain Jane, who do you think you are, mutton dressed as lamb, that's what you would be, the angry words hissed in her ears.*

Morag tried to ignore her mother's criticism, she hummed as she tried outfit after outfit against herself, preening in front of the mirror. In her mind, she pictured herself Susan and Lily shopping together, picking out clothes, trying them on, having lunch, doing things families do together. Susan faded from the picture leaving only Morag and Lily. *I would take care of her*, Morag thought. *I know what she needs. She needs me. A proper family—that's what she needs.*

Sensing someone watching her, she glanced up and caught a young shop assistant trying hard not to laugh. Morag looked in the mirror and bit back angry tears as she saw what the girl could see. A middle aged woman making a full of herself. Red-faced, she rushed out the shop leaving the clothes on the floor in a heap. Stupid *girl*, whispered her mother. *Nobody would look twice at you. Not even if you ran down the main street in your underwear.*

"Bitch," muttered Morag, her nails digging into the palm of her hands. Her mother's endless criticisms followed her everywhere. A woman walking by pulled her child closer to her as Morag muttered, "I wish you would just fuck off and leave me alone."

Morag marched into the Pound Savers store to buy the cleaning products she had originally come for. Thanks to her inheritance, Morag didn't need to scrimp and save when it came to shopping but her mother's miserable ways had rubbed off on her and even now she was reluctant to overspend.

Walking round the aisles, she began picking up a few bits and pieces in anticipation of Susan and Lily coming around the next day. She felt her breathing return to normal and a sense of calm returned. She smiled to herself as she popped some cleaning products into her trolley. She almost walked past the toy aisle before stopping herself. It wouldn't do any harm to pick up a few wee bits and bobs for Lily, just a few things to keep her amused while Susan cleaned and maybe...

"Oh stop it, Morag," she chided herself. "Don't be going too fast, or you will be scaring them away." *Just like you always do*, her mother's voice mocked her, as she picked up some colouring-in books, crayons and an arts and craft set. Her hand hovered over a small rag doll, its big blue eyes and goofy smile made her heart lurch. She hesitated, worried she may be going a bit over the top with the gifts, but the doll called out to her. She reached back and stroked it lovingly, completely unaware of the wide berth other shoppers were now giving her. Her eyes misted over as she imagined Lily's wee face at seeing the doll, a wide accepting smile, the small hand reaching out...

Then look what happened, you stupid bitch, and Morag let the doll dropped back down onto the shelf, abandoned, unwanted, and alone.

Morag's chest tightened, she gasped for breath and tears pricked at her eyes. She had to get out of here, fast. She pushed her trolley to the checkout, throwing her purchases at the cashier, blanking all his obvious attempts at making small talk.

Outside Morag leant against the wall, shopping bags grasped tightly in her hand. The colour drained from her face, and her chest constricted as the memories flooded back. People backed away as she gulped in breaths of fresh air trying to compose herself. "It's done now, Morag, It's all in the past. It's done," she repeated, trying hard to convince herself.

A security guard approached her, a wary look on his face. "Are you alright, Missus? You're a wee bit pale?"

She nodded, "I'm fine, honestly. I'm okay, just a bit of a flush, my age you know..."

His face reddened and Morag almost pitied him.

He mumbled something that sounded like, "Okay... well... if you're sure then..." as he backed away from her, clearly mortified at the idea of dealing with a menopausal middle-aged woman in the midst of a meltdown.

"Thank you, though. Thank you for caring," she smiled back at him.

AN HOUR LATER, and Morag was glad to have arrived home. Kicking the door closed behind her she made her way through to the kitchen, and dropped the shopping bags on the floor. She rubbed at the red welts on her fingers where the handles had been digging into her hands. *Definitely bought more than I meant to*, she chuckled to herself, ignoring the anxiety the spending spree had caused her

She pulled open the top drawer, taking her phone out her bag to hide it away. The NHS logo stared back up at her accusingly. Her fingers hovered over the paper before pushing it to the back of the drawer. Morag bit her lip. She had a morbid fear of being taken in to hospital and never getting out alive. But she would have to bite the bullet. She had to know, especially now she was about to have her family with her. she pushed the phone to the back of the drawer obscuring the letter.

"Tomorrow," she whispered.

Morag moved through to the lounge, her eyes swept the room and for the first time imagined it through the eyes of a stranger. It was awful. What would Susan think when she came round?

"God, I've really let this place go," she muttered.

Nobody had come to visit since her mother had passed away and even before that, they'd had few visitors other than district nurses and the minister coming to tend to mother. The sofa and chairs were littered with old newspapers, dust danced off the furniture and the windows were so filthy it was impossible to tell if it was day or night outside. Mouldy cups and plates covered the coffee table and stale air hovered over the chaos.

Everything was past its best, all worn and shabby. Like her, she thought, it had been worn and used since she was a child. "I'm not wasting my money on any of that modern tat," mother had spat at Morag when she had dared to suggest updating some of the furniture after she'd moved back home.

Her shoulders slumped as she gazed around the room. Where would she even start? What did a proper family house even look like? She wanted it to be perfect for them—her new family. She stamped her feet and cursed. Forcing herself to move, she rushed into the kitchen, a sudden burst of energy taking over her. She found a bin bag under the sink, and began to sweep away as much of the rubbish as she could. But not too much. She had to leave some stuff lying around, it wouldn't do for Susan to think there wasn't any work for her to do here, that she had brought her to the house under false pretences.

Morag stood back and surveyed her handiwork, the room looked slightly better than it had done an hour ago. She peeked into the kitchen.

"Hmm, it could do with a quick once over," she said, massaging her hip joints. she felt tired to the bone. The sudden burst of energy had drained her. She yawned, picked up the nearest bag of rubbish and switched off the light, turning her back on the mounds of dishes and overflowing bins in the far corner. Instead Morag focussed on placing one foot in front of the other in an effort to keep going, trying to shake off the overwhelming feeling of exhaustion.

"You need to keep going, Morag. Come on now, woman," she scolded herself. "You've got family coming, you need to buck your ideas up a bit."

Out in the hallway, she stuffed the bag of rubbish under the stairs, jamming it in with the rest of the clutter she had tried to clear up before—for the others, who never came.

She looked to the upstairs of the house. There were four bedrooms up there: hers, her mothers, and the two spare bedrooms, both of which were empty just waiting to be filled Morag pictured the two rooms filled with life, brightly decorated and full of love and happiness. Full of family—the family that she should always have had. She crossed her fingers and said a little prayer towards the crucifix her mother had loved. Morag was not religious in the slightest but, right now, she could do with all the help she could get.

She made her way up the stairs, her feet leaden, the exhaustion now threatening to crush her. Ignoring it, she pushed open the doors of the two spare rooms, one for Lily and one for Susan. The smallest one for Susan, after all she wouldn't be around for long. She smiled, the rooms were perfect, they would love them. Morag didn't notice the wallpaper waft in the draft from the door and the smell of damp didn't meet her nostrils.

She looked at the door slightly ajar and shuddered. She didn't want Susan seeing that room, her mother's room—she couldn't let her see *that*. Going into her own room to fetch the key for mother's bedroom, she saw her handbag lying on the bed. Peeking out the top was the photograph. She took it out and sat down on the bed, clasping it to her chest.

"Tomorrow's a special day, sweetheart," she whispered. "We're going to be a family again. A proper family, just the way it should always have been. But don't worry my precious, nobody will ever replace you."

She kissed the photograph tenderly and placed it back in her handbag. Her hand brushed against the jar. Pulling it out she unscrewed the lid and tipped it upside down.

The paper hearts fluttered like confetti, coming to rest on her bed. Hearts as fragile as the family she had tried to create. She had only ever tried to care for them, to look out for them. But every one of them had let her down, one way or another. They had all had to leave in the end. They couldn't be her family, if they didn't appreciate her love. They couldn't stay with her if they didn't need her the way families should need each other. Alan had hurt her badly, she had trusted him, thought he was different to the others, but in the end, he was just as bad, if not worse. She had trusted him too much, confided in him, told him things about her life she had never told anyone else. Then he had betrayed her in the worst possible way. He had told her secret.

She held each little heart close, remembering the lost souls they represented. She wrapped Alan's heart around the lock of hair she had taken from him. Before Alan it had been Fiona. Now, she had been special. Such a lovely young woman, real potential to be family But she had been so troubled. In the end, she couldn't be trusted. Morag shook her head, remembering Fiona's threats to tell people about her, trying to humiliate her. Ungrateful little bitch. The accident had been tragic. Fiona had run out of the house... and just before she'd reached home, there had been a hit-and-run—the driver had never been caught.

Morag had just happened to be the one who found her. The one who told police about the black car that came out of nowhere and hit Fiona. The black car that had been found abandoned minutes from where Fiona's body lay. Imagine stealing a car, Morag had chuckled to herself, as she had torn off a small piece of Fiona's blouse. She took the small scrap of bloodied material and held it to her nose, before carefully wrapping it back up in the heart.

Her brows furrowed as she picked up the two black hearts stuck together. Instinctively she clutched them, scrunching them inside her clenched fist. Mother and Father, joined in hellish matrimony. She scowled as she threw them back in the jar and watched them drop to the bottom entwined together forever.

The last two hearts lay on her bed reminding her of the scars she held inside, her own heart scarred by the memories. Her tears soaked the paper hearts, and she allowed the fatigue she had been fighting off to take over, pulling her into a deep sleep.

MORAG WOKE UP to find her room in darkness. She squinted at her watch. The illuminated hands showed it was six-thirty p.m. She jumped up. She had been asleep for almost three hours and she still had lots to do to prepare for Susan's visit tomorrow.

An hour later, she was quietly satisfied the house appeared to be almost presentable. She double-checked her mother's bedroom door was locked and the key hidden safely away.

Feeling parched she went into the kitchen to make herself a cup of tea. She should eat, but she wasn't hungry. Instead, she pulled a packet of digestives from her cupboard and plonked them down on the kitchen table next to her tea. Reaching into the top drawer, she scrabbled about until she found her phone. She switched it on and logged into her other life.

Carla Fitzgerald—happily married mother of two, with her perfect family. This was Morag's online alter ego. Carla had lots of friends, she was a popular lady, everybody loved Carla and her sickly sweet positivity. It was so much easier nowadays, she mused. All she had to do was pick a photograph of the person she wanted to be and create a world around them. Carla served as nothing more than a tool to glimpse into the lives of others, and it was so easy to do. Nobody questioned anything and they all shared everything —from what they ate for dinner to their latest emotional disaster. Their whole lives out there, just for the taking. Morag wished she had more time. She scrolled through the vacuous lives of her new friends, clicking love responses when in reality she wanted to tear down their perfectly filtered lives and snatch their happiness for herself.

Going to the search bar, she pulled up Susan's profile. Susan had told Morag of her worry any online activity would alert Colin to her whereabouts, explaining why she hadn't closed her account down. The picture showed her and Colin on their wedding day. Susan had been smart—her privacy settings wouldn't let Morag look at her page, but that didn't matter, all Morag wanted was the photographs. She zoomed in on the photographs of Lily as a baby, while her mind eradicated Susan and Colin from each of the scenes. She thought of Susan now, alone and vulnerable. She and Lily needed family around them and Morag was just the person to provide it for her, and some proper guidance for the child—the love a child should have. Morag could give her everything Susan could not.

Closing down her page, knowing she would not find him there, she opened up the search engine and typed in Colin Hayes, Susan's ex-husband. Morag had helped Susan complete her benefit applications when she first met her in the library. She had noted the surname on her application was different to the one Susan had on her library card. A little bit of gentle persuasion had led to Susan opening up to Morag about her past. See, she thought, everybody trusts the quiet ones. She had promised not to tell a soul and she hadn't. Susan Bonnar was safe as houses with her. Mrs Sonia Hayes didn't exist.

Morag's search threw up hundreds of articles—links to award ceremonies, video clips and high praise for this well respected officer of the law. Morag read them all, even though she knew most of the words off by heart. He was a good-looking man, but she could see the cold glint in his eyes, even from the grainy reproduced newspaper articles, she could see the cruelty shining from them.

Her favourite article appeared at the top of the search results.

Detective Sergeant Inspector in plea for missing wife and child, the headline screamed. She scanned down the article... DSI Colin Hayes makes an emotional appeal for information leading to the whereabouts of his wife and child who have been missing... Sonia is extremely vulnerable... worried about the safety of his wife and child... if you have any information...' He had not looked after his family had he? Otherwise they would never have left him. It was up to Morag to do it properly now.

The article was over a year old now, and Morag was impressed that Susan had managed to stay under the radar all this time, especially given the influence her husband must have in the force.

"What would you say, DSI Hayes, if you knew where your wife was?"

She pictured Susan's tortured face as she opened up texts from a concerned friend and smiled coldly.

"Family is everything," Morag whispered.

Twenty One

Susan

SUSAN TOPPED UP the meter, thankful her benefits had been paid into her bank account. She turned the television on and plonked Lily down in front of it, knowing her daughter would happily sit glued to it while she put the dinner on. It felt good to have some food in the cupboards she thought as she unpacked her bags absentmindedly. Susan considered the offer Morag had made her as she started preparing their meagre dinner. She looked at the value price tin of hotdogs and beans, not wanting to peer at the nutritional value too closely. She popped a couple of slices of bread into the toaster. The extra money would come in handy that was for sure. She might even be able to save for a deposit somewhere else. Move on, further away this time. Down south maybe thought Susan. Away from her past completely, away from Colin and away from Kris. Her stomach heaved as she remembered his last text. She tried to imagine his reaction if she told him she didn't need his money anymore. She could even offer to pay him back, in cash. Might take her longer to save for a deposit, but at least it would mean she didn't have his threat of Colin hanging over her.

"You are being ridiculous," she thought. Men like Kris were not interested in getting their money back in cash. No, he would be looking at her as an investment—a longer-term cash cow. She felt sick. But she had to leave it to Morag to sort, she had to trust her, she had to trust someone, surely that someone would be Morag? She hadn't told anyone her secret. She had to trust her, she had no other option.

The toast popped at the same time as she heard her phone pinging through a message. She screwed her eyes shut, her breathing shallow.

"Ignore it. Ignore it," she muttered. But she couldn't, he would just keep messaging until she replied. She picked up the phone, it wasn't Kris's number. Her fingers hovered over the delete button before pressing accept.

"He's never going to stop searching for you. You know that, don't you? But don't worry. I'm not going to tell him where you are. Just watch your back though, not everyone is worthy of your trust. A concerned friend. X"

She tried to call the number back but it was unavailable, Susan didn't know whether to be terrified or relieved.

The phone slipped from her fingers and fell to the floor, the screen staring back at her accusingly. Then it rang.

Susan slid to the floor, watching the screen light up—a withheld number from a caller who was clearly not giving up. She stared at the phone, willing it to stop, but it continued to ring. Mindful Lily was next door and would probably come running through if she didn't answer it, Susan tentatively picked it up and pressed reject. Immediately it rang again. She could feel the walls closing in on her. Her chest began to tighten and her breathing grew shallow.

The pan on the hob bubbled, the faint smell of burnt hotdogs and beans lingered in the air.

"Fuck, fuck, fuck! What am I going to do?" Still the phone rang. Her finger stabbed the accept button and she placed the phone next to her ear. There was an ominous silence, she breathed heavily, not trusting herself to say anything.

"Susan, are you there?"

Silence from Susan.

"Susan? It's me, Jess. Are you there?"

"Yeah, I'm here."

"Jesus, I've been ringing you for ages. Are you okay?"

"I'm fine. I was just, erm…" She looked around as she got to her feet. "…burning dinner." She let out a strangled laugh as she yanked the pan off the hob.

"You sound like you've been running a marathon. Either that or doing some kinky sex line," Jess laughed at the other end of the phone.

"How did you get my number?" her voice filled with accusation.

"Whoa! You gave it to me, don't you remember? I said I'd give you a call, see if you wanted to catch up or anything?"

Susan heard hurt in Jess's response and she wracked her brains, she couldn't remember giving Jess her number, but then again, her head had been all over the place recently.

"Sorry, I forgot I gave you it. What is it you're wanting?"

"Well, I'm at a bit of a loose end. Thought you and Lily might like a visitor? Thought I could come round and we could have a chat, y'know, catch up, that sort of stuff."

"I'm sorry, I can't, I've… er… got stuff to do. Lily needs her dinner sorting and I need to tidy up. Er, I'm sorry, maybe we could do it…" she tapered off, not wanting to commit to anything right now.

"Oh, okay then. I just thought that we were round about the same age, you seemed a little bit out of sorts, I'm on my own, thought we might be company for each other, that's all. Sorry. Didn't mean to offend you."

Susan sensed her reply had hurt Jess, so she responded quickly. "Honestly, please, you didn't offend me. I'm grateful you thought of me. It's just, I've had a bit of a long day and if I'm honest, I'm done in tonight. But why don't we meet up for a coffee or something. I'll have Lily with me, mind?" she laughed. "Sorry, no babysitters, so it's a bit of, love me love my kid."

"Brilliant, coffee sounds good. I'll check my shifts and send you a text. Sorry for the call out of the blue, hope you don't think I was being a bit weird, I saw you in the library earlier but didn't want to intrude, you and Lily were engrossed in some arts and crafts. I'm just feeling a bit down in the dumps at the moment, here on my own. Feeling a bit Billy-no-mates."

Now Susan could hear the smile in Jess's reply and felt relieved she hadn't offended the girl, but angry at herself again for being such a sap, always finding herself cajoled into doing things she didn't want to do.

"Don't be daft, I'd love to meet up with you… and thank you, your kindness means a lot."

They said their goodbyes and Susan hung up the phone, not quite sure how to feel. Maybe it would do her good to have a friend around her own age. Maybe things were not so bad after all.

Twenty Two

Jess

JESS LET HERSELF into the flat and, kicked off her shoes and smiled in satisfaction as they clattered off the wall. Susan's rejection of her offer had seriously pissed her off, she had thought they might be friends but, more importantly, she had believed she would be able to wheedle out some more information from Susan about Morag.

Still she had managed to get her to agree to meet her for a coffee tomorrow. Having checked her shifts, she'd fired off a text arranging to meet her at two in the café. Something told Jess she would need to tread carefully with Susan. Morag already had her claws into the woman and Jess didn't want to risk spooking her. Susan wasn't streetwise, Jess had picked up on that almost immediately. There was a vulnerability about her others would be quick to exploit. If she wanted to pump her for information then she was going to have to be subtle.

Her stomach growled and she made a beeline for the fridge. She was starving. Opening the door, she feigned surprise at the lump of mouldy cheese and half-eaten bar of chocolate staring back at her, reminding her she hadn't been shopping in a while. Her stomach grumbled louder in protest. She wasn't much of a big eater, preferring to pick at stuff in the café, or bringing home any leftovers at the end of the night. But she had been chasing her tail all day with no time to pick, and her early finish had meant she'd had no leftovers to bring home.

She slammed the fridge door closed and opened her cupboards, nothing there either. It was too cold outside to head back out to the supermarket for supplies. She clattered the cupboard door closed and headed back into her living room.

Jess threw herself on the sofa. *Bloody hangry.* Hunger and anger was never a good mix for her. It simply fuelled her bitterness at her current situation. It wasn't fair that she was stuck in this shit hole, never having two pennies to rub together and no friends. She couldn't even take that stupid cow, Lynn, in the library's offer up of going to the pub, as she was skint as usual. This wasn't the way her life should have turned out, if only her mum was still around, if only she hadn't gone, if only she hadn't shattered all her illusions. It was no wonder she had ended up having a breakdown.

She wrapped her arms around herself, as she imagined her mum's voice: *You need to be patient Jess, look how far you've come. It's all going to work out in the end.*

"I promise you, mum, I won't let you down," Jess whispered, taking some deep breaths. She lay back on the couch until she felt the tension start to drain away.

In a bid to distract herself from slipping down a dark rabbit hole, Jess picked up her phone and opened up the contact list. Scrolling her way through them she stopped and smiled. Her fingers punched out a text and she threw the phone down on the table and went to take a shower. She didn't bother waiting for a reply—she didn't need to, she knew exactly what the answer would be.

AN HOUR LATER, Jess emerged from her bedroom, dressed in her fleecy pyjamas, her long damp hair bundled up in a hair wrap. She checked the time on her phone, and found a reply to her text. She didn't bother opening it. She gave a small countdown in her head. Bang on eight o'clock, her flat buzzer rang. Bingo, she laughed as she buzzed her caller up.

The living room door creaked, but Jess didn't turn around, she didn't need to. The hesitation sounded as the door creaked again, irritating her.

"For fuck's sake, will you come in and shut the door. Keep the bloody cold out," she snapped. Without turning around, she carried on. "Did you get everything I asked for?"

She already knew he had, the aroma of the Chinese wafted through her tiny flat making her mouth water.

"You know where everything is, go sort it out and bring it through."

All she had to do was click her fingers and he would come running. *He likes doing things for me—it makes him happy,* she told herself, trying to rid herself of the small niggle of guilt at the way she treated him, while at the same time enjoying the feeling of control it gave her. She turned round at the soft shuffle of his feet behind her.

"You get me a drink?"

He nodded, chin pointing down to where a bottle of Irn Bru was wedged firmly under his arm and his hands full of two plates of steaming hot food. Clenched between his teeth he held a bag of prawn crackers and he dropped them at her side before handing her a plate.

"Got, everything you asked me for, Jess. Chicken Chow Mein, spring rolls and salt and chilli chips."

"Fried rice?" she snapped back.

He nodded. "Fried rice too. It came to fifteen forty-five altogether." He stood awkwardly in front of her, refusing to meet her eyes.

"Aye alright, Ronnie. I'll give you the money back, don't be so tight. I've not been paid yet."

"But Jess, y-you still owe m-m-me the m-m-money from…"

He stopped short as her head snapped up and she glared.

"I told you, you'll get the money. What sort of a boyfriend are you if you can't even buy me a nice meal every now and then?" She glared at him, eyes narrowed.

He backed off.

"B-b-boyfriend?" he stammered.

Her smile was cruel, "Yeah, well that's what you call a man and a woman who do Netflix and chill isn't it? A man and woman who have dinner together… boyfriend and girlfriend? Why, don't you want to be my boyfriend, Ronnie?"

She threw him a coy smile and bit down her laugh as his neck flushed red and his mouth opened and closed like a goldfish. *He honestly can't believe all this,* she thought, popping a prawn cracker into her mouth.

Ronnie nodded vigorously and it took all Jess's self-control not to burst out laughing at him. He looked like one of those bloody nodding dogs in the backs of cars.

"Well sit on your backside and eat up, Ronnie, but mind what I said—this is our secret. You can't tell anyone, not a soul."

"I-I-I w-won't," he stuttered.

Jess jabbed her fork dangerously close to his face. "Well just mind you don't, because I know who IT is Ronnie and I can tell IT to find you anytime I choose, so don't you forget that."

Her eyes were trained on his face and she waited for him to respond. Ronnie just nodded, his face white now.

"Eat your dinner then, dafty, before it gets cold," she demanded, and laughed as he began shovelling the food into his mouth.

DINNER FINISHED, AND without prompting Ronnie had cleared up while Jess stretched herself out on the sofa making sure he couldn't sit beside her when he came back. *Proper little lapdog,* she thought.

A shadow fell over her and she peered up to see him standing watching her, a stupid grin plastered across his face. Christ, he actually believes I want to be with him. She recoiled inwardly, while praising herself for her acting skills. She motioned to him to sit on the chair across from her.

"I'm stuffed. I need to stretch out," she exaggerated a yawn and watched him lumber over to the chair.

"So Ronnie, what's this group all about? And that old bint Morag, what's she all about, eh?"

Ronnie fidgeted with his hands and squirmed in his seat.

"She's nice. Morag's nice," he offered. "And the group is good fun. It's good there. We just chat, like family, like a proper family. Morag looks out for us, like family's meant to."

"Like family's meant to…" she mimicked him, ignoring the hurt look in his eyes.

"You'd like it Jess."

"Well, I might if I was allowed to join in," she sneered. "But your precious Morag won't let me. Maybe I'm just not weird enough. Maybe I'm just not enough of a freak." She couldn't help herself— her frustration was rising to the surface again.

"That's not nice Jess. We're not freaks. Morag just looks out for us, that's all… she's…"

"She's a dried up old bitch, Ronnie, that's what she is."

By now Ronnie looked like he was close to tears. Jess bit down on her lip, she was going to have to curb her anger if she wanted to keep him on side.

"I'm sorry Ronnie, I didn't mean it. It's just hard y'know? I feel lonely and it hurt when Morag made it clear she didn't want me around." Jess pretended to wipe a tear away and watched him.

"She helps people. She watches out for them. Maybe she's just got enough people to help and… anyway… I don't like you being mean about her." The last sentence seemed to stumble from his mouth, and she watched head drop to his chest as though embarrassed at standing up to her.

Jess eyed him from across the room. *Oh well, the puppy dog has balls,* she thought with a spark of admiration for him. She clearly wasn't going to achieve much by slagging off Morag. She tried a different tack.

"Well maybe you could put a word in for me," she wheedled. "I mean, I've got no friends, no family. I'm here all on my own, I'm lonely too you know."

Ronnie leapt up from the chair and hurried over to Jess. He put his hand out and touched her on her arm.

"You're not alone, Jess. You've got me. Y-your b-boyfriend."

Jess cringed, she tried not to pull her arm back, but instead peered at him through her fringe and smiled.

"Yeah, I know, Ronnie. But I'm still lonely, I'd like to make new friends. I just don't know why Morag hates me so much."

Ronnie reached over and wrapped his arms around her. His body was stiff, awkward in his attempt to offer comfort without touching her. She almost gagged at the stench of stale sweat from his clothes and moved her face round trying to get some air. He must have read the signals wrong as he lunged forward, his wet lips landing on hers, she could taste the chilli from the chips he had eaten. This was too much for her. She pushed him off, almost causing him to topple the coffee table over. He landed clumsily on his side and blinked up at her, hurt at her actions.

"Shit, shit, shit," Jess muttered.

She dragged herself up to a seated position on the couch and resisted the temptation to wipe away his taste from her lips.

"What the hell do you think you were doing?"

"I'm your boyfriend. I just wanted to k-k-kiss you." His face was scarlet and his eyes downcast.

"Well, you know you aren't meant to throw yourself on a woman like that. That's not how it's done. I think you need to go now." Her voice was firm and her stare cold.

Ronnie looked crestfallen, her hand lifted to touch his arm but she quickly let it drop. She steeled herself.

"I'm sorry Jess, I didn't mean to…"

"Just go, Ronnie," she turned her head away,

He lumbered to his feet, hands out to steady himself and he brushed against her thigh.

"I said fucking go! Take your fucking hands off me and get out!" she yelled.

"I'm s-sorry Jess… I didn't mean to… it was an acci…"

Jess got to her feet. She pushed him towards the door, taking full control of the situation. When they reached the door, she reached up on her tiptoes and whispered in his ear.

"Do not tell a soul, Ronnie. I mean it. You tell anyone and I'll make sure IT sorts you."

She opened the door and pushed him out into the night.

Slamming the door behind her, she took a deep breath, recoiling at how close he had come to actually kissing her. She studied herself in the mirror, imagining she could see her mum staring back at her. Accusingly.

"I'm sorry, Mum. I know I shouldn't use him like this, but what choice have I got? I moved here, trying to do things the right way, Mum, but at every turn something stands in my way. So I had to find a way in somehow. I guess guys like Ronnie are the collateral damage."

She imagined her mum, shaking her head back at her in the mirror. *This is not you, Jess. This isn't how I brought you up.* Her mum's face started to fade away.

"But mum," Jess cried. "Us family, we look out for each other. It's all I'm trying to do."

Twenty Three

Ronnie

RONNIE WOKE UP, tangled in a frenzy of bedsheets. The little sleep he'd had, had been punctuated by vivid dreams of monsters, with Jess's face, attacking him and his mother. At three in the morning, he had dragged himself out of bed to stand guard outside his mother's bedroom listening for the monsters. There had been no sound from behind her door, other than her rasping snore. But Ronnie knew they were not alone. He felt cold air brush by him, as if someone had brought the outside in. He had shivered.

"Hello Ronnie," a malicious whisper in his ear came from nowhere.

"Shh. Don't say a word. We don't want mother to know I'm here, do we?"

Ice-cold fingers curled around his insides, as the voice reminded him his thoughts were never secret.

"Don't even think my name, Ronnie. She'll know. You know she can hear everything inside your head, don't you? You can't keep any secrets from mother, can you?"

He had trembled in fear as his hands had flown upwards, his knuckles diffing deep into his forehead, trying to keep his mother from getting inside his head.

"Good boy, Ronnie, that's a good boy," the voice soothed. "Mother is not good though, is she? Not when she burns you?"

He whimpered.

"I know that's why you dig into your wounds, into your flesh— trying to get rid of them? The evil spirits inside you. Aren't you, Ronnie?"

He nodded—the burns were not enough, he had to keep digging to free himself of them. Poking, prodding, and oblivious to the pain and infection he caused, he couldn't help himself. Even now, his fingers inched towards the scars, anxious to gouge, to rid himself of the voices and the monsters.

"Listen to me, I can help you... I can make it all disappear No more burning, no more hurting. You just need to trust me. It's our secret, okay Ronnie?" The whisper had grown gentle now, softer. Until it faded away into the night.

He had stayed outside his mother's room until he was sure he was alone again. The minutes had ticked by slowly, the house had grown quiet, the shadows his blanket. At dawn, he had tiptoed into her room, hesitantly at first, but growing bolder when nobody jumped out the shadows and the whispers remained quiet. They were alone now.

He could hear the rushing of his heartbeat, the pressure of the last few months build up—the exquisite agony of loving both Jess *and* Morag. Torn between his need to be part of Morag's family, but not wanting to lose Jess. It was starting again, he could feel it, growing stronger, pulling him under. He was drowning and nobody was there to save him.

Staring down at his mother, her pathetic body lost in the tangle of covers, her rancid form almost making him gag. His eyes travelled up towards her face, only there was no face. Just a blank, waxy mask. He reached out tentatively to touch it, to try to pull it back but his hand sank into the black mass.

He tried to pull his hand back, but the mask began to writhe, bubbling up and sucking his hand into a dark vortex that opened up where mother's face had once been. The pressure intensified the more he tried to pull away. He began screaming as the hole grew wider, deeper, consuming his mother's body and her bed. It wanted to consume him, he could feel his body being sucked under, faster, deeper, suffocating him...

"What the fuck are you doing, you fucking little freak?"

His mother's voice pulled him back into the room. He opened his eyes and stared into hers, his mouth drawing in her stinking breath as his lips nearly touched hers, his body flat on top of her.

He threw himself off her, landing on the floor and scrabbling backwards towards the door, terrified of what he had done.

"B-but... y'you... it..."

"You disgusting little creep, sneaking into my room, trying to get your fucking jollies. With your own mother," she sneered, pulling herself up now, the mask gone, her face filled with fury.

"I-I-I w-w-wasn't... it w-w-was..."

"Oh shut the fuck up, you little pervert. Fucking little freak. Should get you locked up for this... I could get you locked up for this."

Her eyes glinted in the early morning darkness—a cruel glint. One which Ronnie knew meant it was time for his punishment.

He crawled over on his hands and knees as she lifted her cigarette and lit it, blowing a ring of smoke towards his face.

He held out his arm and closed his eyes.

RONNIE CRAWLED BACK to his own bed and lay there until morning slipped through a gap in the curtains. He had got up and made his mother's breakfast at the usual time, terrified to deviate from the rules. She hadn't woken up when he went into her room. He hovered around the bed, putting the tray down then picking it back up again, before leaving it beside her bed, afraid to take it away in case she punished him later.

Back in his bedroom, he absently poked around at the freshest burn on his arm. The sharp sting took away his other pain—the pain inside. Sitting on his bed he stared at himself in the mirror and in a moment of clarity saw himself as others must see him. Hair wild, his eyes sunken into a hollow, dirty-looking face. Spots of dried blood crusted where he had cut himself trying to shave. His fingers reached up to touch his cheek, remembering the kiss from the kid. He could see the tremor in his hand. He knew he couldn't take much more, if he didn't get away from her, one of them would kill the other.

His skin still crawled from the names she had called him last night, the things she had said about him. The words clung to his skin. He wouldn't do that. Not to her, not to anybody. He was not a pervert or a freak. He just wanted to feel normal. He wanted the feeling of belonging Morag gave him. Morag didn't make him feel like a freak or a pervert. She understood him. She was the mother he'd always wished he'd had. And Jess? She got him too. She hadn't judged when he had lied about the burns. She hadn't recoiled back in disgust when he had lied about the self-harm. Instead she had listened, and let him talk. Slowly she had prised the truth out of him and she still hadn't turned her back on him. And, when he had gazed deep into her eyes, he saw himself reflected back.

But then he cringed as an image of the night before flashed before his eyes, his clumsy attempt to kiss her. Would she ever speak to him again after that? His mind continued zipping from one thought to another, and his hands grew clammy as the scene played out in slow motion inside his head. The three women in his life were actually destroying him, and he could do nothing to stop it.

Ronnie felt sick, he didn't know what was worse, these rare moments of clarity and focus or the chaos that was his normal reality. However, he did know he had to get out of the house, he felt suffocated, hemmed in, he just needed to breathe. He stood up and listened. The silence was heavy. He pulled his bedroom door closed and crossed the landing to his mother's room. From behind the door, her rhythmic snoring belied the monster who lay beneath the covers.

Cautiously he made his way downstairs, careful not to step on the tread that creaked. He shuffled into the kitchen and picked up his phone. The battery was at ten percent and two bars of signal showed He pulled up the number he knew off by heart and, hands shaking, he slowly typed out the message: 'I'm ready. Can you help me? Please.'

He stared at the message for a moment, knowing if he sent it, he wouldn't be able to stop what came next. His finger hovered over the send button before he closed his eyes tight and let his finger drop. Message sent.

He threw the phone down on the worktop and stood back, watching it. Almost immediately, it buzzed and lit up.

"Of course I'll help you. Come round later. You know where to find me. X"

Twenty Four

Morag

MORAG STUFFED HER phone back into her handbag as she watched Susan and Lily make their way up the path. Checking herself in the mirror for what felt like the hundredth time that morning, she patted down a stray strand of hair and smoothed down her skirt and jumper.

"What are you like, Morag?" she giggled to herself. "Anyone would think you were going on a date."

The truth was, Morag was excited. Unable to sleep she had been up since four a.m., bubbling with anticipation. Even her morning visit to Mother's bedroom had not upset her as much as it usually did.

"Morning, Mother," she had announced breezily, as she pushed open the bedroom door and strode in, full of a newfound confidence. Morag wasn't losing her marbles, she was well aware her mother was long dead and buried, but this ritual of their daily chats had continued long after her coffin had slid through the red velvet curtains.

Normally the memories and her dead mother's control over left her riddled with anxiety. Mother had known everything about her. All her little secrets. And even after her death, she could still reach out and cruelly remind Morag of who she was and everything she had done.

But not this morning. Morag had almost danced into the bedroom. She was walking on air, and even the sour, stale smell of the room couldn't burst her bubble. "We have some friends visiting today, Mother. Nice friends. My new family." She pouted like a small child. "I'm going to look after them, Mother. The way you are supposed to look after your family." She listened with her head cocked, as though hearing her mother's reply.

"No Mother, they are my *friends*. They like me," she said, through gritted teeth. "They don't care about all the other stuff."

Morag carried on this one sided conversation, stopping to listen to the silent replies. "No, Mother I haven't told them, and I shan't tell them. There is no need."

Silence.

"I said, there is NO NEED, Mother! They are family, and family look out for each other. No matter what!"

With her mother's ghost threatening to sour her visit from Susan and Lily, Morag had charged over to the bed and beaten the already burst pillow, imagining her mother's face lying there, as she battered her fists down hard—over and over again. Seeing in her mind's eye the blood splatter as the feathers rose from the bed, fluttering back down to rest. Then quiet.

"See Mother? I told you. I don't need your interfering today, do I? This time, it's your turn to be quiet." She hurried out of the room, slamming the door behind her, turning the key in the lock with a smile of grim satisfaction. "See how you like being locked away," she yelled at the closed door.

She carefully placed the key in her own bedroom drawer alongside her jar and went downstairs to make herself some strong sugary tea. It had taken five cups for her breathing to return to normal. *Interfering bitch, mother. Why can't you just leave me alone?*

The taste triggered a memory of a voice, "Drink it up love, it's good for the shock, you know?" The voice had been kindly. She remembered feeling grateful for the compassion. Only a child herself back then, and she had been in a terrible state when... ·

The shock of hot liquid on her lap brought her back to the present. She cursed herself as she mopped up the tea 'put those silly thoughts away now. You don't need to visit that all over again, you stupid woman. You have Susan and Lily now. Things are going to be better this time round... This time your family will stay with you until the end.'

The letterbox rattled, rescuing her from the dark hole threatening to pull her under. She could hear the breathless giggles of the child on the other side. She made her way into the hall glancing into the living room to make sure the toys she had bought for Lily were placed exactly the way she had wanted them to be. She gave herself one last check in the hall mirror before opening the door with a smile.

"Are you alright, Morag?" asked Susan, as the door opened.

"Yes, of course I am," Morag replied, her mouth stretched in a tight line of irritation.

"You just look a little flustered, that's all?"

"Oh, don't be daft, it's nothing. Just slept in. Rushing about at the tail end. You know what it's like. Come on in." She tried a casual chuckle and Susan gawped at her, so she stood back and let Susan and her daughter step over the threshold.

She gave a quick glance up and down the street to check if anyone had noticed she had visitors. The street was empty. Morag closed the door firmly.

Turning around, she almost bumped into Susan, who still stood there, staring.

"Oh, for goodness' sake. Just go through. Make yourself at home."

Morag was too preoccupied imagining Lily's reaction to the toys she had bought for her to notice the look of hesitation on Susan's face. She ushered them both into the living room.

"Sit down, please both of you. Go on, take a seat."

"Oh, I didn't know you had young family...' Susan began, eyeing the toys arranged on the coffee table.

Morag's face darkened, but she quickly softened her look and, forcing a bright tone, she laughed. "No. No family. I don't. It's just little old me."

"Oh, I'm sorry." said Susan.

Morag bristled. She didn't need this woman's pity or sympathy. "Oh, just one of those things. I never found the rights ones, I suppose."

Morag didn't notice the strange look that crossed Susan's face at her comment—she was too busy staring at Lily now. The child's eyes were like saucers as she'd spotted the toys on the table. Morag worried she might have gone a little bit overboard.

Susan didn't say anything.

"Those are for you Lily," smiled Morag, shyly.

Lily looked at Susan, and then to Morag, and back again, unsure what to do.

"Morag, that's far too much! We only came to find out about the cle…"

"Oh. I'm sorry." Morag's head dropped to her shoulders. "I'm so sorry. I don't have anyone to spoil and I just thought…"

"It's so kind of you, truly it is. I just don't want you thinking I'm here to try and get gifts or to take advantage of you?"

Morag lifted her head, smiling cautiously. "I guess I just went a wee bit overboard. I didn't mean any harm. I just wanted to see her wee face, to make her smile. I can put them away if you want…"

Meanwhile Lily stood quietly watching the exchange between the two women. Her big blue eyes filled with tears when Morag mentioned taking the toys away. Morag smiled. Susan had noticed Lily's reaction too. Morag knew she had won. She persuaded Susan to leave Lily playing. "She's fine, come and I'll show you around."

"I'M SO EMBARRASSED at the state of the place," she had apologised more than once.

"It's really not that bad, Morag. Honestly, a couple of visits and I'm sure I'll have it licked into shape for you, and then it will be easier to maintain."

Morag stopped, she didn't want easier to maintain, she wanted an excuse to keep Susan coming round.

"I'm actually hopeless with housework," she smiled. "Really hopeless. Within days of you fixing it, I'd have it just as bad again. It would be better for me if we could make this a more permanent arrangement?"

"I don't know. I feel like I'm taking advantage of you by taking money from you?"

"You're not, I told you. You would be doing me the favour. I don't want to be getting someone from an agency in, someone I couldn't trust. I hate strangers in my home. Please?"

The sound of Susan's phone vibrating interrupted Morag. She watched as Susan pulled it out, her face paling as she looked at the screen.

"It's him, isn't it? Wanting you to make your decision?"

Susan nodded.

"Well tell him you don't need his money. Tell him you've got a job now and he can just go and pick on someone else."

The tears welled in Susan's eyes. "It's not as easy as that. He knows stuff. Things that could put me and Lily in danger."

In the kitchen, while Lily played happily with her toys in the other room, Susan poured out the whole story to Morag. She told her she had not only left Colin, but she had disappeared, taking his daughter with her. How she had spent the last year constantly looking over her shoulder, waiting for him to find her, scared of her own shadow. Lennoxhill was the first place she had felt safe. Until now.

"He put an appeal out in the papers, and this Kris has a copy of it. If I don't do what he says, he'll tell Colin where I am and... oh, shit, Colin will kill me... We're going to have to leave... We need to go far away from here..." she sobbed.

"Susan, you need to calm down, love. Getting yourself in a state like this isn't going to do anyone any good. You can't just up and leave, dragging that wee mite half way across the country again. You can't keep running forever." She put her arm around the sobbing woman, all the time the cogs ticking in her brain.

Morag got up and stood at the kitchen sink, her back to Susan.

"I told you, I'd take care of him and I will." She gazed out the window. "I might have a plan. Why don't we have a nice cup of tea and see what you think of it?"

Twenty Five

Jess

RONNIE HUDDLED IN the corner of the café, still nursing the mug of tea Jess had pushed into his hands when he'd turned up at the café first thing. When she had received his text message that morning, she had replied, telling him to come to the café partly out of guilt and partly out of curiosity. His tea must be stone cold by now. She watched his hands clasping the mug as if it was the only thing keeping him grounded. His legs jittered under the table, his knees banging the underside and slopping cold tea out over the sides of the mug and onto his hands. This seemed to jolt him back into the present, but Jess recognised the waves of agitation bouncing off him.

Studying him from where she stood behind the counter, Jess cringed at the state of him. He'd been waiting at the door when she'd arrived for her shift, a cold sweat glistening on his brow as he paced up and down the pavement, repeatedly punching one hand into the other. His clothes looked like he had slept in them and she could have fried a breakfast in his hair it was so greasy. Seeing him, she regretted telling him to come to the café, worried his anxiety and strange behaviour was a result of the events the night before. Maybe she had pushed him too far? She tried to push the feelings of guilt away. She had stood watching him, considering turning on her heel and leaving but Ronnie had caught sight of her first and something resembling a smile had crossed his face.

"Jess, you're here. I've been waiting for hours for you," he wavered, sounding close to breaking down.

She had thrown him a warm smile, knowing fine well he had not been waiting for hours at all, but not wanting to upset him any further.

"Alright Ronnie? You must be freezing. Come on in, and I'll get you a cuppa... on the house."

He'd huddled close to her as she fumbled with the shutters, her fingers frozen stiff. Even the sharp winter morning didn't lessen the sour tang coming from him, and her stomach had lurched as she tried not to gag. Garbling nonsense under his breath, he had followed her into the café. Desperate to escape from the odour, she hadn't even tried to make out what he was saying and had instead, made him his tea and sat him out of the way in the furthest corner, where she could watch him without him seeing her. She had warned him to leave her to her work and not get her into trouble by getting under her feet. She'd need to speak to him when things quietened down. There was no way she could risk leaving him in this state.

Already customers were spilling through the door, and she hoped he'd stay put until she had some time to talk to him properly. She needed to know what it was he wanted help with, and she had to make sure he was not about to blurt out all their secrets to bloody Morag.

She went through the motions of serving the steady stream of customers, her mind only half on the job, the other half keeping a close eye on Ronnie, making sure he didn't do a runner—or talk to anyone else. Her stomach tightened as she watched him scratch at his head, his fingers sliding through the thick greasy locks before he stuck a grubby finger into his mouth and extracted something from between his teeth. Whatever it was, he was engrossed in it— examined it by rolling it slowly between his fingers, before secreting it in his pocket. She screwed up her face in disgust. His hands began to clasp and unclasp repeatedly as though he needed to be constantly touching himself for reassurance. She turned away, unable to watch much more.

The morning rush passed quickly and the café, thankfully, stayed quieter than usual. Annie and Mary were not in today as it was pensioners club in the community centre on a Thursday.

"Just a pound for a cup of tea and a cake...*and* a game of bingo," Annie reminded her every week, as though Jess was somehow conning them out of their money when they visited the café.

Marion had called her to say she would be going to the wholesalers and then heading to the hairdresser to get her hair done, so she wouldn't be around either. She recognised an opportunity to speak to Ronnie undisturbed and as the last customer left, she took her chance and locked the door, flicking the sign over to Closed. She would have to make up an excuse if anyone tried to get in and grassed her up to Marion, but she had to speak to Ronnie and she only had half an hour before she would need to prepare for the lunchtime rush.

Pouring them both fresh mugs of tea, she sat beside him and pushed his across the table towards him.

"Here. A fresh cuppa for you. This one must be stone cold by now," she said, smiling as she pulled the old mug away from him.

Ronnie looked up at her, his eyes red rimmed from crying. She could see the dried snot on his face. She dug into her apron pocket and threw a clean hanky over to him. "Christ, Ronnie. Clean yourself up will you? That's disgusting."

He wiped at his face roughly and began to shred the hanky in his hands. She could feel the tremor from his feet under the table.

"I-I-I'm s-s-sorry Jess," he sniffed. "Y-y-you need to help me, p-p-please."

She held his gaze until he turned away. She felt her chest tighten and her cheeks flush, she hated herself for what she was doing to Ronnie. Her feelings towards him were conflicted. On one hand, he disgusted her, but she had enough self-awareness to recognise this was probably a manifestation of her fears about her own mental wellbeing—she didn't ever want to be that person again. On the other hand she pitied him—everyone was using Ronnie, and she was just as bad as the rest of them. Jess pushed those feelings aside. She had to stay strong, and she had to stay focused.

Nobody felt sorry for you Jess, she reminded herself, pulling herself up straight.

"I know, Ronnie. I got your text, remember? I told you to come here, but I don't know what it is you want me to do?"

"I'm scared Jess. The bad feelings are coming back. The voices, the paranoia. I know it's not real, but it feels real to me. I'm scared I'm going to do something Jess... something bad."

"Can you not go to your doctor, then? Tell them?"

He shook his head violently.

"No, they'll put me back in hospital. I don't want to go back there. Please! I need you to help me."

"Ronnie, I can't help you, pal. I'm not a doctor, am I? You need to go get some proper help."

"You can help me. I just need away from my house-away from her. Before It makes me do it again. Like the last time, remember? It made me hurt her. Last night, It was there again. It made me do it, Jess. You've got to help me. Can I come and stay with you?"

"Christ Ronnie, you can't come and stay with me. What about that woman, Morag, from the library? Can she not help you? You're always banging on about how she's like family. Ask her."

He began to shake. "NO! Morag can't help me with this. She'll just make me phone the doctor, and I don't want the doctor. I don't want to go back to hospital. Please Jess, I can't go back, not again. I don't want to be locked up, but she's going to kill me. Last night..." He pushed the table forward almost knocking everything onto the floor.

Jess put her hand out quickly, and stopped the movement. "Okay, keep your hair on for Christ's sake. I only mentioned Morag because you know her better than me."

Ronnie began to cry, muttering about monsters, his mother and masks.

Jess leaned forward and patted his arm.

"Tell me what happened last night, Ronnie."

He didn't notice her eyes narrow as she asked the question.

She heard the uncertainty in his voice as he told her what had happened during the night, his voice breaking, tears threatening throughout. He darted a glance at her face as he told her about the voices, checking for her reaction, but her face remained expressionless.

"If I don't get out of there, she will kill me, I mean it. She's going to tell people I'm a freak… a pervert… I'm not a pervert… I'm not." His chest heaved with sobs now.

"Ronnie, calm down for Christ's sake. I can't help you if you don't calm down."

THIRTY MINUTES LATER, Jess glanced at her watch.

"Right Ronnie, it's time to go now—I've got to get sorted for the lunchtime rush."

She pushed back her chair and stood up waiting for him to do the same. He stayed seated.

"Will it be okay? Do you promise?"

"Yes Ronnie, it will be fine. I've told you it would, haven't I? You need to trust me. I know about this kind of stuff. Just do what I told you, and it will all be okay. I promise. Don't let that bitch of a mother treat you like that. Now, come on, you need to go now, I've got stuff to do."

Ronnie slid out the chair and stood up. He eyed Jess and moved towards her as if to hug her.

She stepped back, "Right. Come on. Don't be getting all soppy with me now. Away you go and I'll catch you later, alright?" She crossed the café to unlock the door and hurried back to the counter, eager to put a barrier between them.

Ronnie shuffled out of the door, turning his head to look at her one last time.

He smiled.

"Catch you later, Jess."

Jess watched as the café door closed behind him, glad he had left and praying to a God she didn't believe in, that Ronnie would take her advice.

Twenty Six

Morag

MORAG MADE LILY a snack and settled her in front of the television, stopping to breathing in the child's scent. She resisted the urge to pick her up and hold her close. To take her and run.

"You curl up here sweetie, eat your lunch and watch your programmes, just while Susan and I have a wee chat?"

Lily smiled back at her, too young to notice Morag's use of her mum's first name.

She looked so perfect lying there, it was almost like she belonged there, belonged in this house. Morag bent over the child, mussing her hair.

"Good girl, my little sweetheart," she breathed.

She closed the living room door gently, tucked the nail scissors and the lock of hair she had just taken into her pocket, and went back into the kitchen where Susan sat just as she had left her, staring into space and stirring her tea absentmindedly. Morag watched her. The woman was a mess. She could be pretty if she would do something with that hair of hers, put some make up on and make a bit of an effort with herself. Still it suited Morag, Susan being so apathetic—she would be more likely to agree to her plans. Easier to mould, much easier that way.

"Susan love? Anybody in there?" Morag tapped her lightly on her shoulder.

Susan gave a start.

"Oh, sorry, I was miles away... and I'm sorry about before, I don't know what came over..."

"Shh, it's alright. You don't need to explain yourself to me. You shouldn't have to explain yourself to anyone pet." She sat, and pulled her chair closer to Susan.

"So, my plan. Would you like to hear it?"

Susan nodded.

"Now, don't shoot it down in flames right away, just listen to what I've got to say first, okay? I think it might just be a way out of your little eh... predicament."

Morag watched Susan's face carefully as she relayed her plan to her. She couldn't tell if the look of shock came from the fear of her ex-husband discovering where she lived or at the proposition she had just made

"Well, what do you think?"

"You want me and Lily to come and live with you, here?" Susan sounded shocked. "But you don't even know us? We don't know you? We can't..."

"I said don't shoot me down in flames. Think about it. It makes perfect sense. You can't be bringing Lily up in that dump you call home."

Susan bristled at the insult.

"Sorry, I didn't mean it like that.' Morag desperately backpedalled now. *Stupid bitch, scaring them away already,* sneered her mother's voice. "I just mean the Waterside estate isn't the nicest place to live is it? It's crawling with lowlife drug addicts and alcoholics."

She forced her voice to soften. "It's no place to bring up a wee one—dirty needles lying about everywhere, fights and God knows what else going on. Surely living here with Lily would be safer for you both. Especially now, if you're worried this Kris person might alert your husband to your whereabouts? This Kris doesn't know me and he doesn't know where I live? Does he?"

Susan shook her head.

"I don't think so."

"See, it's perfect. And it would save you money too. I've no mortgage here to pay, just my food and bills, and our arrangement could still stand, you could do the cleaning and upkeep around the house, and chip in a little for the food but no other costs, no rent or bills? What do you think?"

"But we don't even know you," Susan protested again.

"I'm sure we will soon get to know each other. I'm very easy going, and I love your wee one. Besides the house is big enough, so we wouldn't be under each other's feet. Plenty of room here, a lovely family home..."

"I don't know. It doesn't seem right. I mean what would people say if they saw me turn up at yours and move in? They'd be thinking I was taking advantage of you... it's not like we are family or anything. it just doesn't seem right. This is my mess, and I need to sort it out." Susan made to get up from her chair.

"Susan, please just think about it. You've seen the two spare rooms up there? A room for you and for Lily? They could be yours, your very own." She could hear her voice rise, the panic growing, but she couldn't stop herself.

Susan stood up abruptly. "I don't think so. It's very kind of you. It's just a bit... too much." She made to leave the kitchen. Morag grabbed at her arm.

"Susan, please. We could be a family. Just the three of us. I'm only trying to take care of you. That's what families do..."

"I think perhaps Lily and I should go home now." Susan shook off Morag's hand, moving quickly into the living room, shaking the almost sleeping child, "Come on, Lily, it's time to go."

Morag pressed her palm against her chest, her heart hurt, she couldn't lose them, not now. She watched the younger woman take the child by the hand and it took her every ounce of willpower not to scream out at them.

"Please, Susan, I'm sorry. I didn't mean to upset you. Honestly love, all I want to do is help. I just got a bit carried away.' Her skin felt clammy now, she could feel cold sweat begin to trickle down her spine. 'I'm lonely Susan, that's all. I'm just lonely!"

Susan moved towards the door, "It's fine, I'm not upset... I just think we should leave now. Lily, come on," she snapped at the child, who hovered about over the toys looking at them and back again to her mother. "Leave them. They're not yours."

The girl's face fell.

"It's okay, honestly. Take them, please?"

Susan's eyes flashed with anger as she grabbed hold of Lily.

"Leave them Lily. You have your own toys at home. Now come on."

She brushed by Morag and hurried out the house, dragging the child behind her. Lily turned round and stared at Morag, the tears now streaming down her face.

"I'm sorry," mouthed Morag.

THE FRONT DOOR slammed and Morag slumped to the floor. She sat there until her bones grew cold and stiff. Wearily she pulled herself up and dragged herself into the kitchen. She tapped out a message.

> *More work to be done, I'll be in touch in a couple of weeks with further details.*

Exhausted now, Morag made her way upstairs. In her bedroom, she took out her jar of hearts and wrapped the lock of hair in a baby pink paper heart.

"I'll bring you home precious, don't you worry. You'll soon be home, where you belong."

Twenty Seven

Ronnie

RONNIE CLOSED THE café door behind him and leaned on the wall outside. Jess was right, his mother was a bitch and he couldn't let her keep treating him like this. He tried to ignore the loud buzzing in his head. He thought again about Morag, but he couldn't tell her about what was going on inside his mind. She would be disappointed in him.

Mothers don't want to be disappointed in their children, Ronnie. You can't tell her. She'll think you're a bad boy. She'll send you away, Ronnie.

He peered around him, searching for the owner of the voice in his head, but all he could see were shifting shapes, grey mists all merging into one, weaving their way towards him, tentacles reaching out trying to grasp at him.

The buzzing grew louder.

He slapped the side of his head to get rid of it.

The buzzing became angry now.

He glanced upwards. The sky was dark. Heavy, brooding clouds reached down to draw him in. Gasping for breath, Jess's words wrestled for space inside his skull, mixing with his mother's vicious insults. He punched the side of his head harder now in an attempt to get rid of the angry buzzing, but it was taking over. He wanted to run, but found himself rooted to the spot. Slowly he moved forward, one foot in front of the other, wading his way through quicksand, the ground trying to swallow him whole. He dragged each foot forward, fighting against the monsters who had taken over his world. Ignoring passers-by, he could not see the look of horror on their faces as they crossed the road to avoid him.

"Keep moving, Ronnie, keep moving," he urged himself forward, not knowing where his feet were taking him. His head didn't want him to go home. Too much danger there. He kept moving forward. He couldn't go to the library. Morag might be there. She would know he had spoken to Jess. Morag knew everything. She'd be angry with him.

ANGRY! ANGRY! ANGRY! The voice buzzed in his head.

More people now, crowds of people, busy, buzzy people. Busy, buzzy people going places. I can't hear you. I can't see you. Don't have time, too busy, don't understand...

ANGRY! ANGRY! ANGRY!

The buzzing turned into a roar. They were yelling inside his head now.

DO IT RONNIE! DO IT RONNIE! DO IT RONNIE!

He pushed his way past the people. He had reached the park now, and he didn't want to be there. He wanted to be home. He had to get home.

RUN HOME, RONNIE. RUN LITTLE BOY. The voice laughed hysterically now. *RUN RONNIE, RUN!*

The crowds parted and let him through, a couple of people reached out to him, "Are you alright mate?" "Hey, can I help you?" "Fuck off, freak. You belong in the fucking looney bin." Their voices all merged into one giant cacophony of white noise.

Ronnie ran as fast as he could now. Legs freed from the quicksand, he flew, away from them all. He looked down at all the little ants scurrying about the streets. A grotesque laugh escaped his mouth as he imagined himself stamping on the ants, squashing them all dead to the ground.

He whooped as he ran, the cold wind whipping through his hair, his features fraught with fear. He could not see the dropping jaws and gaping mouths of the people on the streets, their thoughts and their words lost to him.

He found himself at the bottom of his street and came to a sudden halt. He whipped his head round looking for IT. He could feel it coming closer. But there was nothing there. Ronnie spun his head back round to the front then tried to lift his foot, wanting to run, but he couldn't move. Morag and Jess's words merged inside his head, nothing was making sense anymore. His vision blurred as the world around him turned red, he had a bad energy flowing through his body. He pushed one foot in front of the other, forcing himself out of the confusion and deliberately made his way along the street to his house. He heard the whispers of the neighbours as they stared at him from their gardens, he tried to close them out. He needed to get inside and into his room. He needed to make the pain go away. His scars were crying for him to gouge out the pain. He kept walking.

He opened the front door and the first thing he noticed was the whiff of cheap air freshener, the tiny droplets still hanging in the air, choking him in a chemical grip. He edged towards the stairs, trying to ignore the singing coming from the kitchen. His mother's voice singing.

"Ronnie, is that you, you lazy bastard?"

He took the stairs two at a time not stopping until he reached his room. Slamming the bedroom door, he stood with his back against it, trying to shake clear the red mist that had followed him home. His breathing was fast and laboured. Someone was downstairs. Something was downstairs pretending to be his mother. He heard it shout in her voice, calling him names—filthy names, bad names. Nothing made any sense anymore. The noises from downstairs clamoured for his attention. Morag and Jess's faces swam in and out of his sight, morphing into one, before turning into the face of the little girl from the library. His hands tore at his face trying to free himself from the visions but they grew stronger and the noises grew lounder. The little girl's screams tore through him as his mother's laugh grew hysterical. She was hurting the child. His mother was downstairs hurting the little girl. He had to do something.

Ronnie flew out his room and rushed down the stairs, the child's cries growing louder with each step. He pushed his way through the mounds of paper in the hallway as they scattered behind him. She stood in the kitchen, her back to him, bent over something, laughing.

He lunged towards her and she spun round, her face a terrifying blank mask of nothingness.

Ronnie threw out his hand to grab her, to pull her away from the child but she twisted in his grip and danced backwards towards the door. Inside his head, he could hear the child's screams. He advanced on the monster, his vision blurred, his mind focused on one thing only—to save the child. His mother cackled as her face mutated back into her own.

"What the fuck are you doing?" she screamed, but all he could hear were the child's screams. Something snapped inside his head and his world went quiet. A deadly silence descended clearing the red mist. His world became clear—a sharp high definition focus took over from the mist. He watched as his hand reached out towards the table and stared as his fingers, clasped around the knife lying on the plate he had left behind that morning. He showed no emotion as his arm raised, drawing the knife back and bringing it down towards the creature who wore his mother's face.

Ronnie stepped back as she fell to the floor, the child's screams were gone now instead they were coming from his mother's mouth. He gazed around the kitchen. There was no child, just the mess he had left behind and his mother's blood seeping across the floor. He stood still for a moment and watched her, then turned his back and walked away. He opened the front door and stepped out into the winter sunlight, and then he screamed.

THE BLUE LIGHTS bounced off the building. His breathing returned to normal, inside his head was still now. Calm. Ronnie could hear the sirens, and a gentle voice asked if he was okay. The noises sounded like they were coming from under water, or maybe he was under water. He didn't know anything anymore. He watched as a man in a green jumpsuit led his mother out of the house and into the back of an ambulance. She was walking so she couldn't be dead. Unless she's the walking dead, he sniggered. A hand reached out and touched him, he jerked back

"Ronnie, it's okay. I'm here to help you. Are you okay? My name's PC Saunders."

He looked up into the warm eyes of a woman wearing a police uniform. A man stood behind her, his eyes were cold. Ronnie nodded.

"You need to get up, Ronnie. You need to come with us. We have to ask you some questions." She held out her hand to help him up. Ronnie watched the man behind her sigh, he pushed her out the way.

"For Christ sakes, Jen. Just bloody read him his rights and be done with it."

The man grabbed Ronnie roughly and pulled him up.

"Ronnie Whiteside, I am arresting you on suspicion…"

The police officer's voice faded away as Ronnie caught sight of her. He noticed her handbag first. She stood too far back in the crowd for him to see her face, but he would recognise that handbag anywhere.

He smiled as the man finished saying his words, Ronnie had zoned out by now. He didn't struggle. He allowed the man to usher him into the back of the car and pressed his nose against the window, watching her, as they drove away and she turned into a tiny little ant waiting to be crushed.

Twenty Eight

Jess

THE CLOCK ON the wall said two fifteen. Susan had arranged to meet her here at two. Jess tried to quell her irritation at being left waiting. She could feel Marion's eyes boring into her from behind the counter. Jess knew Marion would be raging that she was hanging around the café after she had refused Marion's request for her stay on for the rest of the day.

Normally Jess would have either said yes or made up an excuse as to why she couldn't stay on but today she had simply refused. She knew Marion would be dying to ask her what she was playing at.

Jess didn't turn around, she couldn't face Marion's glare or her questions. She stirred her tea, listening in to the conversation between two customers who were sitting in the corner. Her ears had pricked up at the mention of Ronnie's name and while she could not hear everything the customers were saying, she had made out he had apparently attacked his mother and had been carted off in a police car. At least he was away from Morag. She tried not to think about his fear of being locked up and sectioned again. Couldn't be helped. *Almost done, Mum.*

The sound of the café door opening and the chatter of a child's voice made Jess look up. Susan stood at the door, her brows knitted over eyes that looked red even from this distance. Jess could see something had spooked her. She waved her over.

"What can I get you? Coffee, tea, juice?" she asked, as Susan took a seat next to her.

Susan reached into her handbag for her purse but Jess waved her away. "It's fine, my treat. What do you want, Lily?" She turned to the child who was still chattering away about some toys in the library lady's house, oblivious to the fact her mother was no longer listening to her.

"It's okay. I've got money. Please, here, take it," offered Susan, holding out a couple of pound coins.

Jess shook her head. "No, it's my treat." She smiled, hoping they didn't want any food—she was skint too and didn't hold out much hope of Marion giving her a staff discount.

"Thank you," Susan replied, wringing her hands, "I'll just have a black coffee, please. And some water for Lily. Tap water will do fine."

Jess did not argue with her, relieved Susan hadn't ordered anything too fancy. At the counter, she gave the order to Marion.

"Didn't know you two were friends," said the older woman, pouring coffee into two chipped mugs.

"You don't know everything about me Marion," she retorted. "And can we get mugs that aren't chipped please?"

Marion glared at her, but transferred the coffee into two mugs that were slightly better than the ones she had been trying to palm off on Jess.

"That's four pound," she said, holding out her hand.

"No staff discount?" Jess asked, cheekily.

Marion scowled. Jess gave her the exact money in twenty pence pieces. "We're always looking for change in here, boss," she laughed, turning her back on the woman.

Jess put the drinks on the table and took her seat again. Lily was engrossed in a colouring in book, singing away quietly to herself.

"Thanks," said Susan.

"Welcome. You okay? You look like you've seen a ghost."

"Yeah, yeah. I'm fine."

They sat in awkward silence for a couple of minutes. Now Jess had Susan here, she didn't know what to say. She silently cursed herself for her social awkwardness, her inability to be normal like everyone else.

It was clear Susan didn't intend starting up a conversation, so Jess, remembering the gossip she had heard, asked her if she knew what happened to Ronnie.

"I saw some commotion around his house earlier on, but my mind was on other stuff."

"Poor guy. It's a bloody sin if he's locked up again. Not a nice place to be, I can tell you."

As Susan appraised her, Jess opened up a little hoping it might make the next part of the conversation easier. She told Susan how she had ended up in a psychiatric hospital following a breakdown.

"Oh God, I'm sorry," said Susan once Jess had stopped talking. "That must have been awful."

"Yeah. It wasn't the best time of my life, for sure," Jess replied. "But hey, I got through it, and I'm here to tell the tale."

"What about your family? Do they live around here too?"

Jess's face darkened. "It's only me."

"Same here," replied Susan. "My parents died when I was young. I lived with my grandparents until they died too and then I met... Colin and..." She looked over at Lily who was still absorbed in her colouring. "Well, here I am too, I guess."

Jess smiled, but inside she seethed with jealousy. Susan had had a family, she'd had grandparents who had loved her, at least she had that. And, she'd had a husband. She'd had more in her life than Jess had ever had. Her life hadn't been built on a lie.

She moved away from the subject of family—the memories too painful.

"So, how have you found it living around here? It's bit dullsville, isn't it?"

"It's okay, I guess. Well, it was until recently. Got myself into a bit of bother, and thought I had it all worked out but..." She shrugged her shoulders.

Jess was intrigued as to what Susan's bother had been, but she didn't want to push it. Instead, she turned the conversation round to the library, explaining to Susan she had joined the library to try and rekindle her love for reading as a means of passing her time.

"Yeah, I love the library too. That woman who works there, she is good to Lily and me."

Jess stiffened. "Right, funny that. You're not the first person to say that about her. She seems to have herself quite the little fan club doesn't she?"

"I guess so."

"You and her are quite close though, aren't you?" probed Jess. "Bit weird. She's old enough to be your mum or your gran even."

Susan's face flushed.

"Sorry," said Jess. "I didn't mean to be rude."

"It's okay, no offence taken. You're right though, it is a bit weird…"

Jess sensed there was more to come, she let the silence sit between them.

"Can I tell you something in confidence?"

"Sure," Jess sat forward now, anxious to hear what Susan had to say, hopeful she may have a snippet of helpful information.

Susan recounted her visit to Morag's house earlier.

"There was something creepy about it all. All that banging on about us being family and how family watch out for each other. I only went round to see about a wee part-time cleaning job she wanted me to do, next thing she's asking me and Lily to move in. Christ, she'd even bought Lily a pile of toys." Susan shuddered.

"That *is* creepy," agreed Jess. "Has she not got any family of her own?"

Susan shook her head. "No, she said it was only her, ever since her mum had died. Maybe I'm just being a bit sensitive?"

"No, definitely not, I think you need to watch her. I've seen how she seems to hone in on folk, but only the vulnerable ones. Sorry. Not that I'm saying you are vulnerable or anything, but you know what I mean? Think about the group she runs, all misfits and loners and the things that happen to them."

"What do you mean?" asked Susan

'Well, that Alan guy, the one who lived on your estate? He died of a drug overdose and I heard she found his body. What is a woman like her doing hanging round his flat? Then there's Ronnie, by all accounts he has been sectioned again and she's all over him like a rash. I don't know, something seems off about her. Watch yourself, eh? Family. She's got a bloody cheek. Sad old cow."

Susan didn't reply and Jess didn't push the conversation any further. She had enough information for now.

Lily looked up. "I'm bored mummy, can we go back to the library lady's house and play with the toys please?"

Jess peered over Lily's head at Susan and mouthed, "Be careful."

JESS WAITED UNTIL Susan and Lily had left, and made her way over to the park. Susan's words were playing heavy on her mind. All the talk about family had her missing her mum more than ever. It was almost Christmas and the idea of spending another one alone was killing her. Jess wished more than anything she had family around her.

She was so lost in her thoughts, she didn't notice Radio Joe sat on his usual spot in the park.

"Afternoon," he said. "Penny for them?"

Jess looked up, "Oh, hi, Joe. Don't think my thoughts are even worth that," she smiled. "What you up to? Are you not freezing sitting out here all the time?"

Joe smiled. "Don't feel the cold. I like the fresh air. Better than being stuck in the house all day on my own. Lots of company out here and I always know what's going on."

"S'pose so. Sucks being on your own, eh?"

"You not got any family?" he asked.

"Nope, nobody. Just me. Should have had a family but... well that's the way life goes, I guess."

Joe nodded sagely. "True. Could be worse though, you could be one of the crazies that hang around over there." He nodded in the direction of the library.

"What crazies? Who are you talking about?"

Joe shrugged. "Sometimes you're safer on your own."

"Joe, you're talking in riddles. What are you on about?"

"Doesn't matter. You take care of yourself. Be careful."

Joe got up off the bench and sauntered off. Jess watched him go.

Twenty Nine

Morag

MORAG HANDED OVER a twenty-pound note to the driver and told him to keep the change, he mumbled something about the fare being nineteen pound fifty, and how miserable she was two days before Christmas.

"Ungrateful little man," she muttered under her breath, as she stumbled out the back seat of the taxi. She would not normally have gone to the expense of using a taxi but, after Alan's funeral service, she had been distraught. When she'd come out of the crematorium, the December chill had squeezed the breath from her. She couldn't face the prospect of the two buses she would have to catch to get home from the crematorium. So in an act completely out of character, she had splashed out on a taxi.

She slammed the car door behind her ignoring the driver's grumbles about the season of goodwill her mind still on the service It had been the saddest funeral she'd ever attended. Apart from the minister and herself, the only other mourner had been the young social worker who had tried to help Alan after his gran had gone into care.

They had sat on the uncomfortable pews, the chill seeping through their bodies as the minister rattled through the most basic of services. No hymns, no words of solace and no memories of the boy to whom they were saying goodbye. The social worker had approached Morag after the service to offer her condolences, but she had brushed her away angrily. As far as Morag was concerned, the social worker was part of a system that had failed Alan and others like him. She had no time for social workers—interfering do-gooders at the best of times and worse than useless when they were actually needed.

She had not cried once during the service. Rather she had been consumed with rage to the point her jaw ached from clenching her teeth. He had left her. Just like everyone left her. But it was the note he had left behind that angered her most of all. She had trusted him with her secrets and he had betrayed her. Now she didn't know who to trust and it was almost too late.

The funeral over, Morag had hung around watching as the next funeral party arrived at the crematorium. It was in stark contrast to the one she had just attended. The queue of cars behind the hearse had snaked all the way along the drive and down to the bottom of the street leading into the crematorium. Through narrowed eyes, she had watched as the crowds of mourners spilled out their cars and gravitated towards each other offering words of comfort and condolences. All those families, all that love, there for each other, like proper families.

Partially hidden by the bushes, nobody had noticed her watchful eye. Nobody could see her bitter smile and it was there the truth of her own miserable existence hit her smack between the eyes. When she died, there would be nobody there to mourn her —nobody to miss her, nobody to care. Just an empty crematorium and nobody to whisper their goodbyes as her body slid behind the curtains to burn.

The taxi pulled away and Morag reached out to open her gate. In the gloom of the winter afternoon, she house looked to be shrouded in black, mourning alongside her. She hesitated, not wanting to go inside to the suffocating silence, the memories slipping into her mind to remind her she was alone. But where could she go? She had no close friends, nobody she could call up or visit. She thought about calling Susan but quickly dismissed the idea—she needed to give her more time to come round to her way of thinking. Even Ronnie was out of bounds now—locked up in a secure psychiatric unit. She couldn't even visit him. Loneliness enveloped her. She truly had no one.

With no real alternative, she wearily pushed the gate open and traipsed heavily up the path. Inside the house, she took off her coat and reached into her pocket for her mobile to put it back in the kitchen drawer. She contemplated the phone in her hand, wishing there she had someone she could call, someone to talk to. But she had nobody. Unless… unless…? She drafted out the message and sent it quickly before she could change her mind. The reply came almost immediately. "You're going to have to pay me double. That's not my usual game."

"I'll pay you. Just make sure you get it done in the next few days." Persuasion came at a price, she thought.

"I'll do it the day after Boxing Day."

Morag smiled and put the phone back in the drawer. She had no intention of letting any money pass hands. She'd take care of things her own way.

Her heart was still heavy. The house even more claustrophobic than usual if that was possible. The empty rooms mocked her, her mother's taunts hung heavy in the air. She locked her front door and made her way up the stairs. Lying on her bed, still wearing her outdoor clothes, she reached over to open her drawer. Her hand felt around until it closed around her jar. She lifted it out.

Unscrewing the lid, she shook the hearts out watching them flutter to the bed. Alan's heart, all scrunched up now, along with the others who had left her. She swept them to the side, she had no use for them, not now they had gone.

Placing Ronnie's heart in the palm of her hand, she caressed it slowly, turning it over and over. Her fist closed around it, ready to crumple it up with others who had let her down, but she stopped, not sure she was quite ready to let go of him yet.

She smoothed the heart and gently let it flutter back into the jar. She picked up the last two hearts—the ones she had made for Susan and Lily and smiled as she held them close to her chest. These two were her last chance to bring her family home, to be with her, to be there for her. She creased the larger of the hearts. *A means to an end.* It was the little heart she coveted the most. The clock was ticking.

Twelve months at the most, they had told her yesterday at the hospital. They had shunted her into a cubicle and told her to undress and put on a hospital gown. It had been degrading. On one side of her, she could hear a man she deduced to be called Jimmy given the reprimands shouted in his direction. He had been vehemently denying all use of illicit substances to staff attending to him. On the other side, someone called Tam screamed at the injustice of the bastards trying to incarcerate him while he was off his face. And in the midst of all this chaos, through the gap in the curtains, she had watched in horror as an old woman shuffled across the room gripping onto her rollator walker with a plastic shopping bag from one of the discount food shops wrapped around her leg. The bag failed to do the job the woman had intended it to, as the blood from a burst varicose vein seeped out and left a bloody trail along the floor. By the time the young doctor had come to examine her, Morag had given up all sense of hope. Ill health brought no dignity, this was not the way she intended to go.

The young nurse who had accompanied her along to the consultant's office had been kind, all sympathetic and warm but it had not made the delivery of the news any easier.

"I don't understand why you didn't attend any of your appointments, Miss McLaughlin?"

She shrugged. She did not see the point in giving any explanations to the consultant, he would never understand. None of them would. Why should they understand, none of them knew her, and well, if they did, they would probably think she deserved to die a lonely and painful death. So she stayed silent. Morag had known about her cancer long before any doctor had told her. The tests a year ago had simply been a formality.

She had made the decision not to attend appointments, not to seek out any treatment, because she couldn't see the point. What would be the point in extending a life as lonely as hers? She probably deserved all that was coming to her. But even so, she still didn't want to die on her own. Nobody should die alone. Even Mother and

Father had not died alone. That's why she had spent so long trying to create her family, and now she feared she was too late.

Morag picked up the two black hearts, Mother and Father. She placed them in the palm of her hand and tightened her fists, crushing them hard. Spittle gathered at the corner of her mouth as the curses spewed out. Father had been weak, too afraid to stand up to Mother. Too weak to save her. Useless. And as for her—Mother—she had destroyed Morag. She had denied her the family life she deserved. Mother was to blame for everything Morag had done. She had been forced to try to recreate the family she had been denied. Shame burned deep within her as she remembered. If it hadn't been for them, none of this would have happened. She would have had a proper family, a proper life. They were to blame. Dropping the hearts into a glass trinket dish, she took a lighter from her drawer and watched as the two paper shapes turned to ashes.

"Nothing lasts forever, Mother," she whispered.

MORAG SLIPPED INTO her mother's bedroom. Her nose wrinkled at the scent of lavender, which still lingered in the air even after all these years. The pillows lay shredded where she had left them, but still she could see her mother's face watching her from the bed, taunting her, goading her, reminding her of all her mistakes, reminding her she had nothing.

Adrenaline rushed through her body and she felt a strength surge through her. She marched over to the wardrobe and yanked the door open. Her mother's clothes hung there as she had left them the day she passed. Morag had never even considered throwing them out or handing them on to charity shops. She could not bear the thought of her mother's evil tainting anyone else. She ignored the dresses to her left, the ones hanging in ribbons on their hanger and took out a black dress with her mother's trademark high collar and long sleeves. *It's a sin to flaunt your body.* She could still hear her mother's words hiss in her ear.

She held the dress against her body and turned to look at herself in the mirror. She gasped as her mother's face grinned back at her. She screamed. Flinging the dress on the bed, she grabbed the scissors from the dressing table, and plunged them into the dress over and over again, imagining ripping apart her mother's frail body with each plunge. She made no sound, but the tears were blinding her as she stabbed over and over again, wishing she had done it when the woman had still been alive. Wishing she hadn't taken the easy way out.

If it hadn't been for you, Mother, none of this would have happened, I wouldn't have needed to recreate the family I never had would I? You and father destroyed everything for me. Both of you. Father nearly gave in though, didn't he? You couldn't have that happen, could you? No, so you made him pay. One tiny moment of weakness when he almost gave in to me, when he almost let me go through with it.

But no. You put paid to that didn't you? "Oh, he's run off," you told everyone. You even pretended to be upset, didn't you? You were such a good actor, Mother. Nobody suspected a thing, did they? Mind you, they probably believed he should have run away years ago. They probably felt sorry for him being so browbeaten by you.

But I knew what you did mother. I saw you that day. And what did you do? You forced me to watch as you cut up his body and made me carry it down to the garden to bury him. I even had to plant the bush to hide the evidence, didn't I? What sort of mother does that to her child?

A woman like YOU, Mother. Evil. A mother who locks away her child and tells everyone her daughter is crazy. That is how evil you were. It's no wonder I tried to escape from you. But you had already damaged me, and even when I managed to get away, you were still there behind me, making me do the things I didn't want to do. It was you who made me take…

Morag dropped to the floor, memories racing through her head. She could feel the bile rise and could not stop the flow of hot vomit burning her throat as she heaved until there was nothing left to bring up.

Sitting in the middle of the mess, Morag took a deep breath before pulling herself upright. She had to clean herself up. She had to sort herself out. She needed to get Susan and Lily here, and have them here. She had to bring her family home. She could not die alone and nothing would stand in her way.

Thirty

Jess

JESS PACED THE flat, her thoughts overwhelming her as the walls began to close in. She had spent Christmas Day and Boxing Day with only the ghosts of her past for company, and her emotions like glass, were ready to shatter into tiny pieces at any moment. The box of memories left to her by her mum lay scattered across the living room floor. Each memory reinforcing her need to finish off what she had come to Lennoxhill to do. She had waited a lifetime for this, and now it was time to get justice for her mum and to close the door one final time on the family that had never been hers.

She didn't even have work as a distraction, as Marion had decided to keep the café closed for a couple of days after Christmas.

"No point in opening up. Everyone will be away into town to the sales," she had texted Jess on Christmas Eve.

Jess had sent Susan a text earlier, suggesting they meet up, but Susan hadn't replied. *Maybe she's run out of credit.* Jess wanted to give her the benefit of the doubt, she didn't want to think of yet another rejection in her life. She sensed a kindred spirit in Susan. She seemed to be lost, out on a limb and struggling to find somewhere to belong. *I'll go and see her, some company will do us both good,* she thought, pulling on her jacket and shoes.

Leaving the flat, Jess made her way along the Main Street, taking in the eerie silence of the quiet streets. Marion had been right, most of the shops were closed, and the usually bustling main street lay empty. She reckoned everyone would either still be sleeping off festive hangovers, or away into town to spend their Christmas money. The very thought of it gave Jess the fear. She couldn't understand why people would want to rush to crowded shops to spend money they couldn't afford on useless tat.

As she neared the Waterside Estate, Jess was stricken by how run down and shabby it looked. She hadn't paid that much attention before. She couldn't imagine how someone like Susan coped living in a dump like that. It wasn't like Susan was posh or anything, but it was easy to see she hadn't come from an area like this. Jess shuddered. Although her life hadn't been a bed of roses, she still couldn't imagine spending the rest of her life in a place like this.

She walked up the deserted street, most households still asleep behind closed curtains. She checked her watch. It was not even nine yet—too early for most of the residents of the Waterside Estate. A movement from the block of flats where Susan lived caught her eye. She looked up as a man sauntered out of the entryway. She gave him the once over—he had boy band good looks, but there something about him exuded trouble.

Jess slowed down. A tingle ran down her spine. He might be a dealer. She didn't want to get caught up in any of that shit, she had already been down that road before and had no intention of going back again. She took cover in a row of hedges as the man reached the bottom of the path. Her gut told her to stay hidden until he had gone. A packet rustled, then a soft click, and the slow, creeping reek of cigarette smoke floated by. She held her breath as she peered out from her hiding place. The man had stopped and pulled out his phone. His deep voice broke the silence, "Job's done," he muttered. "She's messed up pretty badly but nothing that needs any hospital treatment. That's me done now, Morag. No more. Get my money to me by the end of the day."

She heard him inhale, then he continued, "If you don't get me the money today, I'll be round to the library to collect it and you wouldn't want anyone at work knowing what you got up to in your spare time, would you?"

Now that's weird, she thought. *What's someone like him calling that old bitch Morag for?* It had to be the same Morag, she was the only Morag who worked in the library.

She listened as the gate clicked closed, and waited until the sound of his footsteps faded into the distance, before untangling herself from the hedge. She made her way up the path and, finding the security door unlocked, made her way into the close, wrinkling her nose at the smell of urine coming from the stairwell.

Jess knocked gently at Susan's door. She could hear muffled sobs coming from the flat. Nobody answered.

Jess put her ear against the door and listened. She could definitely hear someone crying. She knocked again, before opening the letterbox and hissing, "Susan, it's me, Jess. Open the door."

She listened as she heard footsteps shuffle down the hallway. A voice hissed back. "Go away please. Lily's asleep, and I don't want to see anyone."

"Open the door Susan, please? I only want to check you're alright."

Silence.

"Susan, if you don't open the door, I'm going to knock so fucking loudly that I'll wake the bloody dead."

The door inched open slightly, and Jess put her foot in to try to push it open but, as slight as she was, Susan kept it firm. She peered out and, even in the dark gloom of the hallway, Jess tried to hide her shock at the bloody mess of her face.

"Jesus Christ! Susan, let me in. What the hell happened to you? Was it that guy who just left?"

"Please, go away. I'm fine, I fell getting out the shower, okay."

"Don't lie, Susan. Just let me in."

"No. Do me a favour? Go away and leave it. It's nothing to do with you. You'll only make things worse for me. Go!" The door slammed, leaving Jess open mouthed in the close.

She thought about banging Susan's door and telling her what she had overheard. But something stopped her. Instead, she turned and strode away, a plan formulating in her head.

Thirty One

Morag

"ARE YOU SURE this is okay? I mean, what if he finds us here? What if the neighbours tell him where we've gone?"

"It'll be fine, Susan. Nobody knows you're here. Your neighbours all think you done a moonlight flit, don't they? They saw you get into the taxi with your stuff, and the taxi I booked you came from out of town, so there is no trail back to you both. It is a new year Susan, a new start for us all. None of us ever needs to be alone again. We've got each other now." Morag smiled at her.

Morag watched as a flicker of fear crossed Susan's face. "Watch your step Morag. Be careful," she told herself. But she couldn't stop the manic feeling building up inside of her—she didn't want to have to wait. She wanted her family together. Now. *Stupid little bitch, they're not your family.*

"Yes they ARE!"

Morag clasped her hand over her mouth, aware she had blurted her reply to her mother out loud. She looked at Susan and saw her eyebrow raise. Morag laughed. Even to her ears it sounded quite hysterical.

"Silly me. Silly billy old me. Now, what did you tell your neighbours?"

Morag ignored the nervous tic in Susan's eye, but smiled happily when she replied.

"Yeah, I told Mrs Clark across the hall I'd had enough, and we were heading down south. She's the nosiest person on the estate, so if anyone comes snooping, she'll be sure to pass on all the gossip. She can't hold her water that one."

"See? Nothing to worry about then, is there?" Morag replied brightly. "Of course, you are both going to have to lay low for a bit. It'll be fine here. The neighbours are all elderly and keep themselves to themselves. The garden is enclosed, and you and Lily will be able to go outside without worrying about anyone seeing either of you."

"We won't be here for long, I'm sure. It's just until we get back on our feet, that's all. Besides, I'm sure you will soon get tired of us and be desperate for your own space again before long."

Morag ignored the wobble in Susan's voice. "Nonsense. It's all going to work out perfectly Susan. You wait and see. Now drink up the tea I made you—nice and sugary to keep your strength up."

She watched as Susan lifted the cup to her mouth and grimaced slightly as she took a sip. Morag smiled to herself, she hoped she hadn't overdone it with the sugar. She pressed her hands to her mouth trying to suppress a giggle—this was all going exactly how she had planned.

Lily sat on the floor eating her breakfast, eyes glued to some ridiculous pink pig creature on the television. Morag frowned. She would need to put a stop to this nonsense as soon as possible. She hated the way parents used television as a babysitter these days, plonking them in front of screens to vegetate. She was going to have her work cut out with this one.

A clatter interrupted Morag's thoughts. She looked around sharply. Susan's cup lay on the coffee table, the coffee dripping over the edges onto the carpet. Morag smirked.

"I'm so sorry," Susan mumbled. "I don't know what happened, I feel so…" She yawned.

"Don't worry about it," said Morag. "Are you okay?"

"I'm feeling a bit tired to be honest," her words were slurred. "I didn't sleep well last night." Her chin dropped to her chest.

"Oh, you poor thing. Why don't you go for a wee lie down?"

"I can't. What about Lily? I need to…" Her voice tapered off, and she looked as though she was on the verge of collapsing.

"Och, don't you worry about Lily. I can look after her. I'm not at work today anyway. Come on and I'll help you up to your room, you look like you are about to keel over."

Morag helped Susan to her feet, putting her arm around the young woman's waist. Susan gave no resistance.

Lily looked up, a worried glance crossing her face as she saw her mother slumped against Morag.

"Shh," Morag put her fingers to her lips. "Mummy's just a wee bit tired, she'd going to have a lie down. I'll look after you. Properly."

Lily shrugged and turned back to the television, eyes glazing over.

Morag almost floated back down the stairs. Susan was out for the count and now she and Lily could spend some time together, some quality time. First, she had a call to make.

"Hello, it's Morag here. I'm really sorry but I'm not going to be in work this week, I've got a terrible temperature, I think I might be in for the flu... yes. Yes, I'm sure I'll be fine... no, I was due in tomorrow but I'm just letting you know in plenty of time. Yes, okay, I'll call you in a few days. Thank you."

She put the phone down, careful not to slam it back onto the cradle, annoyed at their false concern. They didn't bother about her any other time, why start pretending now?

She stood in the doorway, watching Lily. The child didn't even notice her, her gaze was so focused on the television. Morag had a sudden urge to pick her up and run away with her. She bit the urge down.

No Morag you can't do that, that would be a silly thing to do... remember what happened the last time... She gave herself a shake and adopted a bright voice.

"Right Lily, let's put this nonsense off now."

The child's face fell as Morag marched across the room and snapped off the television.

"I need you to go to your room for an hour for a little nap, and then you and I can have some fun."

"I don't want a nap. I'm a big girl. I'm not a baby now. I don't have naps." She stuck her thumb in her mouth.

"Don't be so cheeky, young lady? You will do as I tell you, when I tell you, is that clear?"

Lily stared at blankly at Morag.

"I said, is that clear?" Morag's voice was shrill and her change in tone alerted Lily to a change in mood. The child's eyes filled with tears. *Damn, I can't have her having a tantrum right now.*

"Shh. Come on now. Don't cry, don't you dare cry. What about a sweetie? I'll give you some special sweeties if you want?"

The tears dried almost instantly. Spoiled little brat. Clearly her mother had been giving into her tantrums. She would soon put an end to that. No child of Morag's would be spoiled. But right now, she would have to give into the tantrums. She couldn't risk Lily seeing anything.

"I'm not like you, Mother. I will look after my child. I will protect her." she muttered darkly.

Morag rushed through to the kitchen, promising Lily she would be back with a treat. Scrabbling in the kitchen drawer, she found what she was searching for—children's antihistamine. Her mother had sworn by it. Not ideal, she thought, but it would keep the child safe for an hour or so. She checked the correct dosage and mentally doubled it, the child would be fine, and after all, it had not done her any harm had it?

She watched as Lily's eyes grew heavy. She picked her up, light as a little feather, and murmured gently into the child's hair. Carrying her upstairs, she laid her down on the bed in the spare room. She gave her a soft kiss on the cheek and locked the door on the way out.

Downstairs, Morag got out her phone. "Come now. Round the back and don't let anyone see you."

Morag went to the walk-in cupboard in the kitchen. On the top shelf she found her father's tool bag. Mother had hidden it away after Father had gone. Morag pulled it down, sneezing as the dust tickled her nose. Rummaging through the bag, she wrenched out the hammer, ignoring the rusty red covering and the short black hairs stuck to it. She began humming as she waited for Kris to arrive.

"PEOPLE REALLY SHOULDN'T underestimate me," Morag smiled to herself, as she locked the shed door. She had surprised herself with her own strength—he had been an absolute pushover. She had asked him to check a leak under her sink while she got her purse to pay him. The sound of the hammer cracking open his skull had caused a small frisson of pleasure. She had been denied the chance to finish her mother off like that. She looked around to check nobody had seen her. Using the sleeve of her jumper, she wiped away the sweat from her face, not noticing the streaks of blood left behind.

"Need to do some gardening, Morag. Get the house ready for springtime. Not that you'll be here to see it, but can't leave a mess behind." She giggled as she made her way upstairs to the shower.

LILY STILL LOOKED quite drowsy when Morag carried her downstairs. She'd already checked on Susan who was still fast asleep. "Lazy little bitch," she'd muttered over the sleeping woman, as she prodded her roughly to make sure she wasn't trying to trick her.

The child tried to snuggle back into the couch, muttering "I'm tired."

"Nonsense, Lily, you cannot possibly be tired. Not after having a nap. Come on now, wake up. Mummy has fun things for us to do."

Lily glanced towards the door, brightening up a little. "Mummy?"

Morag ignored her. "Come on through to the kitchen and we can play schools."

Lily's face brightened and she nodded.

"Yes, I like playing schools. Can I be the teacher?"

Morag shook her head. "No, I don't think so, I'm the grown up, so I'm teacher."

She led Lily into the kitchen and sat her at the table. On the kitchen table lay a pencil, a ruler and some paper.

"Where's the crayons? Mummy always has crayons for school. I don't like this, it's boring," she whined, picking up the pencil and examining it, a look of disgust on her face.

"It's not boring, Lily, it's education and all young ladies must have an education—a proper education."

"I don't want educashon. I want crayons!" Lily's voice raised a notch, and Morag was worried a full-blown tantrum was about to erupt. She didn't want to risk anyone hearing the girl scream. The house might be secluded, but she knew how loud a child's scream could be and how it could carry. She could hear the shrill screams in her head: *noooooooooooooo... leave me alone... you're not my mu...*

"What's wrong with your face?" Lily's voice interrupted.

Morag looked down and the child stared up at her, bemused.

"It's all red and funny," Lily laughed uncertainly.

Morag stared at the child, unsure of herself. Lily wasn't screaming, Morag couldn't see any signs of distress on the child's face. It wasn't... "Oh God, I'm imagining things now."

Lily gawped at her.

"Silly me," she said. "You're right. Schools need crayons and I'm sure I have some here in the drawer."

After an hour of trying to teach the child to write her name neatly, Morag had lost her patience. It was obvious Susan had given little attention to her daughter's educational needs. Lily had been getting increasingly irritable and it had taken Morag all her strength not to rap her knuckles with the ruler. After all, it hadn't done her any harm when mother had rapped her knuckles, had it? No harm at all. Look how well she had done in her life—a job in the library. You couldn't work in the library without an education, now could you? *I told you Mother, I am respected now, and people here know I am clever. You were wrong. I did amount to something after all.*

The child laughed nervously.

"What's so funny?" asked Morag.

"You were talking funny. Talking like a funny lady."

A little more roughly than she intended, Morag lifted Lily from the chair. "Why don't we go and brush your hair? Little girls should be neat and tidy," she snapped.

"Ouch, you hurt me." Lily pulled away from Morag, glaring at her from under wet eyelashes.

A trickle of cold sweat settled between Morag's shoulder blades. This was not how she had planned it at all. She had to get a grip of herself, and quickly, before her plans all fell down the pan again.

Lowering herself to the child's height, she took her hands gently.

"I'm sorry pet. I was just a wee bit upset. I am worried about your mummy, but I shouldn't have taken it out on you."

"Why are you worried about my mummy? I want my mummy..." Her mouth formed into an O—a scream on the tip of her tongue ready to make its escape.

"Shit, shit shit," muttered Morag. "Shh." She drew the child closer. "Don't be silly. Mummy's fine. She's going to be okay. She's worried about grown up things, and not being able to care for you properly. She doesn't want to have to send you away."

Lily's bottom lip trembled. Morag took her tiny face in her hands and spoke gently to her. "Lily, I need you to be a big girl okay?"

The child nodded her eyes wide.

"I am going to make sure mummy doesn't have to send you away. That's why you and mummy have come here to stay for a while. So I can look after you both. If I take care of you, then mummy won't need to send you away, see? But you need to promise me you won't tell mummy you know this. If you tell her she will send you away anyway, so it needs to be our secret."

Lily stared at her, eyes wide now. She nodded again.

"Do you understand, Lily? It's our secret. Just me and you. You can't tell mummy."

Lily dropped her eyes to the floor before looking back up. She put her fingers to her lips.

"Our secret," she whispered.

"Good girl. You are such a good girl. I'm not going to let anyone send you away, not this time, I'll watch out for you. That's what family do. That's what mummies do."

Morag wrapped her arms around the child and held her tight.

"Now let's go do your hair. I know exactly what it should look like."

Thirty Two

Jess

JESS OPENED HER eyes and squinted at the clock on her bedside table. She groaned. She'd only managed two hours sleep. She punched her pillows in frustration. This was killing her. Jess usually slept like a baby, she always had, even in the hospital nothing had affected her sleep. But she had spent most of the night before tossing and turning, trying to work what to do next. Now her head was banging. Thank Christ Marion didn't want her in for a couple of days.

She looked round the room. Everything seemed out of focus. It would be so easy to pull the duvet back over her head and forget the world for the day, but that wouldn't do her any good. She had to push herself, one last time. She would have plenty of thinking time when this was all over.

Picking up her phone, she checked for any messages or missed calls, disappointed to see there were none. Worry niggled at her as she thought about Susan and Lily. She had been trying to contact Susan, but she hadn't returned her calls or messages. Jess had even gone back round to Susan's flat to check up on her, but her neighbour across the landing had taken great delight in informing her Susan had done a runner, somewhere down South, she'd told Jess. Standing at her door with her arms firmly folded across her chest, the woman had relayed her theory around Susan's disappearance. "Reckon she was one of them prossies, so I do, probably a crackhead too, always men coming and going round there. Mind you, she was a bit too stuck up for round here, thought she was better than the rest of us, while she was lying on her back earning her keep." She'd cackled showing a mouthful of decaying teeth.

Looking at the woman in disgust, Jess had retorted, "At least she had the looks to earn something, love. Doubt you could even earn your keep down Glasgow Green these days you old boot." And she had stormed off, leaving the woman open-mouthed. Jess hadn't bought the story about Susan doing a runner down South, she was worried something bad had happened to her, but who could she tell and she could hardly go rushing to the police to report a grown woman missing when there was no real evidence that she was.

She was also fretting over Ronnie. Jess was terrified he wouldn't be able to keep his mouth shut and would blurt everything out to the staff on the ward. She had even tried to visit him but, when she'd called the ward, the nurse had told her Ronnie was a restricted patient and wasn't allowed any visitors. Jess could only hope anything he might say would be written off as paranoid ramblings, and by the time he was well enough for anyone to take any notice of what he was saying, all this would be over.

Jess pulled herself up into a sitting position and picked up her phone. She scrolled through her social media screwing her face up at feeds filled with pictures of happy families—the Christmas memories lingering well into January, mocking her with their exaggerated cheerfulness. She wanted to rip the filters from their lives and show them the ugly truth of life.

A new post in the Lennoxhill Community Page caught her eye. A photograph of a large crowd had already had gathered over two hundred comments. She zoomed in on the photograph, immediately recognising Ronnie's house. Someone had posted the photograph on the day of Ronnie's arrest little over a month ago. Jess only read the first couple of comments.

"See they got the psycho locked up at last."

"Best place fir him—looney bin."

"At least ma weans will be able to play out now."

"Aye, ah saw him, he wiz foamin' at the mouth, ten polis were sittin' on him."

She threw her phone down in disgust. She couldn't get her head round people's ignorance. She recalled how Annie Boyle and her

friend Mary had practically shot through the café door the day after
Ronnie had been lifted for attacking his mum. They were busting a
gut to be the first to break the news of his arrest. Jess hadn't given
them the satisfaction of a reply. She didn't need their gossip. She
already knew what had happened. She smiled at the memory. Poor
Ronnie, locked away, his worst nightmare. Still, he's safer in there
than with that old witch of a mother and away from bloody Morag.
I've done him a favour really.

Awake now, Jess threw back her duvet, jumped out of bed and
quickly got dressed. She had no intention of sitting around all day
getting herself worked up, going stir crazy. Not bothering to stop for
breakfast, she pulled on her jacket and left the house.

Opening the front door, the cold air slapped her. She zipped her
jacket up to the neck, not that it made much difference. The weather
made up her mind—she would go to the main street and pop into
one of the charity shops, to see if she could pick up something a bit
warmer than her summer jacket.

She took a shortcut through the lane at the back of the shops and
came out at the café. She peered through the windows, and saw
Marian deep in conversation with Annie and Mary. *Old crows*. The
three of them would be in their element, three old witches, sitting
there pulling folk's lives apart. She could give them something to talk
about. She could blow them out the water with the stories she had—
it would keep them going for months. She laughed. They'd all find
out sooner rather than later. Whether she'd be round to see it was
another matter.

The door of the charity shop jangled as she pushed it open, and
she wrinkled her nose at the musty smell of dead people's clothes.
The shop assistant looked up and gave her a watery smile. Jess smiled
back, as she made her way over to the women's clothing section.

"Freezing out, isn't it?" she said to the assistant, who smiled
weakly back at her, shrugging his shoulders.

"Nice and warm in here though, eh?" she continued, and received
another shrug in response. *For Christ's sake, they're all bloody weirdos in
this town.* She busied herself with rifling through the rack of winter

coats. A black, military-style, woollen coat caught her eye. Nice one—very eighties chic. She flicked up the price tag—thirty quid? No chance! It was a bloody charity shop, not a designer boutique.

She picked out a plain black one—waterproof and with a hood, priced only ten pounds. She wished she could go shopping and not have to worry about the price. She took the coat over to the assistant who rang it up on the till and stuffed it into a bag without saying a word. She took it back out the bag, shrugging her thin summer jacket off and tossing it across the counter at the assistant.

"Here, take this as a donation. I'm not going to be needing it again."

He nodded and picked it up, shuffling towards the storeroom.

"Have a nice day, why don't you?" Jess yelled, as she slammed the shop door behind her. The sooner she got out of this godforsaken place the better. And, who knows, it might be sooner than she'd thought.

Feeling much warmer in her new jacket, she gave a cheery whistle as she cut across the street and through the park.

"Morning Joe," she called to Radio Joe, who sat on his usual bench. He looked over and waved. *Why's he not over at Morag's poxy group? He must be the only screwball round here who didn't hang around the woman.* She couldn't shake off the feelings of resentment towards the woman.

Jess still seethed at Morag's constant rebuttal of her attempts to join in when she first moved to the town. "Always on the outside looking in, that's me," she mulled, as she wandered through the park, head full of her plans for the future.

In the library, Jess smiled when she saw Lynn McDonald was on duty again, she had a feeling this girl could be quite useful. She approached the desk ready with the excuse she had no credit on her phone and wanted to use the computer suite. Lynn had recognised her and grinned.

"Back again? You better be careful. You'll be known as a regular at this rate."

"Aye. No credit in my phone again, and I've got some work to be doing. Just wanted to see if I can get on the computers? You on your own? No Morag today then?"

Lynn looked up, glanced around, and brought her hand up to her mouth. "She's on the sick."

"That's a shame, hope she's okay," offered Jess, not knowing what else she could say. It would explain the fact she hadn't seen her around for a while though.

But Lynn had just started. She leaned forward. "Between you and me, I don't believe her, though. Some rubbish about a flu bug. Elsie, who took the call, said she sounded perfectly fine to her. I reckon she's up to something."

Jess snorted. "Yeah right. What's a dowdy old spinster like her going to be up to? You think she's got a hot date holed up in the house or something?"

Lynn laughed. "No chance. But I do know she's weird. After you came in the last time, it got me thinking and I've been doing some digging. She's not all she says she is, you know?"

Interest piqued now, Jess leaned forward too. "Oh, nice one. Some gossip! Tell me more!"

Lynn shook her head. "No, not here. Too many nosy gits around. I'm finished at five if you want to hang around, though. We could go for a drink if you want?"

Jess tried to keep the glee out her reply, she didn't want Lynn think she was too keen.

"Yeah, suppose I could go for a couple."

"Great," Lynn smiled, as she handed over the access code for the computer suite. "I'll come and get you once I'm done."

Back turned, Jess gave an imaginary fist pump in her head. She hadn't even had to try.

At five on the dot, Lynn tapped Jess on the shoulder. "Right that's me ready. Let's go."

Jess jumped. She had been lost in the information she'd been browsing.

"Oh, what were you looking at?" Lynn asked, peering over Jess's shoulder.

"Nothing," she snapped, as she quickly shut down the screen, hoping Lynn hadn't seen the headline of the archived newspaper article she had been reading: "Attempted Child Abduction. Police warn parents to be on their guard."

She turned round and saw Lynn's face fall.

"Sorry," Jess apologised quickly. "Force of habit from my younger days. Couldn't do anything without one of my wee brothers peering over my shoulder and telling my ma," she lied.

"It's okay. No worries. Right come on. Let's get to the pub."

THE TOBY JUG was across the road from the library, and the two women had found a table and ordered drinks in less than five minutes after arriving. Jess scanned the room. She had never been in the pub before and, so far, she hadn't seen much to impress her. They had to be the youngest in the bar by about fifty years—it was a real spit-and-sawdust kind of place.

Lynn must have seen the look on Jess's face, as she rushed to defend it.

"It's a bit livelier at the weekend. They have live bands on, and karaoke most weekends. It's a great wee bar."

Not wanting to get off on the wrong foot with her, Jess gave her an apologetic smile, "It's fine, honestly. I was thinking I'd never been in before... Actually, I've not been out to any of the pubs in town. Billy-no-mates, that's me." She forced a laugh, trying to put Lynn at ease.

"Well, we can fix that easy. You are more than welcome to come out with me and the girls any weekend, you know? The more the merrier. We usually start off in here for a few cheap rounds, before we head over the Lennox Arms on Moss Road for a something a bit more upmarket."

Jess had passed the Lennox Arms a few times. It looked a bit posher than this dump—all glass fronts with hanging baskets and small bistro tables outside in the summer. Still, she didn't want to be hanging around with Lynn and her giggling mates. She wasn't here to make friends. She was here to sort things out, once and for all.

She gave a non-committal nod and a smile, before turning the conversation back round to the gossip she had been waiting for.

Two hours later, Jess made her excuses and left a slightly tipsy Lynn, surrounded by some of the girls she had mentioned. Their shrieks were getting shriller and their comments lewder by the minute. Jess smiled at them as she waved her goodbyes. God, as if she would want to hang around a bunch of airheads like them.

Still, it had been a productive enough evening. Lynn had been easy to ply with drinks—she hadn't even realised Jess had switched to coke—and the words were soon spewing out her mouth, without Jess even having to prompt her.

She whistled all the way home.

Thirty Three

Susan

SINCE MOVING IN with Morag, the days and nights had merged into one. Susan had lost all track of time. She couldn't shake off the feeling of lethargy that swamped her. She couldn't understand why she felt this way. She did nothing. She went nowhere.

"I'm so exhausted. Something isn't right," she told Morag. "I think I need to go see the doctor, get my bloods checked or something."

The vehemence of Morag's response had taken her aback. "Nonsense, there is nothing wrong with you. Besides, you can't go to the doctor, can you? Nobody knows you're here. And you can't risk that Kris seeing you and contacting Colin? I'll pick you up a tonic when I'm out. You're just run down after all the stress you've been under."

"But all I ever seem to do is sleep," she had argued. "I'm never this tired. Not even when I first left Colin, and I was totally stressed then. I really do think I should see a doctor, just to be on the safe side. It's affecting how I am with Lily. I'm falling asleep all the time. It's no good... And I've hardly done a thing in here." She waved at the clutter in the living room.

Morag had snapped at her. "There is nothing wrong with you. Don't worry about the house. I've lived with it like this all these years, so another few months isn't going to kill me."

The older woman had clasped her hand over her mouth at her last statement and stifled a giggle, leaving Susan feeling uncomfortable. There was something really creepy about the way she behaved sometimes. Had she made a mistake moving in? Morag's behaviour was becoming weirder by the day.

Morag stared at her, and Susan couldn't help but feel like a fly caught in a spider's web. Morag had said months. Months hadn't been in Susan's plan. A shiver ran down her spine.

She glanced over at Lily, sitting quietly, painstakingly trying to copy some letters Morag had put out for her. The TV screen behind her was black. That in itself rang alarm bells for Susan. Lily adored Peppa Pig and would constantly nag her to watch it. She could not remember hearing her daughter ask for the television once over the last week. Come to think of it, she had not heard Lily whine about anything, which was not like her. Then again, she hadn't been full of her usual smiles and chat either. Instead, she had been replaced by a pale and subdued version of her daughter—a watered down Lily. And as for her hair, Susan had never seen her daughter's unruly mass of curls so severely scraped back off her head and braided into the tightest pigtails. Even the little explosion of colour that had been the staple charity shop buys for her daughter, whose love for clothes was dictated by colour—the brighter, the better—had been replaced by a rather old-fashioned looking wardrobe of sombre dark dresses and skirts, all covering as much of her little body as possible.

"LILY," SUSAN HISSED, not wanting to raise her voice too loud— Morag was upstairs and Susan didn't want her to hear.

Lily ignored her and carried on with her letters, the tip of her tongue peeking out of her mouth as she focused on the task in front of her.

"Lily, come here," she said, louder this time, looking up to the ceiling.

Lily shook her head. "I can't. Got to finish my work." Her head dropped back to the papers in front of her.

"Come on, Lily. Come on, you can have a wee break. Come sit with mum, we can watch Peppa," she wheedled, expecting her daughter to throw herself enthusiastically on to the couch beside her eager for her favourite programme.

Lily's head had snapped up and her eyes opened wide, they were glassy, with tears threatening.

"We're not allowed to watch Peppa. It's not ed-edu-ca-shunal," she stammered.

Susan's jaw dropped.

"Educational! Lily, don't be silly. You are four years old." She laughed, but the hairs on the back of her neck stood to attention. Something felt very off.

"No mummy, please, don't make me watch it. I've got to do my work, I've got to learn how to be proper and write and everything. To be a big girl." The tears started to spill.

"Aww, Lily, love. Come on. Come to mummy and I'll give you a cuddle. C'mon." She patted the seat beside her.

Lily shook her head rapidly.

"Noooooo, mummy please. I don't want to... d-don't want to get taken aw...." The living room door flew open, cutting her words short. Lily's mouth formed a small O, and she quickly put her head down to concentrate on the paper in front of her. Susan saw a tear fall onto the page.

She looked around to find Morag standing at the door, watching them, her eyes narrowed and her face flushed.

"I hope you haven't been disturbing Lily, Susan?" she asked, her voice laced with an undercurrent of venom. "She has homework to do."

"Homework? Morag, she isn't even at school yet."

"Don't answer me back girl. Someone had to take charge of that child's education." Morag's eyes glittered black.

Susan heard the accusation in Morag's words and opened her mouth to argue, but the look on Morag's face changed her mind. Something was going on here and she didn't know what, but her gut told her it wouldn't do her any favours to further anger Morag. So, instead, she tried to smile sweetly.

"No, Morag, not at all. I was saying to Lily how well she is doing and how clever she is. You must have put a lot of work in with her." She sat on her hands to avoid Morag seeing the tremors.

Morag stared at her for a moment then, with a sly grin, said: "Oh, I forgot to mention. I went to the shops earlier, while you were asleep. Apparently some man has been in the town asking about you." She rhymed off a description which sounded enough like Colin to make Susan panic. She felt the colour drain from her face. "Best you lie low for a bit longer eh? Now, let's have a nice cuppa. I'll make it." And Morag bustled out the room, humming to herself.

Once she was gone, Lily looked up and smiled gratefully. Susan's heart broke into tiny pieces as she tried to smile back. She had to find a way to get her and her daughter out of here.

OUTSIDE IN THE hallway, Morag observed mother and daughter unseen. She shook her head. *Stupid woman, she will believe anything.* Morag had not been anywhere near the shops, she hadn't even left the house. She had family to watch out for now.

In the kitchen, as she waited for the kettle to boil, she reached into the drawer and plucked out the sleeping tablets. Crushing three up instead of the usual one, she muttered, "It's for your own good, Susan. Your own good."

Thirty Four

Jess

JESS YAWNED AND stretched. Despite the chill in her bedroom, she felt alive for the first time in a long time. Rubbing her eyes, she looked at the clock. Eleven a.m. She couldn't remember the last time she'd slept so late. She smiled. Today would be a good day. Thanks to Lynn's loose tongue, she had plans for the day, and was eager to get going.

She jumped out of bed and grabbed her dressing gown. In the kitchen, she made herself a coffee and popped her last slice of bread into the toaster, making a shopping list in her head for her way home. Life was good. In fact, life was wonderful, now things were falling into place. Breakfast done, she showered and dressed quickly.

Once outside, she decided to avoid the bus. She reckoned she could walk it in an hour, and the walk would give her the headspace to clear her mind. She made her way down the main street, smiling and nodding a cheery hello to customers she recognised from the café. She popped into Mariana's to grab a coffee to take with her.

"Oh Jess, just the person I wanted to see. Any chance you can stay and do a shift? I've got a really important appointment this afternoon," Marion greeted her. *Typical. Not even a hello, how're you doing?* She guessed exactly what kind of important appointment Marion had—it would either be her nails or her hair.

"Sorry Marion. No can do. Places to go, people to see," she chirped brightly. "I've only come in to grab a latte, to go."

She ignored the scowl on her boss's face. She didn't care. It wouldn't be long before she could tell her to stuff her poxy job, and she would be out of this dump for good.

Marion banged the polystyrene cup on the counter, causing the coffee to slop out through the plastic lid. Jess smiled sweetly.

"Have a good day." She grinned as she left, giving Annie and Mary a cheery wave on her way out. The sneers they threw towards her brightened her day even more.

Outside, she clasped the coffee cup, grateful for the heat. The sky was a brilliant winter blue and her spirits were high, as she made her way along the main street, past the rows of shops and discount supermarket, until she reached the edge of the town. She breathed in deeply, appreciating the clean air, compared to the centre of town— clogged up with exhaust fumes.

She walked along the tree-lined roads with the fancy houses set back in their gardens, small playparks, and roads free from the debris, litter and dog shit she had grown used to seeing in the town centre. She picked at the empty polystyrene cup, allowing the small bobbles of white litter the pavement. She wished she had pockets full of rubbish, a sudden desire to litter the pristine lives of those behind the fancy gates. She scowled as she pictured the charmed lives of those behind the large bay windows and immaculate gardens. It wasn't fair. Why should they have this and she had nothing? 'Why should SHE have this, and I have nothing?' she thought, as a deep fury built up inside her.

She checked the app on her phone and it confirmed she had reached Blackthorn Ave. Approximately one hundred yards along the street was Cedar Drive. Thanks to Lynn and her drunken ramblings the night before, Jess knew exactly where Morag lived. Walking along Blackthorn Avenue, she convinced herself even the air smelt richer here. As she turned the corner onto Cedar Drive, three sandstone detached villas stood proudly in the winter sunshine. Stepping back behind a large hedge to hide from prying eyes, she stood for a moment, taking it all in.

The street was empty, a world away from the continuous revving engines, curses and greetings she heard from her own window each day. Jess breathed in the peace. Driveways lay empty. Curtains lay still, no twitching, or nosy neighbours popping out to watch the drama unfold. She clenched her fists. Her life could have been like this.

Morag's house sat at the end of the road and she made her way slowly towards it, all the time keeping a watchful eye on her surroundings. Satisfied nobody could see her, Jess made her way up the driveway of the house next to Morag's, the large hedge running up the side of the path provided the perfect cover. A noise from Morag's garden stopped her in her tracks. She stood still and listened. She could hear Morag talking in a weird singsong voice.

"See? This is what a little girl should look like. See how pretty you are with that little dress and your hair all done up? Not like those dreadful clothes Susan dresses you in."

"I like the clothes my mummy buys me. They're nice colours."

"That's enough answering back. I've told you. Young ladies listen to their mothers. They don't answer back."

"But you're not my mummy…"

Jess's jaw dropped. There was a child in there and Morag didn't have any children.

Jess inched forward, searching for a gap in the hedge to peer through. She held her breath as the conversation continued.

"I'm a better mother than that lazy article upstairs is. I'm doing a better job than she could ever do. Remember what I told you? If you tell anyone, then Susan will send you away. Is that what you want?"

There was no reply, only the sound of muffled sobs. Jess's heart constricted, poor kid. But where the hell was her mother?

"Your mother is too ill to look after you right now. She's in her bed, so I'm taking care of you. Okay?"

"Yes, Morag"

"Mummy. You call me Mummy when we are at home, remember?"

"But you're not my…"

"LILY!"

"Yes m-m-mummy."

"Good girl. That's mummy's best girl," Morag crooned. "We're the best family ever."

Jess peered through the small gap in the hedge. It was Susan's daughter, Lily, but instead of her usual bright attire, she wore an old-fashioned dark dress with a fussy collar and sleeves down to her little wrists. Her usually wild tangle of curls was scraped back into a painful-looking set of pigtails.

Jess observed them for a while. Morag had a crazed smile painted onto her face while she was shovelling a large mound of earth in the corner. She kept grabbing at Lily, trying to get her to help with one of those little spades you get for the beach. The child tried her best to help, but Jess could see her little shoulders slumped and, even from where she stood, she could see the tears streaking the girl's face.

Stepping back, she drew in a deep breath. Something made her look upwards. A figure stood at the top window looking out, hands pressed to the glass. Jess would have sworn it was Susan.

Thirty Five

Susan

SUSAN STOOD AT the bedroom window, gazing out on Morag and the girl below. The child looked like her Lily, but something looked different about her—her hair, her clothes. Those were not Lily's clothes and that was not Lily's hair. Susan felt the floor sway below her and she gripped onto the window ledge to steady herself. Her stomach churned as the girl looked up at Morag. She could see her bottom lip tremble and it tugged at her heart. She recognised that tremble, and she could almost hear the wails that were bound to follow. Her knuckles whitened as she realised it was Lily.

A movement caught her eye and she glanced over to the left. There, behind the hedge, someone stood watching the scene in the garden. Susan screwed up her eyes. There was something familiar about the person standing on the other side of the hedge, but a foggy haze inside her head meant she couldn't quite place her.

As if feeling her gaze, the woman looked up. Susan stepped back quickly, before moving forward again. Her hand faltered as she raised it to wave, dropping it again in case Morag saw her.

Stumbling away from the window, Susan fell back onto the bed. She closed her eyes willing her mind to focus. She was slipping in and out of reality. She gave up trying to fight it and lay down, and closed her eyes, trying to figure out what had been going on.

Her memories of coming to the house were unclear, like everything else since she had arrived here. She had a strange sensation she was looking in on her life from the outside. She tried to sort her thoughts and memories, running through what she remembered. Morag had arranged it all. Susan and Lily had been in danger, and Morag had left her feeling as if she had no choice other than to flee her home. Had it been Colin hunting her down... or Kris... their faces morphed into one inside her head. She vaguely remembered throwing some clothes in a suitcase and getting into a car.

When they'd arrived at Morag's she had initially been relieved. Morag had been great help with Lily, getting her ready for bed, reading to her, and even dressing her most days. But things had shifted and, from helping out, Morag had slowly taken over, closing Susan out. Lily didn't look the same anymore, either.

She had tried to speak to Morag about the way Lily was dressed, but the woman had dismissed her. 'Nothing for you to worry about, Susan. Sometimes we need to remember children are not fashion accessories. Not little dolls for their mothers to dress up.'

Her look had screamed judgement, and Susan had quickly stopped mentioning it. But Morag had plenty of other criticisms of how Susan had been bringing her daughter up, from the food she had been feeding her, to the television she allowed her to watch. Maybe she was right. After all, hadn't Colin also told her what a terrible mother she was? Perhaps they were better off here. Maybe Lily would have a better chance with Morag looking out for her.

Through the haze, something was niggling away at Susan. Morag and Lily were spending more time together, while she faded into the background, becoming invisible, unwanted. She was being shut out. She had overheard Morag on the phone to her work, calling in sick, yet there didn't seem to be much wrong with her, and Morag seemed to thwart all Susan's efforts at trying to be a mum to Lily.

"You distract the child from her learning," Morag had snapped at her when she'd asked to help.

She remembered trying to leave the house for a walk, only to find the door locked and the key nowhere to be found. Now everything had slowed down, her head full of cotton wool and each movement like wading through treacle. Susan remembered feeling like this once before, when the doctor had prescribed her anti-depressants not long after she had Lily. Realisation hit her like a slow hammer—Morag must have been putting something in her food or drink. It was the only possible explanation for the way she had been feeling since they'd moved in.

Susan forced herself off the bed and back to the window, the figure in the bushes had disappeared, if it had even been a figure at all. She was doubting her own sense of perception. She looked to the corner of the garden, where Morag and Lily were still engrossed in their digging. Perhaps it was time to do some digging of her own.

She forced one foot in front of the other, knowing her time was limited, and Morag could come back in at any point. There were too many rooms for her to check every one, but one room stood out, even in her fuzzy mind. The room with the locked door. Susan had just made it out of her bedroom when a voice yelled up the stairs.

"Susan!"

She stopped in her tracks.

"I'm taking Lily out for a walk now," Morag called.

Susan held her breath and heard Morag whisper to the child, none too quietly, "See? Your mother is lazy. Still in bed at this time."

"Can we wake her?" Lily asked in a small voice. Susan's heart ached.

"No, leave her. We'll have more fun without her," Morag replied, her voice fading as they left the house.

Susan waited until the front door clicked closed. She would have around half an hour before they were back. They had never been away any longer than that. It was as though Morag was hiding both of them away for reasons Susan could not yet work out.

Slipping into Morag's bedroom, she went straight to the dressing table she had seen Morag rummaging in many times. That must be where she kept the key to the room. She pulled the drawer open gently, careful not to disturb the contents. A jar sat on the top of some papers. It looked like it had crumpled up tissue paper and bits of hair in it. Weird. She ignored it for now, scanning the rest of the drawer for the key. Nothing jumped out at her. Running her fingers along the top of the drawer feeling it, she was disappointed to find it empty. Susan was about to give up looking, when she caught sight of Morag's handbag—the old-fashioned Gladstone she always carried—sitting by her bed. Peeking out the top was a black heart keyring with a key attached, one that looked like it might fit the bedroom door.

Making a note of its exact position, Susan grabbed it and shuffled over to the locked door, checking the clock on the wall. She had around twenty minutes left. The key slid into the lock and, taking a deep breath, Susan pushed the door open. The cloying smell of lavender hit her, sticking to her nostrils, but that wasn't what caused her jaw to drop. The bedsheets were not just in disarray, they lay in shreds, the pillows burst and the feathers had spilled out over the floor, the small draught from her opening the door caused them to flutter up in the air and fall back down again. It was far worse than that, though. Words had been written all over the walls in what looked like blood. Someone had scrawled the word BITCH, covering nearly every wall from top to bottom.

Thirty Six

Jess

AS THE SHADOW slipped away from the window, Jess stepped back and began to make her way up the driveway slowly until she reached the main road. She let out the breath she had been holding as the truth of what she had seen hit her. Susan and Lily hadn't disappeared down South after all. They were holed up in there with Morag, but the whole situation stank of something untoward. It didn't make sense. Why would they be staying with Morag? Especially after everything Susan had said about her. Jess felt a familiar bubble in her belly, anger. She and Susan could have been friends and the fact that she was lording it up like Lady Muck in Morag's house was seriously pissing her off. Not only had Morag ignored all her attempts to join in, now she had that snooty bitch and her kid to stay. Her and Susan were probably sitting in the house laughing at her. Yet another rejection pricked at her eyelids and she balled her fists into her eyes to stop the tears from coming. She aimed a futile kick at some rubbish blowing down the street, but it did nothing to relieve the anger building up inside her.

"Chill out, Jess," she told herself. "It's not Susan's fault, and it's definitely not the kid's fault. It's all down to Morag." She repeated this until she reached the Main Street. She stopped, looking around her. She didn't want to go back home just yet, but didn't know what to do with herself. She found herself wandering across the road to the gardens. They were almost deserted—too cold for most folk to be hanging around outside. But Radio Joe sat in his usual spot, transistor glued to his ear. He smiled at her as she approached him, and Jess, desperate for some company right now, sat beside him. If he was surprised at her actions, he didn't show it.

Instead, he threw her a broad grin and offered, "Y'alright?"

"Not really," she muttered.

"What's up?"

"Och, everything and nothing, I suppose. You know how it is? Sick of being on my own, I guess. Sick of life. Just fed up with it all."

"Yeah," he smiled understandingly. "I hear you. Been on my own most of my life. Kinda got used to it... eventually. It's no big deal. Nobody to tell me what to do and when to do it. Just sit here and chill, pass the day with whoever feels like chatting."

"Do you never get fed up with it? With being lonely?"

"Nah, I'm not lonely. I've got all the friends I want or need, but I'm never in anybody's pocket. Free spirit, that's me."

"So, what's your story Joe? How come you spend most of your life out here, sitting on your bench?"

Joe shrugged. "Just the way things worked out. Mum was in and out of psych wards when I was a kid. No dad. So my life was spent being passed from pillar to post. Learned not to rely on anyone too much, especially not family." He smiled. "By the time I reached sixteen, Mum had been taken into care full time—trying to burn down your house to get rid of the devil does that to you. I lived in supported accommodation until I was eighteen, and then got my own council house and, well, here I am. Happy as Larry."

"But what do you do for company, someone to talk to? Or for money?"

"Don't need any more company than I get in here and, as for someone to talk to, I've always got someone in here." He tapped the side of his radio. "And they never answer me back." He winked. "As for money, I've got enough for what I need. I had a job years ago, nothing fancy—only labouring on building sites, but I had an accident and did my back in, so it's just been me and my dole money ever since. I know folk moan it's not enough, but it does me just fine. Got enough to eat, a roof over my head and my friends inside this little box of mine. Don't need anything else."

Jess looked at him with new eyes. He seemed contented enough. Damn, he probably was happier than most people who had ten times what he did. Perhaps she had been wrong to write him off as a weirdo.

"So how come you don't go to the group in the library on a Tuesday?" she asked.

"Not for me," he laughed. "And even if it was, my face didn't fit. She didn't take to me much."

"Who?"

"Morag, the woman who runs it—the older woman who works in the library."

"Yeah, I know that feeling. She doesn't like me either."

"So, why you bothered about that? Don't need anybody's approval to get on in life. Just be yourself, and you'll get by."

"Thing is, Joe, I don't want to be by myself. I had a good mum, a good childhood. Shit happened and then I found myself alone. It's not what I want in life."

"Okay, but you don't need some stupid library group to validate yourself, do you? Be your own person. Besides, that group is jinxed if you ask me."

Jess sat up, alert now.

"Jinxed? How come?"

"Well funny things have happened to folk who've gone to the group over the years."

"What sort of things?"

"About three years ago there was a girl called Fiona—a lovely wee thing, a bit simple but always time for everyone. She got knocked down and killed. Hit and run, they said. But I don't know, it was weird. Morag was the one who found her. Then there was Amy—a single mum with a kid. She went to the group too. Someone tried to snatch her kid, just after she had left the library one night. Again, Morag was the one to find the kid. Always seems to be Morag as the common denominator whenever bad stuff happened to folk."

"But it could be a coincidence, couldn't it?"

"Suppose. But now you've got Alan Aitken a couple of months back—overdose. And Morag found his body. And then Ronnie, he's been locked up again but he'd been doing fine until Morag got her claws into him. Now young Susan and her kid have disappeared off the face of the earth. Seems more than coincidental if you ask me?"

"What, you think Morag had something to do with all that?" she exclaimed

"Never said that, did I? I just said maybe the group's jinxed," he shrugged. "And maybe you are better off out of it. Maybe you should take some time to take stock of what you do have and appreciate it, eh?" Joe stood up, indicating the end of the conversation.

"Got to go. Take care of yourself, eh? And remember what I told you—you don't need anyone to validate you for who you are." He turned away, put the radio up to his ear, flicked up the volume and shambled off.

Jess sat for a while, Mulling over Joe's words in her head. He'd confirmed everything she had suspected—there was something odd about Morag and her group. She had been right. She didn't care about Joe's take on it, it simply strengthened her resolve to discover what was going on with Susan and her kid and get closure on her past for once and for all She pushed Alan and Ronnie to the back of her mind. They were just collateral. What happened to them could have happened at any time, given their lifestyles.

Thirty Seven

Morag

SUSAN STOOD AND stared open mouthed at the sight before her. *What the hell has been going on in here?* The room was carnage. A shiver brushed across her back. *Someone's walking over your future grave,* she thought. And then, a darker thought stuck her. *We're not going to get out of here alive. We're trapped in this house with some batshit crazy woman.*

Her stomach cramped as she fought her rising terror. Her nails dug into the palms of her hands as she frantically tried to think of ways she could safely get Lily out of the house. She didn't know how long she'd been standing there, but the sound of the front door opening and Lily's voice snapped her out of her daydream.

She turned and, closing the door softly behind her, she ran as quietly as she could across the landing back to her bedroom, where she threw herself under the covers, willing her breathing to slow down so Morag would think she was still asleep if she came up. She had forgotten all about the key she left on the floor where she had dropped it.

DOWNSTAIRS, MORAG STOPPED and indicated to Lily to be quiet. She stood at the bottom of the stairs, her head cocked to one side like a bird listening for the worms. It was quiet but she was sure she could hear someone moving around upstairs. She pulled Lily through to the living room where she whispered she should take off her outdoor clothes. She stepped across the room and turned on the television, knowing it would surprise and delight the girl.

"You can watch some television, but it's only this once, as a special treat, do you hear me?" warned Morag. "Sit yourself down on the couch and don't move until I come back into the room. Do not move a muscle. Am I clear Lily?"

"Yes mummy" she mumbled.

"Good girl. Such a special little good girl."

Morag gave Lily's shoulder a squeeze before she left the room and closed the door tightly behind her.

Standing at the bottom of the stairs, Morag listened. All she could hear was the inane chatter of the child's TV programme, but no sound from Lily. She took a deep breath, placed one foot on the bottom step, and slowly climbed the staircase. She glanced towards Susan's bedroom door, it was still closed. She walked towards it and gave a soft knock. No reply. She looked around the landing and her heart lurched. Her mother's bedroom door was slightly ajar. Creeping across the landing, her hands were shaking with fury. She pushed the door open gently and stepped inside. Just as she had left it. As she moved towards the bed, she felt something under her foot, she glanced down and saw the key to the door.

Morag bent down, picked up the key and pocketed it. Next, she went to her own bedroom. Her handbag lay where she had left it. Nothing looked out of place.

She left her room and knocked on Susan's door again, a little louder this time. Still no reply. Morag turned the handle slowly and pushed the door open. In the dim light, she could see Susan's shape under the covers. She crept over and reached out her hand, touching the top of the duvet. "Susan," she murmured. "Are you awake?" No reply.

She took a step back and watched the shape on the bed. She had felt the body underneath the blankets trembling. Morag knew Susan was not asleep.

AFTER CHECKING EVERYTHING was where it should be, and locking the door again, Morag made her way back downstairs. Opening the living room door, she smiled to see Lily had fallen asleep. It would give her some time to think. Turning the television off, she slipped a cover over the sleeping child and left her sleeping while she went into the kitchen.

A fresh swell of rage rose within her. Susan was spoiling all her plans for them to be together, to be family. Why couldn't she do what she was told? Why did she have to be like all the rest of them, sticking her nose in where it wasn't wanted? Always questioning her, always disobeying her. Family didn't do that, family did what they were told. They were all the same, ungrateful little bitches. *Nobody wants to be with you Morag. You're going to die on your own.* 'Shut up, mother,' she replied, under her breath. 'I am not going to die on my own. I am not like you. I am going to sort this out once and for all.'

She pulled open the bottom drawer and reached into the back, pulling out the phone. She slipped open the cover and quickly changed over the sim card. 'Oh, if only those young ones appreciated I'm not quite as stupid and behind the times as they think I am,' she laughed to herself. With the new sim card in—the one she used to send the texts purportedly from Colin—she quickly stabbed out a message. "I know where you are, BITCH, and I'm coming to get you."

Morag knew Susan had no credit in her phone to reply or to call anyone else and she would not risk calling the police given her ex-husband's profession. Sending this message to Susan would achieve little other than to freak her out, make her even more dependent on me, Morag grinned.

Next, she logged into her fake Facebook account. She scrolled down the page and a post from Lynn McDonald caught her eye—a photo of a group of women in the Toby Jug stared back at her. Morag pinched the photo to zoom in. In the corner, as though trying to hide herself away, sat the girl who worked in the café. Jess. Morag's mind ticked over. What was Jess doing hanging out with her colleagues?

Invisible hands gripped at her stomach. She had a bad feeling. She didn't like this at all. Things would have to move a little faster than she had planned. It wasn't ideal, but time was running out, and she didn't want anyone to spoil her final exit.

Thirty Eight

Susan

SUSAN LAY PERFECTLY still under her duvet until she was sure Morag had left the room and gone downstairs. Her heart pounded so hard, it felt as though it would burst out her chest. She had convinced herself Morag must have seen her heart pound as she stood watching her earlier. Her mind whirred as she thought about everything going on—the bedroom, her exhaustion, Morag's odd behaviour. None of it was right. In fact, it was downright sinister. She had to get her and Lily out of there, and soon.

Pulling back the duvet, she swung her legs round to the floor. Her head spun and a wave of nausea hit her, memories of hangovers from nights trying to drown out the horror that was her marriage. *God, I wish I did have a bloody hangover. I wish I was back there, at least then I knew what I was dealing with.* The tears sprung to her eyes as she thought of how messed up her life had become. Abused by her ex-husband, some sleaze bag trying to pimp her out, and now trapped in the hammer house of horrors with some crazy old woman. You couldn't make this shit up.

She gave herself a shake and forced herself to her feet. Padding across the room, she opened the door slowly and peered out. Nobody there, her eyes landed on the bedroom and a memory fell into place. *The key, shit, the key, I didn't lock the door behind me.* Her eyes scanned the hallway frantically as she groped in all her pockets for the key. Nothing. She closed the bedroom door and prayed Morag would not guess she had been in the room. Susan hoped the older woman would think she had simply forgotten to lock it herself.

She stepped over the threshold and tiptoed across the landing to the bathroom. Inside, she locked the door, and turned on the taps.

Frantically she looked around, searching for anything she could use as a weapon, but other than a worn out old loofah and a bottle of bubble bath she could see nothing of any use. Susan clutched onto the sink trying to quell the rising panic. Looking up into the bathroom cabinet mirror, she cringed at her reflection—a gaunt face, straggly hair plastered against it, and bags under her eyes she could carry a month's shopping in. She tapped the glass, thinking she could smash it and use it as a weapon and bit down her lip in frustration as the dull thud told her it was self-adhesive mirror roll.

Frustrated, she yanked the cabinet door open. Perhaps there might be a razor or something, anything, she could use. A row of brown pill bottles stared back at her. Picking one up, she read the label. It was faded with age, but she could see the name: Mary McLaughlin and the prescription name, Zolpidem. Susan guessed Mary must have been Morag's mother, but why did she have all these bottles of sleeping tablets?

She picked another one up, finding it empty. And another, and another. All but one were empty. 'That crazy old bitch must have them stashed away somewhere and that's what she's been using to drug me,' she thought. She wanted to yell in frustration but clamped her hand over her mouth. She had to play this game carefully if she wanted out of here with her daughter.

Susan gave a final glance in the mirror and tried to set her face into something resembling normal. She had to let Morag think she didn't suspect anything.

Downstairs, Susan stopped outside the living room. She could hear Morag murmuring something to her daughter, she couldn't quite make out what she was saying but Lily's response was crystal clear and it shook her to the core.

"Yes, Mummy. Of course I love you, Mummy." She wanted to burst into the room, snatch her daughter and run. Instead, she went back to the staircase and made herself trip over the last couple of steps.

"Ouch!" she yelled loudly, looking towards the living room door. It opened and Morag peered out, her eyes narrowing suspiciously when she saw Susan.

"I'm so clumsy," laughed Susan, hoping Morag could not detect the tremor in her voice.

Morag shrugged and turned back into the living room.

Susan shuffled in after her, her shoulders rounded as she tried to make herself appear as non-threatening as possible. Lily sat at the coffee table with paper and pens. She was studiously copying something from a book in front of her. Susan could see the tip of her tongue poking through her lips as she concentrated. Lily didn't even acknowledge her entrance. Her heart sank at the sight of her usually bubbly little girl so docile and compliant, with all the spirit gone from her. She looked towards Morag.

"Do you mind if I get a drink of water, please? I'm so thirsty."

"Help yourself. You know where the kitchen is."

"Lily, do you want some juice, sweetie?" Lily did not look up.

"Lily?" she repeated.

Morag interrupted her. "She doesn't want anything. She has her school work to complete. She didn't finish it yesterday and this is her punishment."

"School work? She's only four!" exclaimed Susan, watching her daughter, who remained focused on the paper in front of her.

"Old enough to learn the right way in life. And old enough not to be mollycoddled and treated like a baby," snapped Morag. "If you want a drink, I suggest you go and get yourself one. I will look after the child."

In the kitchen, Susan ran the tap and filled her glass. She drank greedily—she hadn't lied, her mouth was parched. It must be the sleeping tablets. Her eyes scanned the kitchen and, listening out to make sure Morag was still in the living room, she turned the tap back on hard and began opening the kitchen drawers, sweeping her hands through the contents trying to find any evidence of tablets or anything else Morag might be hiding. She stopped at a sharp cough and turned her head around guiltily.

"Looking for something?" Morag swept across the room and turned off the tap.

"No... I was... eh... I..."

Morag was behind her, grabbing a clump of Susan's hair and pulling her close to her face.

"I know you've been in the room."

"I h-haven't... I..."

"Don't lie to me Susan. I cannot abide liars."

"I-I'm not..."

"You're making things worse. Lies always make things worse. Mother always knows when you're lying and we all know what happens to bad dirty liars, don't we?" She let go of Susan's hair with a rough shove.

"P-please... just..."

"Shut up!" Morag's hand stung as it slapped off her cheek. Susan's eyes watered, and she moved to draw away, but Morag stared blankly at her now. "You're nothing but a dirty little tramp... coming in here with... nobody will want you... alone... always alone... little bitch..." The words were spewing out her mouth, making no sense at all.

Susan saw her chance. She slowly edged backwards, all the time watching Morag, but the woman seemed to be on a different planet. Susan got to the kitchen door, slowly and surely, ready for any attack from Morag. She made it to the living room door. Lily was still at the table, seemingly oblivious to events unfolding around her.

"Lily," she hissed loudly. "Come on, we need to get out of here now. Quick."

Lily ignored her.

"Lily," cried Susan. "Now, come on quickly!" She roared this time.

Lily looked up at her, her eyes vacant. "No, Susan. We can't go anywhere. Mummy wouldn't like it." She put her head back down and carried on writing.

"I'm your mummy Lily. Come on. Now!" She ran over and swooped down, dragging her daughter by the arm.

"No!" Lily screamed.

She clamped her hand over her daughter's mouth, terrified at what this woman had done to her. Her hand drew back quickly as a small set of teeth clamped down hard.

She dropped her daughter in shock, tears blinding her now.

"Susan, please leave me alone. Mummy will be angry. Now do as you are told and leave me," parroted Lily in a dead, robotic voice.

"Lily," sobbed Susan. "Please honey, I'm your mummy. Please. You need to come with me. We need to go, Morag… she's not well. She's going to hurt us…" She grabbed Lily by the wrist and dragged her, this time ignoring her protestations and her screams. She had one goal in mind—to get them both out of this house.

She reached the front door and held on to Lily more tightly now as the child wriggled and kicked against her, trying to escape. She loosened her grip slightly as she tried to open the front door. Hand grasping the handle, she pushed it down, the door started to open just as her hand let go of Lily's.

She turned around to grab her daughter again, head bent down as she swooped to pick her up. As she raised her head, something cracked against her skull and the world went dark. As she went down, she could hear Morag croon, "It's alright pet, Mummy's got you now."

Thirty Nine

Susan

SUSAN'S EYES SNAPPED open. She blinked a couple of times as the flashbacks intensified—visions of Morag and her daughter, of Morag refusing to let them leave, Morag… Susan reached up, letting her fingers run over the back of her head. She winced as they met the lump, but she was grateful to feel no sticky residue of blood left behind when she took her hand away. Her mouth was like sandpaper and waves of nausea added to her misery. She looked around, trying to work out where she was.

She could feel a bed underneath her. A bedroom then. It looked familiar, but strange at the same time. Morag's face came screaming into her vision and it hit her, the crazy old witch had locked them in her house. Frantically, her eyes darted around the room, but she couldn't see anybody there. A surge of adrenalin rushed through her body, telling her to run.

Slowly she lifted her head from the pillow, wincing as the room began to spin. Gulping in deep breaths, she rode out the feeling until she could sit upright. She tried to swing her legs around, but something prevented them moving. She tried again, straining harder. There was something attached to her leg. Something heavy and cold. She lifted up the covers and saw the cuff. Thrashing wildly in panic, she grabbed at her leg pulling it in a futile attempt to escape. As much as she twisted, turned and thrashed, all she achieved was an increasing feeling of panic and utter hopelessness.

"Help, help, help…" she screamed, until her throat became hoarse. Nobody would hear her. Throwing herself back on the bed Susan wept.

She became aware of a shadow pass over her. She opened her eyes reluctantly, only to see Morag towering over her, a look of fury across her face.

Susan opened her mouth and screamed defiantly, stopping abruptly when Morag delivered another stinging blow to her face.

"Shut up, you stupid little bitch. You will wake the child. What sort of a mother are you?"

Susan opened her mouth to make a retort, but Morag was in full flow now.

"You are my family now. This is my home and you will do what you are told... nothing but a dirty little tramp... bringing shame on the family..." She punctuated each phrase with a blow to Susan's body.

"Please Morag. Please, I'm begging you. Stop it."

Morag stopped and stared, her brows furrowed and eyes narrowing.

"This is all your fault," she hissed. "Why couldn't you have just done as you were told? Why did you have to go snooping? You are not supposed to snoop on your family, you ungrateful little bitch. Just like all the rest of them. But, I'm not going to let you stop me. I am not going to die alone. I will not. I will have my family around me."

Susan cowered on the bed, paralysed, her lips refusing to move. Her eyes darted around the room. Lily. Where was Lily? She couldn't see her daughter.

"Where is Lily? Where is my daughter?" she cried.

"Lily is safe. *My* daughter is safe. And her mummy knows how to care for her."

Sweat beaded on Susan's forehead as Morag paced around the room, muttering incoherently, her eyes wild. Susan strained to listen for any sign of her daughter being close by, but could hear nothing other than Morag's ranting. Her skin crawled and she could feel the muscles in her body tightening, telling her to escape. Susan leaned forward and yanked hard at the cuff around her ankle, but it held fast. She pulled herself up on the bed and yanked hard at the chain.

If she could only get off the bed, maybe she could overpower Morag… Her eyes frantically searched the room for something to defend herself with if she did get free. There was nothing. There was no way out. She screamed in frustration, stopping Morag in her tracks. Susan watched in terror as the woman spun round and flew across the room towards her.

Morag pushed Susan onto the bed and leaned in so close, Susan could almost taste her breath and feel her saliva spray across her face.

"All this is your fault," Morag hissed. "You've caused all of this, Susan. You should have done as you were told. Why couldn't you have just been like family are meant to be? Now you both need to come with me."

"Where?" Susan asked. "Where are you taking us? Please Morag, let us go, I won't tell anyone." The panic made her voice shrill.

Morag's nose touched Susan's, her hands pinning her down on the bed as she spat: "I'm dying Susan. And you and Lily are coming with me."

Forty

Jess

JESS WOKE UP, rolling her neck in an attempt to loosen off the knots. Sleep had haunted her with images of her mum's face and Radio Joe's words coming out of her mouth, against a backdrop of her wasted years, her meltdowns and her car crash lifestyle. But she knew who to blame. Grabbing her pillow, she launched it across the room.

"You bitch! I gave you every chance to put things right, but you turned your back on me every time.'"

She grabbed the small bedside lamp and hurled it across the room too, revelling in the sound of the mirror shattering.

"I know everything about you, bitch. And now you're going to listen to me!"

Her anger sated for now, she had a shower and spent a little longer than usual getting ready. Today she wanted to leave a lasting impression. Everyone would remember her and she wanted to look her best. But she had something else to put right before her final outing. She ripped a sheet of paper from the notebook on her bedside table and began to write a letter.

'Dear Ronnie, I hope you're doing okay and you're getting better every day, There's no easy way to say this so I'll be as straight with you as I can. I'm sorry Ronnie, I used you. I manipulated you for my own ends, and I only hope, one day, you will understand why I did what I did. I hope you will find it in your heart to forgive me. When you get out of hospital, Ronnie, get out of Lennoxhill pal. Get away from your mum and this poisoned, small town mentality. Move on, and make a new life for yourself. With the right support, I know

you can do it. I only wish I'd had the right support. Maybe then things wouldn't have turned out the way they did. Look after yourself pal. I'm sorry. Love Jess. xx'

Her tears dripped onto the envelope as she allowed herself a moment of remorse for using Ronnie the way she had. She affixed a second-class stamp knowing, by the time it reached him in the secure unit, she would have finished what she came here to do.

Satisfied she had dealt with her task, Jess pulled on her coat and made her way outside. For the last time. The winter blue sky promised all kinds of hope. Her heart smiled. She felt lighter than she had for a long time. Today would be her day, the day of reckoning. There was just one other part of her life in Lennoxhill she wanted to bring to a close first.

She made her way down the Main Street for the last time, pausing at the door of the café and peering through the window. Annie and Mary were in their usual seats, their faces twisted in bitterness, as they no doubt tore someone else to shreds.

"Perfect."

Jess pushed the café door open and breathed in the familiar aroma of coffee and grease. Thank God she wouldn't have to come back here. Marion glanced up from the counter and smiled.

"Jess! Just the person I wanted to see. How are you fixed for covering for me for a bit, eh? I've got an important…"

Jess didn't let her finish her sentence. She strolled up to the counter, placed her hands flat down, and leaned forward.

"Nope. Not doing it Marion, not now and not ever. I'm just coming to tell you I'm quitting, as of right now."

"What do you mean quitting… from now… you can't do that… I've…"

"Frankly, Marion, I couldn't give a shit what you've got to do or what you've got to say. I'm out of here and out of this dump of a town."

She turned her back on Marion, who stood at the counter mouth flapping. "And close your mouth, Marion. You look like a bloody goldfish," she threw over her shoulder.

She approached Annie and Mary, whose heads had almost swivelled round a full circle to watch the drama unfold, looks of unmistakable glee on their faces. Arms crossed Jess towered over them.

"You want to know something?" She didn't wait for a reply. "You two have been the worst thing about working here."

Their jaws dropped in unison, and Annie spluttered: "Who do you think you're talking to?"

"I'll tell you, will I? I am talking to two dried up old bags who are probably the rudest and most judgemental women I have ever met in my life. Mary, you're just an old windbag who has no friends or family and it is no wonder. But Annie fucking Boyle. You are the worst. It's no wonder you couldn't find a job when you left The Overton. I wouldn't pay you to look after my dog, never mind work in a hospital. If I were your daughter, I would be embarrassed to call you mother. You are ignorant, uneducated and a bully."

Mary opened her mouth to argue, while Annie screeched at Marion to put Jess out of the café.

Jess held up her hand. "Don't bother, I'm leaving. And the best thing about it is never seeing your hacket old faces again. Couple of bitches that you are!" And with that Jess stormed out of the café, making sure she slammed the door as hard as she could.

Once outside, she gave a small fist pump and grinned to herself—things were getting better by the minute.

She spied Radio Joe sitting in his usual spot and made her way over to him.

"Hey Joe, I wanted to thank you for yesterday."

He squinted up at her. "What did I do?"

"Och, you know. Just helping me sort things out in my head that's all. You were right, it's time I stopped focusing on what I don't have, think about what I do have, and stop seeking other people's approval. Time to accept myself for who I am, and let the past go."

"Aye, well, it's usually the best way, hen."

"It's the only way Joe, the only way. See you around, pal."

"Take care of yourself, hen. And just be happy with your choices in life," he shouted after her.

"Too right, Joe. Too damn right," she whispered, smiling as she strode out the park and made her way out the town for the last time.

Today the journey to Morag's house seemed quicker. Jess had a spring in her step, a renewed determination. She stopped at the driveway and peered up at the house. A brief thought of what could have been flitted through her mind again, but she dismissed it. She had a job to do. The curtains twitched as she strode up the driveway. She rattled the door knocker loudly, stood back, and waited.

Forty One

Morag – *Then*

MY MEMORIES OF my childhood are of a house shrouded in silence and religion. I learned to speak only when spoken to especially around Mother. She never knew the prayers I said were not the ones she taught me from the bible—I prayed for a family who loved me. My mother's God never answered me, confirming my belief He did not exist. Father, bless him, tried a little harder, but he couldn't hide his strained smile, and his nervous, flitting glances to the door, waiting on her coming and catching us out meant it was easier to fit into her rules, to be who she wanted us to be.

Yet, in the playground, in amongst the buzz and the chatter, I searched for my voice. I wanted to be a part of it all—the huddled giggles and whispers, the tales of sleepovers and parties, I'd push my way in, but when I got there, my mouth dried up and my lips glued together. Instead, I listened and drank in their lives. I stole their homes, their lives and their families and weaved them into my own hopes and dreams for the future. I learned to live through others.

In my last year in primary school, Mother surprised me and invited two girls from my class for tea. I watched on in horror as she spewed out lie after lie about me. "Oh do you still sleep in beside with your parents, too?" she'd asked them, and when they shook their heads, she turned to me and said, "I'll bet they don't still wet the bed either."

I watched their little rosebud lips form into giggles they tried to hide behind their hands, I caught their sharp side-glances as they left the house and their huddled heads and shoulders heaving with laughter as they reached the bottom of the drive.

Children can be cruel. Mother's lies ran through the school, and soon I became the butt of everyone's taunting and humiliation. I began to retreat into myself and to my books—there I could escape into a world where Mother didn't exist.

Secondary school brought new opportunities as I took the lives I'd stolen and used them to create a new life for myself. I could be whoever I wanted to be. I shed Morag at the school gates every morning, only picking her back up when the bell rang at the end of the day. I had already created a whole host of characters to choose from. I'd had plenty of time to study, after all, from the lives absorbed from others and from the characters in my books. I was adopted, my real parents were dead, they died in a car crash. No, they couldn't come round to my house, my mum was terminally ill and my dad had to work away to pay for her care. If they realised I was lying they didn't seem to care, at least not the ones I hung around with.

Back home, Mother's relentless tirade continued as I grew older and my body began to change. "Ugly little freak," she would hiss at me, as I lay curled up in the chair reading. I'd look at my father, waiting for him to come to my defence but he just stared at the newspaper in his lap. Punishments were meted out for misdemeanours I didn't even know I was committing—flaunting my body when leaving the bathroom wrapped in a towel, or wearing my clothes inappropriately, or for being filthy and untidy, or for thinking sinful thoughts depending on the expression she perceived on my face. It was easier to accept them all, but inside, I seethed. Inside, I pictured her dead.

By fourteen, I lived two separate lives. I revelled in my alter ego at school, and retreated into the world of books at home. Before long, I was sneaking out the window after my parents had gone to bed. Creating my alter ego from a stash of stolen clothes and make up stored at new friends' houses. If Mother could have seen me! I didn't care, the other me—the real me— was free to be whoever she wanted to be, and it made being Morag so much more bearable.

At parties, I was the life and soul the first one to get drunk, the first to smoke, and the first to try anything going round. Never sex though—no matter how hard I tried to leave Morag behind, my mother's warnings about sin and my body never left my head. Nobody ever guessed, they were usually too drunk to recognise the lines I drew.

I could have lived this life forever and I would have, if *that* night hadn't happened. I'd gone to a party as usual, but the noise, the smoke, the crowds had left me with a migraine, and the alcohol had made it worse. Wanting some fresh air, I squeezed my way through the bodies packed into every available space in the house—teenage sweat mingled with cheap body spray making me want to gag. Nobody paid any attention to me. They never saw me leave. Making my own way home was nothing new to me. None of my new friends lived close to me. The Waterside Estate was at the other end of the town and I considered taking a shortcut through the park, but even the rebellious Morag was not that stupid.

The sky was black and cold. The kind of cold that makes it hurt to breathe. It's funny the things you remember. I walked fast, focused only on getting home and into my bed. I had just passed by the last of the shops and made my way along Moss Road towards the Rosehill Estate where we lived. About a mile outside of town, during the day, the walk felt like no distance. However, time stretched at night. The trees at the side of the road whispered my name, branches reaching out in the wind and caressing me as I strode by. The streetlights were the old-fashioned dim lights painting the street a misty yellow. The road was deserted. I stopped a couple of times, footsteps echoing behind me, but each time I swung round to check I wasn't being followed, the footsteps stopped and only darkness stared back at me. I had almost reached the end of Moss Road, about to turn into Blackthorn Way, when it happened.

Dirty fingers covered my mouth, a gruff voice rasped in my ear. "Don't scream. Don't move. Tell anyone, and I'll come back and kill you."

I didn't move. I lay still for what seemed like forever. Eventually I crawled out of the bushes where he'd left me. I stumbled home, and somehow made my way upstairs and stripped off my clothes, stuffing them into a plastic bag I would get rid of the next day.

I didn't go to any parties after that, friends drifted away and I slipped back into my old life. Back to being Morag. It was easier that way.

Forty Two

Morag – *Then*

AROUND FIVE MONTHS later mother grabbed at me as I came out the bathroom. I felt her fingers dig deep into the tops of my arms as she dragged me into my bedroom. I imagined the bruises she would leave behind. My towel slipped away as she threw me across the bed. The swell of my stomach was clear.

She leaned over me, her nose almost touching mine—possibly the closest we had physically been for years. "Filthy little slut," she hissed, as her fingers prodded my stomach. "Who have you been with? Who have you been spreading your legs for? Whore."

Tell anyone, and I'll come back and kill you. My lips stayed glued together, the words refusing to come out. The truth would have meant nothing to her anyway—she would have made it my fault, regardless. My refusal to speak sent her into a fury. Climbing up on my bed, she straddled my hips and began punching at my swollen belly. My head rang with the sound of my baby's tears. I stared up at the ceiling waiting for her attack to be over.

The following day she and father came into my bedroom. Kneeling at the bottom of my bed, they prayed. I imagine mother prayed to the devil as she begged my body to rid itself of my unborn child. She left, saying nothing other than to give my father instructions. I sat in my room, as the sound of father fixing a lock to the outside of my bedroom door penetrated my thoughts. I rubbed my belly and watched a spider in the corner of the ceiling methodically spin its web.

Not long after father had fitted the lock, I overheard my mother on the phone in the hallway.

"Morag will not be coming back to the school... no, we have decided to move her... most unsuitable..." The person on the other end must have protested, as I heard her say: "No, we're quite certain... she will be going to Oakburn."

My eyes widened, Oakburn was the girls-only private school in Glasgow. One of the best schools in the area. How could my parents afford the fees? A small bubble of excitement rippled as I imagined the world of opportunities presented to me by a private school. I could travel the world. Get out of here. Maybe I'd be a boarder and not need to stay here anymore.

I should have known better. I never went to Oakburn. I never went back to any school. Home had become my prison. Locked up, I became dependent on Mother for everything, which meant I received nothing.

As my belly grew rounder, Mother's fury grew exponentially darker. She would sit on the toilet watching me bathe, lip curled and her cruel eyes staring at my ever-expanding stomach, while she read aloud from the Bible.

The flutterings inside me gradually became full-blown kicks as my baby began to make its presence felt. A stirring of love grew inside me and at night, I fell asleep hugging my belly, whispering stories of the family we would be.

My room was bare, other than a Bible, some tissues and a calendar on the wall. I tore the tissues into strips and worried them in my hands. Soon I was tearing out shapes and fashioning tiny figures. My own little family, a tissue heart representing my baby.

Every day mother would tick off the date in the calendar and I watched as the days counted down towards the black cross on the 1st of September. I guessed it to be the day my baby was due.

On the 24th July, I woke with cramps in my stomach. With each cramp came a pain that consumed my whole being, more intense than I could ever have imagined.

"My baby's coming," I whimpered, as my mother came into my room shortly after midnight.

Her eyes stabbed me and her mouth tightened. Saying nothing, she left the room, leaving me alone with my pain. I let out an anguished, but hopeless scream. Nobody would hear me, the thick walls of these old Victorian houses kept everything firmly behind closed doors.

As my screams died to whimpers, mother pushed open the door, flicked on the light, and stared at me.

"Mum. It hurts," I wailed, as my body screamed at me to push.

"Shut up, you little tramp. Of course it hurts. It's the Devil's child tearing its way out of you. Now keep quiet. If you don't, I will tape your bloody mouth shut."

I did not doubt her.

She mopped my brow with damp towels and, as she leaned over me, I caught a glimpse of a tear in her eye. My heart leapt. Maybe a grandchild would change her, change us. That night is my only memory of her ever touching my skin, other than to slap or beat me. I wanted to reach out and hold onto her, I wanted her to be my mum. I was fifteen and I was about to give birth. I needed my mum.

At one point, my bedroom door slid open and I caught sight of my father's worried face peering in. Only for a second though. Mother swung round with a "Get to your bed. I've got this under control."

I bit down on my tongue and clutched my mother's hand, as my body forced me to give one last push. Something slipped from between my legs and gave a mew like a tiny kitten. Mother turned away from me, reaching down with a towel in her hands. I tried to lift my head to see what was going on, but all I could see was Mother's back as she busied herself between my legs. Her hand reached out and picked up scissors, and I heard a small snip. She quickly wrapped up the tiny bundle and stood up.

"My baby, mum. Please, let me see my baby."

She looked down at the tiny bundle in her arms and back at me. She stepped forward hesitantly, as though she wasn't quite sure. She pushed the bundle towards me and I reached out my arms to hold my baby. But she snatched it away out of my reach.

"Lie back," she snapped.

I obeyed, and she pushed the bundle under my face. I caught sight of small rosebud lips, and tiny eyes squeezed shut as though they were asleep. Not a sound.

Mother pulled the bundle back, turned and left without saying a word.

I never saw my baby again.

Forty Three

Morag – *Then*

THE DATES ON the calendar were never crossed off again. At fifteen, I had become a mum and motherless in a matter of hours.

"It was for the best... six weeks early... nothing we could have done... it's your own fault... punishment... God's plan..." Mother's words trickled through my consciousness. I must have asked her if it was a boy or a girl. "Doesn't matter what it was... gone now... not important." I sunk back into my oblivion, ready to stay there.

One day, without warning, I woke to bright sunlight flooding my room. The curtains had been flung open. I blinked. Mother stood over my bed.

"Get up now. You've spent enough time idling around in your bed, feeling sorry for yourself."

I pulled the covers over my head. I wanted to be dead, but she was having none of it. Yanking the covers down, she pulled me up roughly.

"Get up. Now."

With no choice, I pushed myself onto my feet, the room swayed around me and I grabbed onto the bedside table to steady myself. She dragged me across the room and out onto the landing.

"Get in the bath and clean yourself. You stink," she spat, as she pushed me into the bathroom, throwing a towel in behind me. I sat on the floor and buried my face in the towel. The door rattled with a hard kick

"Get in the bath. NOW!"

I sat in the bath until the water grew cold, and then watched it drain away, I imagined myself dissolving in the bath water and disappearing down the plug hole. But of course I didn't. I stayed whole and here, with nowhere to run to, nowhere to escape to. I ran back into my room and dressed quickly before Mother decided to come up and see what was taking me so long. As I made my way downstairs. I could hear her voice in the kitchen and I pushed the door open. Nothing much had changed since they had locked me away. Father sat in the corner, shoulders slumped. He seemed to have shrunk to half the size he had been before. She was killing him slowly.

Mother stood at the sink with her back to me, all the while directing a stream of instructions at my father, who had completely zoned out. She must have heard me come in. She spun around and ran her eyes over me.

"You'll do," she said, as though choosing a cut of meat from the butcher for dinner. I moved over to sit at the table.

"What do you think you're doing? You've got chores to do." She threw a black bin bag towards me. "Put that out in the black bin."

I picked it up and went to the door.

"If anyone asks, you've been in hospital," she snapped.

"Why am I meant to have been in hospital? Did you tell them about the bab—"

"Do. Not. Mention that again. Never. Do you hear me?"

I nodded.

"A mental hospital. That's where they think you've been." She turned her back on me.

"What about school... my exams...?"

"School? I don't think so, Morag. That ship sailed when you spread your legs."

I took the bag outside. Thankfully, nobody was around. The dark circles under my eyes stood out on my pale face, and although I'd washed my hair in the bath, it had dried in fat rat's tails. Job done, I wandered around the garden, welcoming the sun on my face. At least outside I could pretend I was free.

At the hedge at the back of the garden, something caught my eye. I walked over and found a small stone, it was in the shape of a heart and had a cross crudely painted on it. I picked it up and turned it over in my hand. Something had been written on the back, I screwed up my eyes and peered closer. 25th July 1980. I let it drop to the earth and I cried.

Forty Four

Morag – *Then*

THE NEXT COUPLE of years saw me confined to the house. Only, this time, the prison was of my own making. Anxiety crippled me and the thought of anyone looking at me was overwhelming. It was easier to stay where I was. Chores, books and silence were my life now. All fight had fled. Birthdays and Christmases came and went with no celebrations and no presents.

I had already turned eighteen when everything changed again. I had finished my chores for the day and sat in the garden reading. The raised voices coming from the house startled me. Nobody ever shouted in our house. I heard my father yell, "You should never have done that. It was cruel. I can't stand this anymore."

Mother shouted something in return, but I couldn't make out what she said. I tuned out and tried to lose myself in my book.

It must have been around half an hour later when a shadow loomed over me. I looked up, surprised to see my mother standing there. She seemed different, dishevelled almost.

"Inside. Now," she hissed, pulling me to my feet. Her eyes darted all over the place. I followed her into the house, not quite knowing what to expect. She went into the living room and I went in after her. The curtains were drawn and the television blared in the corner. Butterflies fluttered in my stomach—the television was never on during the day in our house. I could see father sitting in his favourite chair, his back to us. He didn't turn around.

"You need to help me sort out this mess." Her voice drew my attention. I scanned the room. It was spotless, exactly how I'd left it that morning.

"What mess?" I giggled nervously. Nothing made any sense.

"There's been an accident."

She pushed me forward and I stumbled. As I fell, I grabbed at the back of father's chair to stop myself. I missed the chair, and hit his head. It fell forward slightly, and still he said nothing.

"There is no mess." I said as I righted myself, I was feeling confused now.

"That bloody mess!" Her voice become shrill, a wobble of panic running through it. I felt sick. She pushed me forward again and this time I kept my balance, I inched my way around father's chair, expecting him to look up at me and shrug. He didn't move. I kept on walking. My jaw dropped, his face didn't look right. Where were his eyes, his nose? What was the sticky stuff all over his face? I leaned forward and stared at the figure then back at my mother. I looked back again, it had my father's clothes on, it had the same colour of hair and the wedding band on his finger looked like his, so who was this? What was this?

"Mum?"

She said nothing.

"MUM!"

She didn't move.

I looked down and saw the hammer lying on the floor.

Forty Five

Morag – *Then*

I STOOD FOR what seemed like forever, trying to marry up the bloodied, battered face with that of my father. Mother stood rooted to the spot.

"What have you done?"

She stared right through me.

I grabbed her, shaking her. "What the fuck have you done?"

Even swearing did not shock her into action.

"I need to phone an ambulance… the police… someone." I started to back away from her. She reached out and grabbed me.

"He was going to leave me. Nobody leaves me. Nobody leaves me!"

"You've killed him! You can't bloody kill someone because they are going to leave you!" I screamed at her, ready to run. This seemed to jerk her awake and her eyes snapped open as though noticing me for the first time.

I tried to free myself but her fingers tightened their grip. "You're not leaving. You are going to help me clear up this mess."

And that's how, at eighteen years old, I found myself helping my mother drag my father's battered body into the bathroom and over the next two days I sat downstairs in the sitting room with the television blaring as she painstakingly cut him up into tiny pieces. Then she made me help her bury my father beside the garden shed.

Happy families indeed.

I now had two stone hearts in the little mound of earth she had created.

After that day mother became progressively crueller, as though a dam of vitriol had opened. She'd wake me in the middle of the night and drag me to my knees to pray. She refused to let me sleep. She would taunt me about my father, driving me insane to the point I began to think it was I who had killed him and not her. She would leave packets of pills on my bed with notes telling me to kill myself. I would go for a bath and open razorblades would be left at the side. I'll admit, I was sorely tempted at times.

I should have run after the incident with Father. I should have taken my chances then. But she had ground me down to nothing. Or, at least, into believing I was nothing and nobody would believe me.

"I will tell them you killed your father and threatened me. They all think you are crazy anyway. It's me they'll believe, not you! I'll dig up your baby and show them the bones. Tell them you killed that, too."

Not long after the incident with Father, I had heard her on the phone.

"Jim's left us," her voice wobbled. "He couldn't take living with her... her illness anymore. She has never been right since she left hospital." Her voice dropped to a whisper and she stared at me as she caught me listening in. She didn't stop though. Eyes fixed on me, she continued her conversation. "It was the stress of living with her... bizarre behaviour. He's met someone else... no. No. I couldn't do that! I couldn't put her back in hospital. No...no! She's my daughter. It's my job to look after her. Thank you. Yes, we'll be fine. Yes I'll be at church. Morag? No, she's too unpredictable, best not... Bye then. See you Sunday."

She placed the receiver gently and fixed me with a smile that cut me in half.

Forty Six

Morag – *Then*

WITH NOWHERE ELSE to go and nobody to turn to, I had no choice but to stay there and live under mother's roof with all it entailed. The nights were dark and there were times I seriously contemplated taking the easy way out. I rolled the pills around in my hand trying to work out how many it would take to do the job. I caressed my skin with the razor blades she left out, imagining the blade digging deeper, my life draining away with the bathwater. But something inside me was stronger than that, something kept me going.

I snapped the day after my nineteenth birthday. She gave me a birthday present—a day late. It was the first present I ever remember getting from her. I sat staring at the package, neatly wrapped with a pink bow around it. She stood over me watching.

"Well, open it."

I ripped the paper open, my cheeks lifted and my mouth formed a small smile. My excitement was short-lived. A silver photo frame nestled inside the wrapping paper. I turned it over, confused. We weren't the kind of family who had any family photographs and mother would never splash out on a painting. I turned the frame over slowly. A photograph stared back up at me. A baby, but not my baby, it was one of those old sepia photos from the Victorian times, a woman holding a sleeping baby. I knew exactly what it was though. The baby was not sleeping. Mother had made me watch a documentary a month earlier about how the Victorians took photographs of their stillborn babies. I let the frame slip through my fingers and crash to the ground, the glass shattering into hundreds of tiny shards. I vomited. She laughed.

I packed myself a small grab bag and put it at the bottom of my wardrobe. In my bedside drawer, I had all the sleeping tablets she had left for me, wrapped up safely in tissue, in case I'd needed them. They would do the trick. I knew there would be money in the biscuit tin in the kitchen. I wanted to take the stone hearts from the garden but I couldn't bring myself to move them. Instead I took my tissue hearts, found an empty jar to put them in, and stuffed them in my bag. I took the photograph of the baby too. I couldn't leave it with mother.

Next day, I tried to act as though nothing had happened. Inside my stomach churned. I made dinner as usual, and crushed up some of the tablets into hers. After she had eaten, I crushed up some more into her tea. My nails dug into the palm of my hands as I watched her drink it.

At one point she screwed up her face, "You can't even make a proper cup of tea."

I held my breath, terrified she would pour it down the sink, but she was too lazy to get up and do that. She grimaced as she drank the rest of it, but drained every drop.

Her eyes began to lose focus. She reached out towards me. "Aaaa don fee we…"

She keeled over sideways onto the couch and within minutes she was snoring heavily. I prodded at her to make sure she wasn't faking it, satisfied she was dead to the world, I ran upstairs, grabbed my bag and emptied the contents of the biscuit tin into it. Just over two hundred pounds, enough to get me out of there.

Legs shaking, I tiptoed to the front door, convinced she would lurch out of the living room and grab me. I lifted the latch on the door and placed one foot over the doorstep. Glancing around the hallway one last time, I stepped over the threshold, closed the door softly behind me, and ran for my life.

Forty Seven

Morag – Then
Two Years Later

A NEW CITY meant I could reinvent myself all over again. When I left home, I'd gone to Edinburgh, where I had managed to find myself a small bedsit in Muirhouse on the outskirts of the city. I had escaped, nobody knew me here and nobody cared about a stranger in their midst. It was nothing like where I'd come from and it was ten times as bad as the Waterside estate. My neighbours in the four-in-a-block where I lived spent their lives passed out from shooting up or were too busy scoring their next fix to bother about me, and that suited me fine. I found myself a part time job in a bar. Nothing fancy, just a working man's pub on the edge of the estate. With live bands at the weekend and a regular clientele, I found myself a new niche and a new identity, far removed from the life I had escaped.

I'd been working in the bar a couple of months when I got chatting to one of the regulars—a girl called Stacey. At twenty, she was the same age as me, but she was everything I wasn't—tall, pretty and with bags of confidence despite her circumstances.

Stacey had fallen out with her family when she took up with a guy they didn't approve of. He'd dumped her in the end, and left her on her own. She was perfect. Stacey and I became friends. Well, that's what she led me to believe. How was I to know she would freak out when she arrived home from work one night to find me on her doorstep? How did I know her address? Why was I following her? Why did she have to ask such awkward questions? I was only looking out for her.

After a month, she'd had enough. She told me to leave her alone. I only went round again to ask her to change her mind. She didn't have to tell my boss in the bar, he didn't have to sack me. That night I cried as I scrunched up the paper heart with Stacey's name on it.

With no job and no friends, I had no reason to stay. Time to move on. This time to Leith. Luckily, I'd built up some savings and my landlord gave me my deposit back on my flat, so I managed to find somewhere a little bit nicer to stay. Well, just with a better class of addicts. They kept themselves indoors mostly, and slumped bodies in the stairwell were not as big an issue anymore. I got to know some of them, bumping into them in the communal garden sharing a joint. There had been one boy—a poor looking soul. He lived upstairs from me. I still don't understand why he got bored with me so quickly. I cried when I heard he had died from an overdose. Well, they do say you need to be careful where you buy your drugs from, don't they?

I stayed away from bars this time, and had managed to find a part time job in the small community library. I think they felt sorry for me as I spent so much time there, and when a job came up as an assistant, they asked me if I wanted it. I jumped at the chance. It was my dream come true, surrounded by books all day and getting paid for it.

I settled quickly into my new job and could easily have spent the rest of my life there. Until my life was thrown into turmoil once more. It was a Saturday morning and my weekend on, my favourite day. Saturday was family day in the library. I loved to watch them all.

They came in at opening time. They were new to the area. They were looking to be a part of their community and the library seemed the best place to start, they said. They were mum, dad and their two perfect children—a little girl of about four years old and a new baby boy. The perfect family. I hated them on sight.

With a smile painted on, I helped them complete a family membership for the library and made the appropriate cooing noises at the baby. But it was the little girl who caught my eye. A mass of blonde curls and big baby blue eyes. Her name was Lily. The name I had chosen to give my baby if it had been a girl. I watched them as they wandered over to the children's section, him with his arm wrapped protectively around his wife, the little girl's hand tucked into her mother's—a perfect fit. Something stabbed me deep in my chest. I recognised it for what it was. Envy. I envied what they had and mourned the loss of something I would never have.

I reached into my handbag, surreptitiously peeking around to make sure nobody could see me, and pulled out my jar. Digging my fingers in, I plucked out the tiny little heart for my own baby and caressed it in my fingers, remembering and wishing, biting my lip to stop the tears from flowing.

"Excuse me?" A voice interrupted me. I let the heart flutter to the floor, starting as I peered up. I didn't see the mother, only the blonde curls peeking over the counter.

"Can you tell me where the ladies is please, Lily needs to go." She smiled down at the child.

I pointed over in the direction of the toilets trying not to let my feelings show. "It's over there."

"Thanks."

"Lily. What a pretty name for a pretty little girl."

The woman looked at me and smiled tightly, I'm sure her grip on the child's arm grew firmer.

I watched as they strolled away. The girl glanced over her shoulder and threw me a smile.

"Hi, Lily," I mouthed, as I raised my hand and waved to her.

After that, they were regular visitors to the library. The little girl's smiles grew wider as she began to recognise me, and I always made sure I had a wee treat or two in my bag for her. The day I had brought in a Rag Doll for Lily, her mother had overreacted a little.

"No. Thank you," she had said with her lips pursed, pretending to smile. Lily's eyes had widened with pleasure at the sight of the doll, but dulled over quickly at her mother's refusal. I tucked the doll back into my handbag next to my hearts. It could wait.

The family lived in a beautiful Victorian townhouse in Morningside. You might be wondering how I knew this? Well, I had to check these things out, didn't I? I had to make sure Lily was being looked after properly. Children need someone to watch out for them. That's all I was doing, looking after my Lily. I wouldn't hurt anyone.

Hours of my time were lost, sitting on the wall across from their home—out of sight. I didn't want them to think I was snooping on them, did I? My heart hurt to watch their normal family routines—the smiles and hugs that should have been mine. I bit back my tears as I watched the curtains close at night-time. It should have been me up there reading Lily her favourite bedtime story. It should be me kissing her gently on the forehead and whispering, "Sleep tight, little one." Me. Not them.

The hours grew into days. My frustrations growing stronger. They didn't deserve Lily. They were shallow and materialistic, they couldn't love her the way I could.

It was nearly two months later when my chance came. The family were in the park. I just happened to be passing. Of course I didn't know they went there every Thursday. As I watched Lily, I could feel her sadness as she trudged up and down the slide. Her mummy and daddy too busy fussing over the baby to care. They should have been telling her how clever she was. They should have been watching her.

Lily had been trying to attract their attention, but furious screams came from the pram. The baby was always screaming, demanding their attention, leaving Lily out in the cold. They turned their backs on her. She climbed up the slide and down again, repeating her actions, her little mouth turned down at the corners. She had given up asking her parents to watch. So I watched her instead, my hand inside my handbag, caressing the doll I had bought for her.

My heart quickened as I imagined the look on her face if she found me waiting at the bottom of the slide for her. I crept out of the bushes, keeping one eye on her mummy and daddy. They didn't even notice. I stood at the bottom of the slide and watched as her little pink shoes came flying towards me. I held out the doll in my hand. She reached the bottom and gazed up at me, her mouth opened and I put my fingers to my lips.

"Shh. Don't bother Mummy and Daddy while they are sorting the baby out."

She shrugged. I pressed the doll into her hand, reached out, and took her other hand.

"Why don't we go get some sweeties?"

She glanced towards her parents and looked back at me, her brows furrowed.

"It's okay. They said to take you, and we can bring them some sweeties back too." My hand covered her little fist and my heart melted. "Come on. Let's be quick."

She looked over at her parents again. My grasp tightened around her hand, I ignored her wince, annoyed at her ungratefulness. I was being nice to her, she didn't need to be such an ungrateful little brat. I yanked at her arm, anxious to get her away. She let out a yelp, and I placed my other hand across her mouth, very gently. I wouldn't hurt Lily. Half-walking and half-running, we had nearly made it out the gates when a hand clasped my shoulder, swinging me round. It was him. Lily's daddy.

"What the fuck do you think you are doing?" he snarled. His eyes glittered with rage.

I dropped Lily's hand and she ran into her mother's arms, burying herself into her legs. The doll lay on its back, glassy eyes staring up at us all.

"You shouldn't swear in front of your child." I stared back at him defiantly.

He shook me. "I asked you, what the fuck do you think you are doing?" His grip became tighter, I could feel the bruises start to form at the top of my arms, he reminded me of mother. I started to sink back into the old Morag—scared, terrified. I shrank backwards. I opened my mouth, but no words would come out.

"I-I-I-I w-w-was..." I stuttered.

"You were what? Trying to steal my fucking kid, you fucking weirdo." He stepped back slightly and his grip loosened. I took my chance. I squirmed free and I ran.

I replayed the scene in my head all night as I waited for the police to knock on my door. Or worse still, I waited for Lily's dad to knock on my door. The look on his face earlier had screamed murder. But nothing came.

By the next day, I had created a different narrative in my head. I hadn't done anything wrong. If I had, someone would have come for me. Wouldn't they?

Ready to leave for work, I had already thrown on my jacket and slipped my feet into my shoes, when my phone rang. My stomach plummeted. Nobody ever called me. Mother. Perhaps she had tracked me down. Or someone else had. What if something had happened to her and this was the call to tell me the good news that she was dead. A small giggle rose in my throat at the idea of that. I swallowed it down. The phone kept ringing, shrill, and insistent. I wanted to leave it. I couldn't leave it.

I held the receiver to my ear. I said nothing.

"Hello?"

I breathed deeply.

"Morag, is that you?"

I let out a sigh of relief. It was only Bob, my manager at the library.

"Hi Bob. Yeah, it's me, sorry. I'm on my way in. I'd already left when the phone started ringing and I had to unlock…" I stopped, aware I was gibbering. "Am I late?" I asked, afraid I had messed up this job.

Bob coughed on the other end of the line, his voice strangled. "No, no Morag. You're not late, but eh… Well… it's a bit awkward to be honest."

My mouth went dry. Mother must have found out where I was working and called them, she would have told them all sorts of lies about me.

"If it's about my mother, I just want to…"

He cut me off. "No Morag. It's not about your mother. We have received a complaint about you. Mr and Mrs McAllister…"

The name rang a bell, but I couldn't place it.

"Lily's parents…" I sunk to the floor as his words trickled down the line. "…won't take it any further… But, you can't come back. They will call the police. I'm sorry to say, your contract is terminated." She didn't hear any sorrow in his voice. "Best if you don't come in today, or any other day. You will be paid what we owe you, and we will make arrangements for any of your belongings to be sent on." He hesitated before continuing, almost in a whisper, "And if I were you, I'd get out the area as fast as you can, they know where you live. Goodbye." The line went dead.

An hour later, my bags were packed and I picked up the phone.

"Mother, it is me… Morag… Can I come home?"

Forty Eight

Morag – *Then*
Two years later

I HAD RETURNED home, tail between my legs. At twenty-three, back where I had started. Any hope I'd had Mother might have mellowed in the intervening years had been short lived. She was frailer, but her tongue was as sharp as ever. She took a great delight in taunting me about my sudden return.

"You'll never have anyone Morag. You're nothing but a freak. A cheap little tart. No wonder you couldn't even be a mother."

I found a job in the local library. Thankfully, they didn't bother to check the fake references I gave them. I tried to fit in with the others—I wanted to be different from the girl I had been before. I tried to be their friends, I spent time getting to know them and the things they likes. I'd take small gifts in for them, gifts I'd put a lot of thought into. None of them appreciated them. This along with mother and her constant demands meant my life returned to how it had been the day I left. My colleagues stopped inviting me anywhere, and soon I became invisible again. It was just Mother and me. Alone. I suppose I could have stood up to her, answered her back, refused to give into her demands. But I didn't. Deep down I think I was glad she needed me at last.

However, the final straw came when I returned home from work to find mother sitting in my room with my jar on the dresser. The jar was empty and a pile of ashes settled next to the lighter. I snapped. She had taken them away from me again.

I was furious.

That night I watched her from the doorway as she fell asleep. I shook her gently, I didn't want her to miss anything.

I put the pillow over her face and watched impassively as she took her last breath. She didn't struggle much. Perhaps she knew there was no point.

I knew nobody would be suspicious—I had seen the letter from the hospital. She had been diagnosed with cancer and hadn't got long to live.

They removed her body and we buried her. Her church friends and neighbours drawing me disapproving looks. I was the crazy one after all. That's what they believed.

After the funeral, I thought about clearing her room, removing all traces of her from the house, but I couldn't bring myself to do it. Instead, each night I took a dress from her wardrobe and ripped it to shreds, wishing I'd had the courage to do it to her when she was still alive.

MORAG JUMPED AS a loud bang infiltrated her memories. She tried to drown it out, but it was insistent. Someone was at the door.

Forty Nine

Morag

MORAG SHUFFLED TO the front door, she ached all over and her heart felt heavy. *How had things come to this?*. Exhaustion washed over her. *I just want to sleep now, to lay my head down on my pillow surrounded by my family.* She glanced upstairs, *it's not too late for them though,* her voice of reason whispered, *let them go Morag, you don't have to do this.*

"I can't, I've spent my whole life on my own, everyone pointing and staring at me. It's too late, I've made my mind up." Somewhere in the recesses of her mind she heard her mother's wicked laugh. The door rattled again, louder this time. Peering through the peephole, Morag recognised the girl from the café standing on her doorstep. She stiffened and peered over her shoulder half expecting to see Susan and Lily rush down the stairs.

Of course there was nobody there, the house was silent. She crossed her fingers it would stay that way, at least until she got rid of that girl outside. Her blouse stuck to her back, her hands felt clammy. She briefly considered pretending she wasn't in, but the knocking grew louder. It was persistent. If she didn't answer, the rattling was bound to draw attention.

Morag took a deep breath and yanked the front door open.

"Yes?"

The look she gave Jess should have turned the girl to stone, instead she was met by a long stare, and what seemed like an eternity of silence as the girl stared back at her, head tilted. Morag shivered at the sharp glint in her steely grey eyes. There was something so familiar there. She might be young, but there was something overly confident, arrogant almost, in the way she stared back at her.

"Can I help you? I'm a bit busy to be standing here on my doorstep playing staring games."

Jess took a step forward and Morag matched her with a step back, pushing the door closed slightly. Jess placed a foot in the doorway, preventing her from closing it any further.

"Oh, you can indeed," she sneered. "Are you not going to invite me in?"

"Invite you in? Why on earth would I do that? What is it you want?"

"I think we would be better talking indoors." Jess pushed forward a little more.

"I'm not inviting you in. I don't invite strangers into my home thank you very much." She attempted to push the door closed, but Jess's slight size belied her strength, and she pushed it back harder, almost causing Morag to stumble.

"Oh, I'm no stranger, Morag. No matter how much you wish I was. You've made that clear for a long time!"

"If you don't leave immediately, I'll call the police."

"Really? Call the police, will you? No, Morag, I really don't think you will. Not with everything you have to hide. Now, why don't you let me in, and we can have a nice little chat. You and I have so much to catch up on. And what I've got to say is something I think you'd best hear sitting down." She stepped across the threshold, forcing Morag backwards further, and slammed the door behind her.

Feeling as though she had no choice, Morag led the way into the living room.

"Nice place you've got here, Morag." Jess's eyes roamed around the room, not bothering to hide her critical gaze at the mess everywhere.

"What is it you want? I have no money you know. So if you've come to rob me you're wasting your time!"

"Rob you? You really think that's why I'm here?" Jess laughed, mirthlessly. "I'm not here to rob you, you silly cow. But I am here to talk about all the things you've stolen from me." She plonked herself on the sofa. "Why don't you shout your guests down? It's a bit rude leaving them upstairs, isn't it?" She glanced at the ceiling. Morag felt the fear bubbling in her gut. Everything was unravelling. Who was this girl, to come in here like this? She wasn't wanted here.

"I-I-I don't have any idea what you're talking about."

"Really? Are you sure about that Morag? So, Susan, and her kid, Lily, aren't upstairs then? Just you here is it?" She eyeballed Morag as though daring her to lie.

"How do you know that?"

"Oh, Morag. There's lots about you I know, don't you worry about that. Your secrets didn't die with Alan, after all." Her wink was pure maliciousness.

"Alan? What do you mean? Who is Alan?"

"Oh, don't play the innocent with me, Morag. Alan Aitken. You know fine well who I'm talking about. You got his note, didn't you?"

Morag's face drained of all colour, but the girl was relentless now.

"Oh, close your mouth, for fuck's sake, you're going to catch flies. Alan and I grew close, so we did. He told me lots about you, Morag. He filled in some of the gaps for me. Shame he had to leave us like that, eh? Still, at least he went out with a smile on his face. I made sure of it."

"I-I-I…"

"What's wrong, Morag? Cat got your tongue? You've gone a right funny colour there. You okay?" Jess laughed at her now, moving towards the door. "How about I shout Susan and the kid down, I'm sure they would love to hear what I've got to tell them, eh?"

"No, please, don't do that!" Morag wailed.

She pushed herself further into the sofa as Jess turned and flew towards her.

Jess leaned in, Morag could smell the tell-tale minty breath of someone trying to hide the smell of cigarettes.

"It's okay. I know *all* your secrets, remember? So you may as well just admit they're both upstairs."

Morag shook her head wildly, unformed words stuttering from her mouth.

Crack. Jess's hand flew off the side of her face.

"Don't even try to lie to me. Seriously, don't even dare. It's fine. I'm going to leave them up there for a bit. I'll get to them when I'm ready, don't you worry. First you and me are going to have a little chat. One, I reckon we are long overdue."

Morag slumped to the side, she couldn't speak. She had no idea why Jess had turned up and why she had burst in like this. Maybe she was ill? Maybe she was one of those people you read about in the paper? A psychopath? But the way the girl looked at her told her not. Though it also warned her to be wary. Jess knew something. What, she wasn't quite sure, but the fact that she knew Alan and all about the note rang alarm bells already. What had he told her? She finally found the courage to speak.

"Alan... how did you know Alan? How did you know about the note?" she stammered.

Jess stared at her, eyeing her up like a predator ready to pounce on its prey. Her eyes looked crazed yet her stare challenged her, judged her even. Morag cowered back further.

"How did I know Alan? Well, I made it my job to get to know all your little waifs and strays. I couldn't work out why they all gravitated towards you. And when you wouldn't let me into your little clique, I wanted to know why."

"I-I-I don't know w-what you mean? Let you in? I didn't stop you..."

"Shut up, you fucking liar," Jess lifted her hand and swung it towards her, letting it drop at the last minute.

Morag's breathe quickened.

"Stop your fucking lying! Listen to me! For once in your life, you WILL listen to me."

Morag shrunk back into the chair, she kept her mouth firmly closed, terrified the wrong word would trigger another attack. The girl was clearly unhinged. She tried to calm her breathing and listen as Jess rambled on about how she had befriended Alan. How she had found out he was all alone in the world, apart from Morag. He'd told her how Morag watched out for him. How Morag told him he was like family to her. How she was going to look after him. How they were going to be together forever.

Morag bit her tongue, she wanted to scream and shout at Jess— tell her she had got it all wrong, tell her she hadn't manipulated Alan. She had been looking out for him. He was like family. Why couldn't any of them understand.

"Family, eh?" spat Jess. "Shame you never looked out for the family you had!"

"I don't know what you mean? Alan *was* like family. I was looking out for him. He had nobody else. I was only trying to help him."

"No, you were fucking manipulating him. You didn't want to be alone, so you dragged him down, you were every bit as bad as those other wasters who pretended they were his friend. You all used him Morag."

The girl was pacing the floor now, anger radiating from her pores. Morag looked around, trying to work out if she could get up and make a run for it but Jess seemed to have read her mind. She marched back over to Morag and lunged over her once again.

"He told me everything. All your secrets. How you are so scared of being alone, you would do anything. But he also told me how you had started to control his life, Morag. You decided when he would go out, who he would see. You wanted to mould and shape him into something he wasn't. He might have had a shit life, but until you came along, at least it was *his* shit life. He tried to make changes, he wanted out of the life he had, and along you came—Morag to the rescue, eh?"

Jess carried on, barely stopping for breath.

"Alan wanted to change, he wanted out the hole he had found himself in, and he thought you were there to help him. But all you wanted to do was stop his dependency on the drugs and make him dependent on you."

Morag shook her head, "I didn't... I only..."

"Save it for someone who gives a shit."

Morag dropped her head to her chest, she didn't want to hear what Jess had to say anymore. She felt a sharp tug as the girl's fingers grasped a clump of her hair and pulled her head up again.

"Pay attention, Morag. Being alone isn't your only fear is it? Oh no, you are a bit of a dark horse, aren't you? Alan told me lots more things about you. How you used to stay in Edinburgh. You helped a few addicts out there didn't you? And the stalking? Following folk around, spying on them? Not so squeaky-clean, are you? But best of all was trying to snatch a kid? To replace the one you lost. What kind of freak steals someone else's kid?"

"I don't know what you're talking about. That's nonsense, all of it. Nonsense… just the stupid ramblings of some drugged up loser!"

"Oh, I don't think so, Morag. See, I had a few friends from my own time in hospital who owed me some favours, and let's just say their talents are wasted. You can find out anything if you want it bad enough. So yes, I know that you did live and work over in Edinburgh, and you were run out of town after trying to snatch a wee girl. You had to run back home to your mummy. See, I already knew your dirty little secret, Morag. Alan simply confirmed it all."

Morag said nothing. The girl knew too much, there was no point in her pretending.

"So, anyway. Back to the here and now. Alan wanted out, he'd had enough. He wanted away from you. Said he would do anything. Anything Morag, he even said he'd rather be dead than end up depending on a freak like you. He asked me to help him and I did. I sourced some of the best gear—top quality it was. Not like that shit he was used to pumping himself full of. Trouble was, it was so pure, it fucked him. Killed him outright. Shame, eh? At least he escaped you though."

Morag vomited and the room went black.

Fifty

Jess

JESS TOWERED OVER Morag. Her fingers drummed against her thigh as she fought back the queasy feeling in her gut. She could feel her mum's eyes boring into her, lips pursed as she crossed her arms and shook her head. Jess didn't know how to stop herself.

"Let's get you cleaned up. Think you passed out there. You've been out cold for almost an hour. Must be my storytelling skills, eh? Always loved a good story as a kid, I did." Her sarcasm was at odds with the gentle caress of the cloth against the older woman's face.

Morag spluttered and tried to push Jess off her, she let go of the cloth and gripped Morag's wrists hard stamping down on her own weakness. *Sorry mum.*

"Now, now. Why don't you settle yourself down a bit? I've still got plenty left to tell you. You can either do it the easy way, or the hard way." She smiled as she brandished a set of cable ties from her pocket.

"Thought so. You don't want to be all tied up, do you? Not like them upstairs, eh? Oh, don't look so panicked, Morag. You really have gone a funny colour there, you know? They're fine, by the way. I went up and checked on them while you were having your wee nap. The kid is out for the count and think Susan is still feeling a bit sleepy. Those tablets you've been giving her have really fucked her over, haven't they? Naughty Morag. Still not learned your lesson have you? But it's fine, they will be down when they wake up. I made sure to unlock the leg cuffs you put on Susan. That really wasn't very nice of you was it? She waved the key in front of Morag's face. 'And leaving this lying around on your dressing table? Well, that's plain stupid."

"I don't know what you are talking about," sobbed Morag. "Please can you just let me go. I'll give you whatever you want, anything. Please will you let me go."

"Anything I want? Eh? Anything? Are you sure?"

Morag nodded. "Anything," she gasped.

Jess gave a harsh laugh and leaned in closer. "There is nothing you could give me that would make up for..." She stopped abruptly, feeling the tears sting her eyes.

"Make up for what? What is it you think I've done? Please tell me. If you tell me, I can put it right."

Jess snapped back into herself, pushing Morag back onto the couch.

"Listen to me. Just listen, and don't you dare say a word."

Morag was clearly terrified to move, obviously recognising the crazed glaze in Jess' eyes. She stayed where she was and listened, slack mouthed, as Jess told her how she had targeted and picked off each of the people Morag had chosen to be her family. First of all Alan and then Ronnie. Jess described how she had manipulated Ronnie into thinking his mum was trying to kill him. How she had worked on him over the months, even breaking into his house one night and pretending to be the voices in his head. How she had done it, aware he would eventually break and end back up in hospital.

"You see, Morag? Ronnie and I had grown close, I reckon he was a little bit in love with me, he would have done anything for me. It is so easy to manipulate people into doing what you want when they love you, isn't it? Especially when they have nobody else in their lives. Or maybe you wouldn't know."

Jess crouched, rocking back on her heels. She burned with energy, she was in charge, and enjoying the power she had over Morag. The fear in the older woman's face gave her a huge buzz. She was also acutely aware Susan and Lily were still upstairs and that none of this was their fault. She didn't know what to do with them, but she did not want to let them go just yet. She felt Morag's gaze on her.

"What ya looking at, Grandma?" And she couldn't help but laugh hysterically.

Morag's chin dropped to her chest. She said nothing.

"So, there you go. Another one's gone and left you. Poor Ronnie, all locked up in the madhouse again. Safely out of your grasp. Don't worry though, he'll be fine. They'll sort out his meds, and he'll be back out in no time at all. But it makes no difference to you, because you are going to be well gone by the time he's out. I did him a favour really. He hadn't been taking his meds properly, his mother was a complete psycho, just like you, who would have destroyed him. So call it my community service, eh?"

Jess pulled herself up and sat next to Morag. Curling her legs up on the couch, she turned to face her.

"So, it's finally time for us to get to know each other a little better, now." She grinned. "Where's your own mum Morag?"

"She's… she's…"

"Spit it out woman, she's what?"

"She's dead."

"Shame. What was she like?"

"Jess, please tell me what this is all about? What's my mother got to do with anything. Why are you here, doing this?"

"Tell me. What was your mum like?"

"She… well she… she was strict, she…"

"My mum was the best mum in the world," said Jess, cutting Morag off. "She loved me with all her heart, would have done anything for me."

"Is she dead Jess?" Morag asked, her tone affecting a sort of kindness.

Jess swallowed hard.

She nodded and whispered in a falsely childlike voice, "Yes, she's dead. She left me. She went and died when I was just ten years old. Mummy went and left me all by myself."

"I'm sorry to hear that."

"Fucking sorry? Really? Not as fucking sorry as I was. Want to know what happened? Do you?" She didn't give Morag a chance to respond.

"I don't even know where my story begins anymore. So, I'll start back when I was ten years old and the day that plays on a continual loop, like a bad movie, inside my head, slowly driving me insane."

Jess took a deep breath and continued, "I'd passed a test in class, top of the class, top marks, gold star, the lot. I ran home, bursting to tell my mum, to see her face light up. Wanting to hear her say, 'You've done good, really good, I'm proud of you.' That's what I lived for then, to make her proud." She wiped away a stray tear.

"You see Morag, back then, Mum brought my world alive. She chased away shadows I didn't even know existed. We stayed with Mum's dad, my grandfather. It should have been fun, an extended family muddling along together, supporting each other, but it wasn't like that. Grandad was nothing like my mum, she was like a rainbow, while he was a dour granite." Jess stopped to draw breath. "Are you listening to me?" She prodded Morag in the side.

Morag yelped and nodded.

"Mum would take me off to the seaside, probably to get me out that house. Even now the smell of summer reminds me of her. The taste of a fish supper sends me back to the beach. Everything Morag, every bloody thing reminds me of my mum. Anyway, I'm rambling." Jess let out a sharp laugh.

"Let's get back to my story. So there I was, back home and yelling on mum dying to tell her my news. I wasn't worried when she didn't answer. The house was huge, and she didn't always hear me, especially if she was tending to Grandad. So, I ran through the kitchen, the smell of home baking stopping me in my tracks. I snatched a biscuit from the rack where they were cooling, and stuffed it into my mouth. I was so busy stuffing my face I didn't even see the letter propped up on the kitchen table. If I'd seen it, I might have pressed pause and stopped where I was forever. But I didn't see it, I didn't see my name scribbled on the front. I didn't catch the scent of Mum's perfume clinging to the envelope, I just kept moving.

"I ran upstairs calling her. But there was only silence. I didn't see the shadows creeping out the walls, I didn't notice the colour fading from my world. I came to was Grandad's. I hesitated at the door, I hated going in there, it stank. The smell of age, decay and death. The smell of Grandad.

"I knocked softly, not wanting to barge in, in case I caught Mum washing him or helping him onto the loo. I'd done that once before, and Mum had been horrified. I'd been mortified, too. All his saggy grey skin hanging there. Gross. Mum had yelled at me to leave. At the time I'd been too young to notice the expression on my mum's face. Too young to understand what was really happening. I listened at the door, but couldn't hear anything. I tried again, a little louder. Then I heard a muffled grunt from behind the door.

"My Grandad. The colours were fading faster now. 'Can I come in?' I had mumbled at first and then again, a little louder when I heard no reply.

"Another grunt, which sounded like 'Come in.' I pushed the door open and peered inside. The room was dark, the curtains drawn and the dark heavy furniture added a solemn air to the place. It smelled black, forcing its way up my nostrils and making me want to gag.

"Grandad?' My voice had been shaky. 'Is my mum here?' 'Come in properly, girl,' Grandad replied, his voice thick and rough, not his usual sharp, stabbing words. My first thought was he must be ill. The room felt strange—it was cold. Panic bubbled in my belly. I had a sudden desire to rewind back to the oranges and yellows of the seaside.

"The ground became quicksand, pulling me under, pulling me in. The panic bubbled up faster, I tried to pull myself back, but dark fingers were prodding me from behind, pushing me forward until I stumbled into the room.

"I felt sick. I knew something wasn't right. My heart was hammering and I wanted to scream, but my tongue was stuck to the roof of my mouth. My eyes were darting crazily around the room, searching for the oranges, the greens, the ocean blues. Where were the colours? Where was my mum? I was drowning in the shadows. Dancing shadows. I couldn't understand what I was seeing. Why was my mum up there? Why was she dancing like that?

"I strained my neck to look up, all the while wanting to turn the other way, but I couldn't. My eyes were drawn to it. Like a magnet pulling at me. A rope hung down from a large beam in the ceiling. I thought to myself that I'd never seen those beams before. I just wanted to keep staring at them. I didn't want to see the rope. I didn't want my eyes to travel down its length. I didn't want to see the noose at the end of the rope. And I most definitely didn't want to see the noose wrapped around Mum's neck. Or to follow her body down and see her feet twitching as her last breath escaped her. That's when the switch flipped and my world became grey.'

Fifty One

HER HEART RACED, sharp pains shot through her chest. She tried to control the tremor in her body and swallow back the sobs desperate to escape.

She watched as Jess rocked back and forward, her body shuddering as she let go her tears. Morag wanted to reach out and hold her, she needed a mother almost as much as Morag had needed a child. She wished more than anything she could go back and change things—that she had welcomed Jess into the group and into her life. She could have been the one. *We could have been a family.*

"Jess," she murmured, shuffling forward. "I'm so sorry, sweetheart. You poor, poor child." She tried to twist herself around to attempt to embrace her. She softened as Jess cooried into her. "There, there," she soothed. "I'll look after you, my special girl. My little precious. We can be a family."

Jess's body stiffened instantly and Morag held her breath. Jess jerked her head up, cracking Morag's chin and causing her to bite her tongue.

"Family? You're a bit too fucking late for that," she spat, grabbing Morag by the throat and squeezing hard.

"Stop! Please, stop. I was only trying to…"

"Trying's no use now. You're too late. Besides, I've not finished my story yet." Jess drew back from Morag, hesitantly removing her hand, but keeping her eyes firmly focused on her.

"I want you to listen really careful now. This part's important."

She tilted her head and raised her eyebrows. "Well?"

Morag nodded, the bloodied saliva salty in her mouth.

Jess smiled.

"Well, since you are sitting comfortably, I'll begin."

Jess recounted her life with her grandfather until his death when she was fourteen. Her face twisted as she told of the aunt who turned up at the funeral and told Jess she would be going to live with her.

"I'd never met her before," Jess said.

Morag had decided it was easier to let the girl talk, get it all out. She listened as Jess recalled her aunt's resentment. 'She hated me. Said I reminded her of my mum and all the trouble she had brought to the family. She refused to explain what she meant. I stayed there until I was sixteen and she chucked me out. Gave me a box with letters and stuff of my mum's and told me never to come back. I stayed at friend's houses for a while, grabbing a bed where I could, but nobody ever wanted me around for too long. Eventually I had to declare myself homeless, and ended up in a scatter flat in the Southside of Glasgow. Only then did I pluck up the courage to go through my mum's stuff. And that's when my whole life crashed around my ears. And I mean crashed. Exploded. Kaboom! I ended up in hospital, Morag, in the nuthouse. I left there with a diagnosis of PTSD and Borderline Personality Disorder. I prefer to call it a fucking genetic malfunction.' Jess slumped back as though exhausted with her outburst. Morag's heart hurt for her but she was also starting to panic, Susan and Lily were still upstairs and she didn't know how she was going to resolve the situation. There was no way she would be able to take them all with her.

"Jess sweetheart, I am so sorry that all this has happened to you, I wish I could do something to make it right but I really don't understand what all this has got to do with me? Why are you here?"

"Shut the fuck up... I am coming to that bit. First, I think it's time to bring your visitors down now. I reckon they will be up for a good story, given all the crap you've fed them."

"No. Please, leave them. Please don't hurt them..."

"Hurt them? What the fuck do you take me for Morag? Why would I hurt them? You have done a good enough job of that yourself. It's you I want to hurt, not them."

The single punch she aimed wasn't even that hard. Enough to stun Morag into a pained silence, and leave her weakened and cowering.

"Now stay there and don't fucking move." She prodded Morag hard, ignoring her moans of pain.

Fifty Two

JESS RAN UPSTAIRS. Her energy was almost manic, she felt wired. She pushed open the door of Morag's mother's bedroom, her eyes widened at the sight of the bloody walls and shredded bedsheets. Susan lay motionless in the midst of it all. Jess rushed over and shook her. "Susan? Wake up, it's me… Jess."

Susan stirred, her eyes still closed. "Please leave me alone, don't hurt me. Please, I'll do whatever you want…"

"Susan, it's me, it's Jess. I'm not going to hurt you. Please wake up. I need you to come downstairs… quickly."

Susan uncurled herself from the foetal position she had been lying in. her hair was lank and plastered to her face and the dark circles under her eyes contrasted against her pale face. Jess tried to hide the look of shock on her face.

"Wha… how… why are you here? How did you get in? Where's Lily… Lily… oh my God… is Lily hurt?" She got up too fast and fell back over and began crawling her way off the bed, crying for her daughter.

"Calm down, Susan. Lily is fine. She's in her room. She's sleeping. I'm here to help you, not hurt you. Come on now."

She reached down and took Susan's hand and pulled her to her feet.

"Stop it, you're hurting me."

Jess took a deep breath and slowed herself down, she was going to spook Susan if she kept on rushing her.

She dropped the tone of her voice. "Put your arm around my shoulder. Come on, like this."

She picked up Susan's arm. It was a dead weight, but she placed it around her shoulder and held her by the wrist to secure her. "Come on. It's nearly over now," she said softly, leading Susan to the bedroom door.

"Lily! Please, let me get Lily."

"She's best staying where she is. She's fine, honestly. Check for yourself." She dragged Susan over to the small box room and pushed the door open. Lily was fast asleep on top of the covers, one arm curled around herself and her thumb stuck in her mouth. A gentle snore came from her mouth.

"What's happened to her hair?" Susan wailed. "Her beautiful hair," she began to dry-heave.

"Shh. We'll sort her hair once we're out of here. It will be fine. First, I need you to be quiet, I don't want Lily to wake up right now. We'll come and get her in a bit. Trust me, it will be okay."

Glancing back at the sleeping child, Susan allowed Jess to lead her down the stairs, stumbling as she reached the bottom. Jess pulled her up gently and took her into the living room.

"What the—?" shrieked Susan. "What have you done?" She tried to pull herself away from Jess, but didn't have the strength.

"Shh. Just sit here." Jess plonked Susan down on the armchair and turned to Morag.

The older woman was on her knees, her face flushed and tear-stained, a pathetic mess, trying to shuffle her way towards the door.

Jess moved in front of her.

"Where the fuck do you think you are going?" her temper was rising again, she used her foot to push Morag back, doing her best to ignore Susan's squeals of protest.

"Story time isn't finished. I told you to stay where you were."

Jess reached down and yanked Morag by the hair, ignoring her screams. She pulled her back towards the couch and shoved her onto it.

"Jess, what are you doing?" Susan exclaimed. "Please stop it, this isn't helping anything. Just leave her please. Let me get Lily and let's leave… please?"

"Susan be quiet. She doesn't deserve your sympathy or your pity. She's had you locked up here for the last two months. And she's been trying to take Lily away from you."

"Two months? I've not been here two months?"

Jess looked over her shoulder and nodded at her. "Yep, two months, everyone thought you'd done a runner, or that guy who'd been hanging round your house had chopped you up and fed you to the fishes. Nobody's seen him since you've been gone either?"

She shrugged as Susan folded into herself. The red mist had descended again and she just wanted this over with.

"Right, Morag, now Susan is here we can finish the story. Susan, you've not missed too much, I can give you a brief synopsis if you like, to bring you up to speed."

Jess watched Susan's eyes widen as she repeated what she had already told Morag.

"And now it's almost the finale." Jess sat on the chair furthest away from them both. She took a deep breath and began the end of her story.

Reaching into her back pocket, she pulled out a sheet of paper, folded into a tiny square. She slowly unfolded it, all the while staring at Morag.

"So, I was feeling settled in my new home, thinking maybe just maybe this was a new start for me. I've not looked at any of my mum's stuff before—didn't have the guts to do it—but I wanted to blow away the cobwebs, start afresh and all that." She gave a strangled laugh.

"There were loads of photographs of me and mum, on the beach, out walking, old school reports and home-made Mother's Day cards, the usual keepsakes. Then there were a pile of letters. I flicked through most of the official looking ones before, I found the envelope with my name on it. I knew right away it was Mum's handwriting. I wish I had never opened that letter. Really, I wish I hadn't. And you," she spat towards Morag. "You're going to fucking wish I hadn't either."

She coughed then began to read from the paper in her hand, not noticing her fat tears dripping onto the paper.

Jess, my love, my precious girl. I am so sorry, sorry that I had to leave you and it breaks my heart knowing that you will someday find out the truth from this letter.

I had to go Jess darling, I couldn't face waiting until you were older to tell you, to risk you hating me. You are not who you think you are, Jess. We were never who you thought we were. Our lives were one big fat lie. You always used to ask me about your dad, Jess. I didn't know what to tell you. I didn't know how to tell you. So I guess I took the coward's way out. Your Gran and Grandad are not my parents.

They "bought" me as a baby. It was all very respectable—like a church arranged adoption, that's what they told me. Your Gran, well your adoptive Gran became ill early on in her life. She had dementia, a particularly vicious strain and that's when things began to go wrong, love. Your grandad had mostly ignored me up until then. I worked out that it had been Gran who wanted a child, not him. But once she became ill, I became useful to him. I became her carer Jess, I cared for her right up until the day she died. You were only little, you won't remember much about her but I've left some photographs for you. She was a lovely woman. But because of her dementia, she wasn't the wife your grandad was looking for. And so he turned to me to take her place. It's killing me to say this Jess, your grandad was your dad. He only stopped raping me the day he found out I was pregnant with you.

She couldn't read any more and let the letter drop to the floor. She could recite the words from memory, having read it so often, but still its contents kicked her in the stomach every time.

The two women stared at her. Susan had tears streaming down her face. Morag was trying to form some words.

"Well? Speak up Morag," sneered Jess, wiping away her tears with the back of her hand. "Something to say, have you?"

"I-I-I still don't know what this has got to do with me?" Morag stuttered.

Jess laughed hysterically. "Really, are you that fucking stupid, *Grandma*?" she roared.

"If I'd been your grandmother, Jess, none of this would have happened to you. I'd have looked after you." Her shoulders dropped. "I never got the chance to be a grandma, I never had any children."

"Are you sure about that?" sneered Jess.

Morag nodded, tears streaming down her face.

Jess crouched at her feet and rocked on her heels.

"Oh, but you did, *Grandma*, and your daughter was my mother!"

"No, no, it's not true... my baby died... my baby's dead!" Morag cried.

"Nope. Wrong again. Your baby didn't die. Your baby was taken and adopted through the 'Good People of the Parish'. That is what all the other envelopes contained, Morag—birth certificate, letters between your mother and my so-called '*grandparents*'." She made inverted commas in the air at this statement. "I've got them all back at my flat, I could show you, but there really isn't much point. In your heart, you've always known. Besides, you're not going to be around long enough for it to matter now, anyway."

Morag began to wail—a high pitched keening noise. "My baby... my baby... That bitch. My own mother stole my baby."

Jess moved back a little to avoid the woman's arms as she thrashed about. She tried hard to reach inside and feel some pity for her, some warmth towards the woman who was her own flesh and blood. But her heart was empty. This woman was to blame for her mum's suicide. For her hideous birth. For everything her life had become. She had to pay.

She stood and aimed her foot at Morag. She couldn't do it, she couldn't bring herself to do it.

"Stop, Please don't hurt me," cried Morag. "Please stop. If I am your Grandma, please, let me be your Grandma! We can be together... we can..."

Jess let her babble on incoherently about family and not being alone at the end. When she'd had enough, Jess reached down and slapped her hard across the face. She wanted her to stop talking. She didn't want to hear her.

"Family? Are you fucking kidding me? You wouldn't even let me be a part of your fucking group of weirdos. No offence, Susan," she threw back at the woman staring opened mouthed on the chair. "You, Morag, are not my family. You never will be. It's because of you my mum is dead, because of you I ended up abusing every kind of drug I could get my hands on, and letting others use and abuse me, until I snapped and ended up in the fucking nut house. So. No. You. Do. Not. Get. To. Step. In. And. Play. Happy. Families. Now." She screamed these last words into Morag's face, her spittle landing like raindrops on Morag's chin.

"But hey, you're not going to die alone after all," Jess smirked. "That's what you're so scared of, isn't it? Well, don't you worry, Grandma dearest. I'm going to be right here with you."

Susan shrunk back into the chair.

"Please Jess. Please just let me and Lily go. I don't want to be a part of this. Please."

"Shut the fuck up with your whining. I'm doing this for you too, you know? This bitch has been playing you. She was going to kill herself and take you and Lily with her. She's been playing you all along."

Jess reached over to the table and picked up the phone she had taken from the kitchen drawer, tossing it over to Susan.

"Lily20 is the password. Open up the messenger and you'll see some interesting messages between her and Kris. Read the rest of them too. Her twisted mind fucks with everyone she meets. See what sort of sick bitch my Grandma really is. Nice, kindly old woman, isn't she?"

Susan punched in the password and Jess watched as her face dropped when she read through the messages. Jess smiled when she realised she was telling the truth.

"Morag, is this true? Why? Why would you do this?" sobbed Susan. "I trusted you."

"You don't deserve that child," Morag snapped. "Too wrapped up in your own little world, taking her away from her daddy and her world. You were even considering selling your body at one point. Don't you remember? You were not fit to be a mother. I would have been a better mother to Lily. I'd have made sure she had everything she needed."

"You bitch," snarled Susan, as she jumped off her chair and leapt towards Morag, aiming a punch at the woman's face.

Jess stepped forward and pulled her back.

"Enough, Susan. There's no point. There's a better way to hurt her. Just leave her."

"See Morag, it's not nice when everyone leaves you is it? It's not nice being alone. I wanted you to understand exactly what being abandoned feels like—how it feels to know someone has deliberately made the choice to leave you, and that they are about to blow your world apart. Is that how you felt when you read Alan's note, Morag? I only wish I could have seen your face when you read it. That's why getting Ronnie locked up again was so much fun—sad little sod would do anything to keep me happy, so he would. It was too easy. You see Ronnie told me what you were doing, so did Alan. Drawing them in, making them dependent on you. Just because you wanted to be needed. The night you lured Ronnie to the park, playing on his paranoia, you were deliberately sending him round the bloody twist, Morag, how fucking sick is that? All because you were jealous of his friendship with me. You knew what would happen if his paranoia took over. You knew he would attack his mother and end up locked away for it. I finished that one off for you. But you would rather have him locked away than have him choose to leave you. And now, well now, the last of your 'family' is about to watch you leave."

Jess stepped back and reached for her rucksack. She pulled out Morag's jar and waved it in front of her. "Thought I didn't know about this? Your jar of hearts. Your family?" She threw it towards her, aiming for her head and making her target.

"Yours and Lily's names are in there Susan. The only ones not crumpled up. Mine never even made the crumpled up pile. Hey, that's family for you, I guess. You can choose your friends and all that, eh?"

"Please Jess. You've said your piece. It wasn't my fault. But I am sorry. Please don't leave me," cried Morag.

Fifty Three

HER HAND CLUTCHED the door frame as she watched them get into the taxi. Susan hurried Lily into the back seat before turning round. She had to stop herself from tearing down the path after them and into the taxi. But she couldn't go, not yet. She had to see this through.

Just go please, before I lose my nerve. Her smile was tight as she waved them off. Jess waited until the taxi was out of sight.

They were safe now. That was all that mattered.

She clicked the door closed and contemplated her next task.

She had made Susan a promise. Or rather Susan had forced her into making it.

They were gone now though, they'd never know.

Jess walked across the hall and pushed the living room door open. Morag sat in the chair where she had left her. The older woman's face was stained with tears but thankfully there was no sign of bruising from their earlier scuffle. She stood at the doorway and watched her for a moment. This was her flesh and blood, her grandmother. The only connection she had to family.

It's her fault you're in this mess though, she thought, balling her fists. It would be so easy, the woman was skin and bone, she was dying in front of her. Two minutes and she could be gone. And revenge would have been served.

"Don't hurt her Jess. What's the point? You'll only get caught and end up in jail. What's the point in that?" Susan's parting words echoed in her mind. She had tried to convince Susan to see things from her point of view, but she was adamant.

"Jess, can't you see? She's as much a victim as you are. Think about what she went through, her mum taking her baby and letting her believe it was dead. The years of emotional abuse she went through? And now look Jess, she is dying and she is dying alone without a family, no matter what she has done to us, it doesn't take away the fact she is going to die alone. There's your revenge, don't let it ruin the rest of your life."

"If it hadn't been for her then my mum would still have been here and none of this would have happened," she'd retorted.

"Jess, if it hadn't been for Morag, you wouldn't have been here. And you don't know that anything else would have been different anyway. We can't see into the past any more than we can see into the future. Morag's already paid in the worst possible way, Jess. Don't be another victim of this whole mess."

Jess had caved eventually and, if she was honest, she had been relieved. She didn't want to hurt Morag, not because of who she was, but because that wasn't who she was. She'd started out her journey wanting payback for her mum's death, but something deep inside told her what she had really wanted was to find her family, to belong again and that's why Morag's rejection of her had hurt so much.

Jess had agreed with Susan on the condition that she took the three thousand pounds they had found in hidden away in the kitchen drawer, underneath the letter from Morag's consultant confirming there was nothing else that could be done. Morag was dying. Susan hadn't wanted the money.

"I just want to get away from here, start again."

"Take it. You deserve it. Take it, and make a new start for you and Lily. Get away from here.' Jess had insisted.

The two women had talked for hours, about their past and how they would move on in the future. When Susan had asked Jess to join her and Lily, she shook her head. Susan wouldn't take no for an answer and had worn her down. Jess would never tell her that inside she was delighted. She wasn't quite ready to let all of her guards down just yet.

Fifty Four

FOR THE NEXT four days and nights Jess sat with the woman who was her grandmother. And they talked. At first Jess had refused to listen to anything Morag had to say, she didn't want to give her the chance to worm her way under her skin. But eventually she relented, this was the only chance she was going to get to spend time with her last known living relative.

Listening to Morag's story properly, Jess couldn't help but pity the woman. Her life had been shit. There was no denying that. She could empathise but she didn't think she had the strength to forgive the dying woman for everything she had done and the lives she had destroyed. And hell would freeze over before Jess would give her the one thing she knew she wanted. Family.

"I'll not leave you to die alone," she had told Morag. "I'm not that cruel or heartless. My mum brought me up better than that." She couldn't resist the dig. "But you are not dying as my Gran. I'll stay with you but I won't allow you to claim me as yours. You gave up that right a long time ago."

Days and nights merged into one and Morag's breathing became slower, more laboured. When the tell-tale rattle of death sounded, Jess had wanted to call the doctor or an ambulance but Morag's vice-like grip belied her condition.

"No…" she wheezed. "No doctors, no ambulances and no hospital. It's all written down, my consultant and GP both know it's what I wanted, nobody will blame you."

Jess turned away, she didn't want Morag to see the pain in her eyes.

"Nobody will know you were here," Morag whispered. "Just clear up after yourself and leave when I'm gone. I'm truly sorry, Jess. I wish I could turn back the clock. I wish I'd had the guts to stand up to my mum when I was younger. You are right. None of this might ever have happened."

Morag's final breath came during the night. She died alone in her bed as Jess slept downstairs on the sofa. Standing over her dead body, Jess felt like she had just stepped off the wildest rollercoaster, only to realise she felt nothing.

On autopilot she went round the house clearing away all signs of herself, Susan and Lily. Her final task was the hardest, Morag's jar of hearts, it was the one thing she had agreed to do for Morag and she wouldn't let her down. Not over this. She took the paper hearts and held them in the palm of her hand, a shiver of pity for each person they represented.

As per Morag's wish, she took them out into the back garden and buried them under the evergreen bush in the corner. She then sent Susan a text promising her that she would make her way to the Borders to be with her and Lily.

Jess waited until it was dark and slipped out the front door, allowing it to click closed behind her. She never looked back.

Epilogue

Six months later

THE PUB WAS quiet. The two women finished their meal. They smiled at something the girl sitting between them said. They had settled—content in the quiet rural village on the Scottish borders. Nobody bothered them and they bothered nobody.

The bartender raised the TV remote control and turned up the volume as the Scottish news headlines came on. The women glanced up, before returning to their meal, but the words of the newsreader stopped them dead.

"Today in Aberdeen, the trial of DSI Colin Hayes continues… a plea of not guilty to a string of domestic offences and the murder of his partner… the court also heard that his wife and child who went missing three years ago have never been traced… refuse to rule out further charges relating to their disappearance."

The two women looked at each other across the table, their mouths turned up into smiles as they clinked glasses.

"Cheers, and here's to the family we choose for ourselves."

One year later

LENNOXHILL CEMETERY. The child watched from the car. They had told her to stay there while they 'paid their respects'. She was too young to understand what paying respects was but she was happy, she had a packet of crisps and fizzy juice as a treat. Plus she had got an extra day off school to come away for the day with her mum and Jacey. She smiled to herself. Grownups were silly, Jacey had been Jess before, but Mummy had told her they were playing pretend, and so they all had new names.

Mummy was now called Dianna. They let her keep her name though. She was glad. She liked the name Lily, she was the only Lily in her class, not like Abbey Brown, there were already four Abbey's in her class.

OUTSIDE THE TWO women stood by the grave. Compared to the others around it, this one was overgrown and untidy. No pots of flowers or stone angels adorned this final resting place. It looked as though nobody had been near it.

"Still on her own," the taller of the women, called Jacey, smiled. Dianna nodded.

"See, I told you, you got your revenge after all, and you're still here."

Jacey knelt down and pulled some of the weeds away from the headstone—just the most basic of markers, nothing fancy. Her name and year of birth and death.

She took the flowers she had picked up at the garage on the outskirts of town and placed them by the grave. "I forgive you, Morag. It's time for me to let go and move on."

She stood and wiped away at a tear threatening to fall. She saw Dianna stare at her.

"I'm not crying, you are!" she sniffed.

Dianna smiled.

"Sure, Jess, if you say so. Now come on, hurry up. Ronnie will be waiting for us. He's dying to show us his new flat and have us meet his support worker."

ACKNOWLEDGEMENTS

A book is never a solo journey and I have more people to thank than I could ever fit into a few pages.

First of all, thanks to Sean and all the team at Red Dog for taking a chance on me, twice now! It is an honour to be a part of the kennel, thank you all for all of your support.

To Noelle Holten, Sarah Hardy, Claire Knight and Kate Eveleigh for being my beta readers. Your words of wisdom and encouragement have meant the world to me throughout the writing process. I can never thank you all enough.

For those who have read and reviewed my books and sent me lovely messages; the book groups who have invited me along to speak to them, to everyone who has taken the time to write and share a review, it really does mean everything to me. Once your book is out there, it is no longer yours, it belongs to the reader and so words of encouragement have kept me going when the self-doubt starts to creep in.

A special thank you to Mary Picken and Anne Cater, for being you—your friendship is priceless.

Graham Smith, I'll be forever grateful for your encouragement.

Susie Lynes and Angela Marsons, two of the fiercest women whose support has been immense, I want to be you two when I grow up!

To my Ceartas team, especially Patricia Ovens, you keep my feet on the ground always! And Ronnie, hope you're still talking to me!

Susan Bonner, Morag McLaughlin and Lynn MacDonald, thank you for letting me borrow your names, remember, it's only fiction!

To my Harrogate Babes, Angela, Katie and Eileen and their lockdown launches, laughs and support.

But my biggest thanks as always is to my family for all their love, support and belief in me! Dad, you instilled my love of reading, hope heaven has a bookshop.

And to you the reader, thank you for reading.

ABOUT THE AUTHOR

By day Sharon Bairden is the Services Manager in a small, local independent advocacy service and has a passion for human rights; by night she has a passion for all things criminal.

She blogs at Chapterinmylife and is delighted to be crossing over to the other side of the fence to become a writer.

Sharon lives on the outskirts of Glasgow, has two grown up children, a grandson, a Golden Labrador and a cat. She spends most of her spare time doing all things bookish, from reading to attending as many book festivals and launches as she can.

She has been known to step out of her comfort zone on the odd occasion and has walked over burning coals and broken glass – but not at the same time!

CPSIA information can be obtained
at www.ICGtesting.com
Printed in the USA
BVHW031006061021
618260BV00013B/180/J